PRAISE FOR S

T0221580

Valencia and Valentine

"Despite themes of loneliness, loss, and mental illness, Krause manages to infuse her tale with charm and gentle humor."

—*Booklist*

"Suzy Krause's debut novel, *Valencia and Valentine*, is a warm and unexpected treat."

—*POPSUGAR*

"*Valencia and Valentine* is a beguiling and charming first novel by Suzy Krause."

—Authorlink

"A singularly unique, superbly scripted, and inherently entertaining novel by an author with a distinctively reader-engaging narrative storytelling style . . ."

—Midwest Book Review

Sorry I Missed You

"A high-energy, feel-good story about the ghosts of our past and the importance of human connections."

—*Kirkus Reviews*

"*Sorry I Missed You* is so quirky and original, full of humor, wit, and warmth. I loved how three such different women forged a genuine friendship—and, of course, that mystery. A real page-turner."

—Josie Silver, *New York Times* bestselling author of *One Day in December*

"A quirky, original story about unexpected friendship and the power of hope, *Sorry I Missed You* is a gem of a book."
—Phaedra Patrick, internationally bestselling author of *The Curious Charms of Arthur Pepper* and *The Library of Lost and Found*

I THINK WE'VE BEEN HERE BEFORE

ALSO BY SUZY KRAUSE

Valencia and Valentine

Sorry I Missed You

I THINK WE'VE BEEN HERE BEFORE

A NOVEL

Suzy Krause

LAKE UNION
PUBLISHING

Text copyright © 2024 by Elena Krause
All rights reserved.

No part of this book may be reproduced, or stored in a retrieval system, or transmitted in any form or by any means, electronic, mechanical, photocopying, recording, or otherwise, without express written permission of the publisher.

Published by Lake Union Publishing, Seattle

www.apub.com

Amazon, the Amazon logo, and Lake Union Publishing are trademarks of Amazon.com, Inc., or its affiliates.

ISBN-13: 9781662517525 (paperback)
ISBN-13: 9781662517532 (digital)

Cover design by Philip Pascuzzo
Cover image: © Vladimir Illievski, © Goce Illievski / Stocksy; © CSA-Archive, © Pialhovik / Getty

Printed in the United States of America

For my grandma Enid, who read my first two books out loud to my grandpa Glen and who preordered this book direct from me before I'd even started writing it

OCTOBER

1

Having your heart broken is like finding out you have bedbugs—not in an emotional sense, but practically. Both broken hearts and bedbugs require extreme treatment. You can't just wash your sheets and think that's enough. Not only is it not enough, you've likely made the problem worse by carting your dirty laundry all over the place.

You can get your house fumigated (this could be a metaphor for therapy), but even that won't be enough, because the memories will be as bad as the bugs themselves. They'll continue to plague you whether they're there or not, crawling all over your legs and feet as you lie awake at night, unable to sleep. When you put on that T-shirt, you'll feel them running up your neck into your hair. They'll make their home in all the quiet, innocuous places in your life, burrowing into memories and holidays and songs and smells, and every time you think you've gotten rid of the last one, you'll discover that you were an idiot to think there would ever be a last one.

That's not how bedbugs work, and it's not how broken hearts work.

No, a broken heart requires more than a trip to the dumpster or a visit from a licensed exterminator. You have to get rid of the mattress, the rug, the other furniture, the pillows, the clothing in the closet. The closet.

The house.

Replace it all. New Everything.

Nora doesn't know that starting over like this is a privilege reserved almost exclusively for the young. She doesn't know that metaphorical fumigation is often the *only* option when you're, say, forty, and you have a job and a mortgage and responsibilities and friends and New Everything is just a lot of work, a lot of money you don't have. She doesn't think about it because she doesn't have to; she simply does what young people do, what young people are uniquely able to do: in the face of her first real broken heart, she gets on an airplane and finds New Everything.

She finds a fifth-floor apartment on Greifswalder Strasse and a view of reddish-brown rooftops out the slanted ceiling window. Thin daisy curtains and unframed band posters and fake chrysanthemums in a dollar store vase by the sink. Two roommates, one from the States and one from Germany.

She finds a new language and a new currency. Air that feels and smells new and people who interact with each other in a new way and new things to look at (mostly buildings, all of them ironically very old, with giant, brightly colored murals painted all over them).

She finds a new coffee shop, named Begonia, on a street with a long, hyphenated name she doesn't know how to pronounce yet. It's a modern place, lots of tile and wood, a neon-pink sign behind the counter spelling out its name in sharp calligraphy. You can buy indie electronica albums with your freshly squeezed orange juice, and you can sit by the window and watch all the fascinating strangers walk by on the sidewalk outside. Everything here feels like it is trying specifically, pointedly, to be the opposite of where she grew up—a rural Saskatchewan village full of quiet, blond Norwegian Canadians; no lights, neon or traffic; no indie electronica albums. No sidewalks, even.

She appreciates the effort Berlin has made to help her feel emphatically *not* at home. Maybe her brain can be persuaded that this is not just a new beginning, but that it is *the* beginning. Nora's beginning. That nothing has ever happened to her before, that she came into existence in Berlin at nineteen years old, has never been in love, has never been hurt.

Maybe an alternative to what feels impossible—healing a broken heart—could be to convince it that it had never been broken to begin with, that it, the heart itself, is new.

She found Begonia through a work-abroad program recommended to her by her high school guidance counselor, an opportunity that had sounded, at the time, laughable, impossible, torturous. After all, Nora had a boyfriend at the time, and he was the love of her life, and moving that far away from him would kill both of them! They would literally *die* if they were separated, as though Cupid's arrow had pierced them through major arteries and could never be removed without fatal blood loss.

Now she knows: he would've been fine. Cupid had merely grazed him, and his wound healed insultingly fast.

(Is there anything more humiliating than one-sided romance?)

She's early for her meeting with Begonia's owner, soon to be her boss, so she buys a coffee, no cream or sugar, and sits in a soft velvet chair by the window, admiring the mural on the building across the street, a vibrant display of birds, penguins and blue jays and hawks and pheasants and falcons, one of those paintings with so many fantastic details you'd need days to notice them all—and she'll have time to do this. This is comforting. She will spend enough time here for this mural to become familiar. Maybe the knowledge of this is why it already seems like something she's seen before, something that makes her feel at home.

The door opens and Nora sits up straight.

She senses his presence, like he's bad weather or air-conditioning, something that changes the atmosphere and makes her skin prickle. When she looks, she's half expecting something paranormal or extraterrestrial, something shining or radiating—but it's just a man.

He's tall but not giant, wearing a black T-shirt with the word Spoon written across the front. Handsome but not supernaturally so, not someone whose presence should cause this much inner chaos. But she can feel him and more than that: she knows him from somewhere. Not recognizes, not like he's someone she walked past on the street earlier or someone who went to the same high school as her but ran in different circles; she *knows* him.

She begins flying around inside her brain, sorting through mental filing cabinets, trying to find the memories that correspond with his face, coming up short. This man is as familiar as her childhood home, a place she lived in that now lives in her. She has kissed him. Held his hand, cried on his shoulder. His presence is comforting and calming; he's safe. These aren't memories; she doesn't remember any of this at all. They're just facts, things she knows, fluttering into her mind as though they've been written on scraps of paper and stuffed into her ears.

But there's so much *missing*. She has no idea who he is. She doesn't know where she met him or anything concrete about him. It's all just some kind of visceral, emotional déjà vu. She starts to say his name, but as she opens her mouth, she realizes she doesn't know it.

Everything is new. Everything is opposite and unexpected and different, except this man. He's as old as her reflection in the mirror.

How?

He seems to sense her eyes on him and glances at her. She should feel embarrassed that she's been caught staring, but she doesn't, and this is strange too.

Soon he turns, coffee in hand, surveying the space. Then, to her delight and horror, exactly the same amount of both, he walks over to her table.

She sips her coffee, trying to play it cool, though she's realizing now how out of her depth she is. She grew up in a village; everyone she'd ever known she met as a kid. Small towns don't lend themselves to meet-cutes, chance encounters, mystery dates. Attractive strangers who approach you in coffee shops. Those are things that happen to beautiful people in big cities. Small towns are for childhood friends who fall in love slowly, without noticing it, and end up married, almost accidentally.

How stupid of her. She'd flown halfway across the world to forget a boy and possibly meet a new one without realizing this all-important fact: she doesn't know how to flirt with strangers.

"Nora?"

He's smiling at her. He knows her name.

"Yes," she says. She sounds almost reverent, like she's having a mystical experience. Maybe she is.

"I'm Jacob." The name doesn't ring a bell. He sets his coffee down and reaches across to shake her hand as he sits. The handshake is electric, like it's their first time touching, but it's also comfortable, like they've been touching for decades. Maybe the strange sense of intimacy she had upon seeing him is normal, the way everyone feels when they meet someone attractive. Maybe he felt it too. Maybe that's what love at first sight is, false familiarity, a future so beautiful and vivid that you can see it and feel it all the way from the past.

"Did you get Ida's email?"

Oh. This explanation is so obvious as to be embarrassing. Ida, the owner of Begonia. So, okay, that's how this man knows Nora's name—but what about the rest of it?

"No," she says.

He looks alarmed. "So you don't have a clue who I am . . . ?"

"Not a clue." It comes out ruder, and much louder, than she'd intended. "Sorry."

"Why are you the one apologizing?" He's scrambling out of his seat, his face flushed, as though he's been caught doing something illegal. She notices his German accent, but, unlike anyone else she has encountered here thus far, it fades to the background when he speaks to her, like she's already so accustomed to it that it's unnoticeable, the way it probably would if they were an old married couple. "I need a do-over." He takes a few steps backward, his face serious and businesslike. He makes a show of looking around the room as though trying to find someone. His

7

eyes land on her. Another little jolt of electricity. The calm assurance of familiarity. She'd assumed all her life that these things couldn't coexist, that they'd cancel each other out, like an ice cube in boiling water. But there they were, very happy together, right inside her chest. "Excuse me," he says, his face still red. "Hello, are you Nora?"

She nods, laughing self-consciously. One of the baristas is watching the whole thing with the annoyed expression of a person who has taken a public service job without any desire to be in proximity of said public.

"My name is Jacob. I'm here for your job orientation. Ida, the owner of this fine establishment, could not be here today, as she is not feeling well. I wish I had arrived earlier so I could buy your coffee—nice to see you're so prompt, though!" Big exhale, his shoulders settle. "Is it all right if I sit with you, or shall I conduct this meeting from that table over there?"

She pretends to consider this. "I think it's fine if we sit at the same table," she says.

He nods. "I probably do come off more professionally when I'm not yelling across the room," he says.

"Same."

He sits again, slower this time, as though the previous interaction took a little bite out of his self-confidence.

"So. How's Berlin treating you so far? Ida mentioned you only arrived a few days ago."

"Last week, yes. And it's really good." She's stumbling over her words and has to remind herself to slow down. "Berlin is. Really good."

"Wonderful." He sips his coffee.

"Do you work here, then?" She needs clues. Where is this man from? Why is he so familiar?

"I work here very part-time while I'm in school. Ida is a family friend of my mother's, so I've been doing this for . . . five years now?"

This isn't helpful. "Oh. And, so, where are you from?"

"Here. And I know you're from Canada, but not which part . . . ?"

"Southwest Saskatchewan," she says.

8

He nods. "Ah," he says, as though he's familiar with southwest Saskatchewan. This would be strange. No one is familiar with southwest Saskatchewan.

"Have you been there?"

But he disappoints her again. "No. Is it close to Montreal? My sister's going to school there."

"I think it'd be a thirty- or forty-hour drive to Montreal from my house."

He looks impressed, as though the vastness of her home country reflects positively on Nora herself, like she'd had some part in it.

The orientation goes quickly. They talk at the table; then he walks her around behind the counter and introduces her to her new coworkers, a couple of rainbow-haired teenagers. (This interaction, if you wrote it down on paper, would appear perfectly pleasant and polite, but afterward Nora felt there was a subtext she couldn't quite grasp, and she wasn't sure if it was a cultural thing or if she had, without realizing it, reached that age where high school–aged kids inexplicably loathe you.)

When the meeting is over, she has one more moment, as he says goodbye, of disorientation, an overwhelming urge to hug him, even kiss him, as though that's how they always say goodbye. But he leaves and it passes.

She is sure now that she doesn't actually know this person. It was in her head, maybe something similar to jet lag. Maybe she recognized him to make herself feel better, a reaction to unfamiliarity overload, like how your body stops feeling cold when you're about to freeze to death—starts to actually feel hot.

She doesn't know that as he walks to his car, he's working through a similar set of questions. *Where do I know her from? Why did she feel like someone I've loved before? Why did that feel like a reunion rather than a meeting?*

But he, too, will write it off as a trick of the mind, like the time a hypnotist at a birthday party, in the middle of July on a swelteringly hot day, was able to make him believe he was very cold.

2

Hilda stands at the head of the table as if she's going to say grace, her fingers knit tightly together, her shoulders hiked up by her ears. What she's going to say is the opposite of grace; it's more of a curse.

She looks at the precious faces around the table—her husband, Marlen, his beautiful, sad smile; her father, Iver, half-asleep, leaning dangerously to the side like a house built on a swamp. Across from them, her sister, Irene, and Irene's husband, Hank, one of those couples that have started to look like brother and sister, their faces crumpled into matching frowns (Hilda wonders whether they fought on the way here, but she doesn't want to pry). At the end of the table, Irene and Hank's twelve-year-old son, Ole, stares despondently at the lutefisk (a Norwegian staple, his grandfather's favorite thing about every major holiday, and Irene makes Ole try it every year in hope that one of these times he will discover that he loves the gelatinous, lye-soaked fish. But the smell of it makes him gag and ruins everything else on the table by proxy).

Nora, Hilda and Marlen's daughter, is in Berlin. She left just in time to miss this. It's like she knew. Her cat, left behind in the move, skulks under the table, rubbing against Hilda's legs. No one but Nora has ever really liked this cat, but this cat has never cared. She carries herself with an air of superiority; you can feel the derision in her eyes when she deigns to look at you. Still, her presence is comforting. Exactly where she has always been, doing exactly what she has always done.

Something—maybe the only thing—completely unaffected by the bad news.

"Thank you all for coming," Hilda says, her voice somewhere way back in her throat. She's like a jack-in-the-box, wound tight, each word another twist of the crank. "We're . . . so . . . blessed—" There it is. She explodes into tears and her family recoils in surprise, trading alarmed glances. *These don't seem like* we're so blessed *tears, do they?*

It takes her a few minutes to regain her composure. Marlen reaches up and tugs lightly on the sleeve of her blouse, and she unlaces her fingers, slipping one of her hands into his. He won't make eye contact with anyone, and Ole starts squirming nervously.

"Sorry," she says. "I promised myself I wouldn't do that." She can't stop shaking, so she picks up her wineglass with her free hand, as if to make a toast, and clutches it tightly against her stomach. It's cool and solid, something to remind her that she is *here, now.* "Marlen and I have some sad news." Another long pause, agonizing for everyone. She inhales. "Okay. So, earlier this summer, Marlen started to feel off. Just tired and—kind of sick? We wondered . . . but he wouldn't go see a doctor at first." She checks herself. *A bit accusatory. Rein that in.* "I mean, we didn't think it was necessary, at first. Then one night, he found a lump." She watches the light bulb go on in everyone's heads. But, of course, she has to actually say the word for it to be real; you can't be vague with these kinds of announcements. She plunges clumsily ahead. "He actually said to me, 'I wonder if this is—*you know*—or something.' I remember saying to him, 'Marlen, sometimes we wonder because we really do wonder, but sometimes we wonder because we already know . . .'"

She pauses. Her family is gaping at her. She's gone about this in a really stupid way—but they don't understand how hard it is to get these words out. She means to just say it, but then she can't.

"Marlen has . . . a tumor. And it's benign."

"Malignant," Marlen whispers.

She stares at him, like she's offended. "What did *I* say?"

11

"You said *benign*."

"No, I wouldn't say that."

"You did, though."

"I'm sure I said *malignant*." Her voice cracks on the word.

Marlen is unsure of himself. Hilda's a confident woman, and with good reason. She's incredibly smart and usually right. "You probably did." He's still whispering, but the room is silent, so everyone hears their exchange anyway.

Hilda's lost now. She sets the glass back on the table. She doesn't need to touch anything to know where and when she is, because now she is sure that she has never been anywhere else but here, in this awful moment. She lets out a big sigh, suddenly done crying, just too tired. The words come flowing out. "Well, anyway. It's the bad one. Malignant. It's cancer. And it's not good cancer, if you know what I mean? I didn't know there was 'good cancer,' but apparently there's 'good cancer' and 'bad cancer,' and 'bad cancer that pretends to be okay at first,' according to Marlen's doctor. Who's a quack, *I* think."

She adds this last part in only a slightly softer voice, then glances at Marlen, who shakes his head at the ceiling. Marlen likes his doctor. *Rein it in.* She picks up the glass again and tries to take a drink, but the glass is empty and she laughs at herself, an angry-sounding laugh that makes her leaning father sit up straight.

She wonders why it had been so hard to get the words out before; it's too easy now. She pulls at the neck of her blouse, straightens her necklace, the one Nora gave her, a cheap silver locket.

She clears her throat again. Hilda doesn't usually ramble or fidget, and her smiles don't usually scream. She's soft spoken and soft lived, dignified in the face of anything, like a portrait of a person in a pretty gold frame. The adults begin to squirm along with Ole. "So anyway. Now we're having conversations about treatments and advance directives and end-of-life care . . . We're sorry we didn't say anything until now. We just wanted to wait until we had good news. But." She gives another short, hysterical-sounding laugh, and then her face falls and she sits abruptly, leaving the rest unspoken. *We never got any.*

She looks over at Marlen. She doesn't want to be angry at him right now, but she can't help it. He's still holding her hand, and she's holding it right back, but in her head she's raging. This is what marriage looks like after so many years. She can hold his hand and feel comforted by him even as she wants to shove his face into the Jell-O salad.

Everyone stares miserably at the bird on the table. It lies there, between the corn and the lutefisk, waiting for someone to cut it up and eat it, but no one moves. It might have breathed a sigh of relief and gone on its way had it not already spent four hours in the oven.

Marlen feels like he should say something, too, but what? This whole thing is uncomfortable, takes them to a place of vulnerability that feels inappropriate, like having the doctor do his annual physical in front of his family. He's not a crier—he's an entertainer. A teacher. The guy with the trivia. He'd known his wife was going to tell the family his news tonight; he'd given her the go-ahead, and it had been his idea for her to tell them instead of him. He just hadn't realized she was going to do it right up front like this, the opening act. He feels her thin fingers between his and squeezes them lightly. She's still upset with him, he can tell, but she squeezes back, her fingers brushing against the long scratch in the webbing between his thumb and pointer finger—a lovely parting gift from Nora's cat when he dropped her off at the neighbor's house yesterday. Its home until Nora gets home from Berlin. Good riddance to that cat. It had always hated him, even though he was the one who fed it most of the time.

"Well," he ventures, "since it's Thanksgiving, should we do our usual thing where we go around the table and say one thing we're thankful for? And then you can each give one guess where the cancer is? Winner gets—"

At this, Hilda bursts into a new round of tears. "Stop it, just *stop* it, Marlen!"

Everyone begins intently studying the things on the table, the silverware, the napkins with the gold-foil autumn leaves around the edges, Hilda's fancy plates that live in the china cabinet and appear only at Thanksgiving, Christmas, and Easter.

Hilda breathes through a sob like it's a contraction, her mouth in a tiny circle. She can't stand Marlen's attitude. He's been cracking jokes since that first appointment, on the way there, on the way home. Jokes about going bald, about tumors, about caskets and cremation. He has the nerve to make jokes about his own corpse—which, at that point, will be more *her* dead husband's body than *his* corpse. Doesn't he understand that this is why it's so crass? You don't make jokes about widows' dead husbands, even when you're the dead husband. It's cruel.

He sulks. What's worse than a terminal cancer diagnosis? Not being allowed to crack jokes about your terminal cancer diagnosis, that's what. Surely his wife knows this is his coping mechanism. Is he not allowed a coping mechanism? Then again, she's upset with him because he won't let her call Nora and tell her "the news," as she calls it. *The news.* Like he's expecting a baby. He doesn't want to tell his only child he's dying and not be able to hug her right after. Is that so terrible? Poor kid's just moved abroad, left everything familiar behind. That stupid boy. That stupid cat.

"I'm so sorry, you guys." Irene is the first to break the awkward silence. Her voice is appropriately soft, full of horror and comfort and pain. "Please let us know how we can be helpful. We'll do whatever we can. We love you guys."

Hilda tries to say thank you, but no sound comes out. Irene reads her lips and nods. They all know this is just the first of many difficult conversations, but for now no one knows what else to say.

"I just need everyone to promise me you'll play good music at my funeral." Marlen gives Hilda a playful little poke, indicating that he *knows* this bothers her—he does—he just needs the mood to be a little lighter. "I want 'Blue Eyes Crying in the Rain' when they wheel me in, 'Baby's in Black' on my way out."

And this time, for some reason, she concedes. She feels herself come down a bit. "You just can't help yourself, can you?" she says quietly.

"I sure can't," says Marlen. He knows she didn't mean that the way he heard it. He hears everything a little differently these days, one of the symptoms of terminal cancer.

They dish their plates, and everyone picks at their food carefully, like paleontologists looking for minuscule dinosaur bones in the mashed potatoes. They're all having some version of the same thoughts, though no one says them out loud because they know they sound slightly unhinged. They're thinking, *This all feels very familiar.* They're thinking, *Maybe when something so awful happens, it feels like it's happened before because you spend so much time over the course of your life imagining awful things happening to you or hearing about them happening to other people.* They're thinking, *Wouldn't everyone else at this table think I was so strange for thinking these things?*

Under the table, Nora's cat settles on Hilda's toes.

3

When Nora gets back to her apartment, her roommates are on the couch, looking at something on a phone.

Nora doesn't know these women very well yet; they're often gone by the time she's awake in the morning, and Petra comes home after she's asleep at night, if she comes home at all. They found each other online, something that had caused Nora's parents excruciating anxiety but doesn't seem like a huge deal to Nora, who has met many people online and knows of many other people who have met many people online. Petra is from Hamburg and is studying molecular medicine at Humboldt; Sonja is from San Diego and is getting her bachelor of music at the University of the Arts. Sonja is warm, flighty, gossipy, outgoing. She has black hair and beautiful green eyes.

Petra is terrifying.

She has a low voice, severe vocal fry, and a way of looking over the rim of her glasses with an air of hokey self-importance. Her face is small, her features sharp, and she speaks with a thick German accent.

But they are exactly as advertised, and that's pretty much all you can ask of people you meet on the internet. That's what Nora said to her mother on the phone the first night. *They're who they said they were.*

(Hilda said she was glad to hear it, but she still sounded anxious and will probably stay anxious until the day Nora moves out.)

"There she is," Petra says when Nora comes through the door. She speaks gruffly, as though they've been waiting awhile. She turns the screen so Nora can see it. "We are buying; it is your welcome-to-the-apartment meal. What do you want?" Her voice is sharp, her words enunciated crisply.

Nora gingerly accepts the phone and examines the screen. The header at the top reads WILLKOMMEN IM SCHNITZELKÖNIG, and the entire take-out menu is, predictably, written in German. "I'm sorry—I don't know what any of this says."

"Right." Petra rolls her eyes, and for a second Nora thinks she's rolling her eyes at *her*, for not knowing German after having lived in Germany for all of one week. But then she adds, in her deadpan croak, "Of course not. Why should you?"

She begins to translate the menu, reading much too fast, then peers over those thick black glasses like a school principal or a judge. Nora panics and chooses a random number—#85—how does one kitchen produce this many combinations of dishes?—and Petra, with no commentary on her choice, leaves the room to make the call. Nora sinks into the scratchy green armchair the other girls found at a flea market the week before Nora's arrival, and her cat jumps onto her lap. She hugs it to her chest. She'd originally planned on leaving the cat back in Saskatchewan with a high school friend, but at the last minute the friend had gotten a job in the city and moved into an apartment there that didn't allow pets. Nora's mom hates this cat, so it wasn't an option to leave it at home. Nora was happy enough to bring it along, but she hadn't expected to feel so dependent on it.

The dependence is one-sided; the cat tolerates the hug for only a moment before it scrambles away, annoyed.

"You'll get used to Petra," Sonja says, her voice low. "She's extreme."

"Oh? I hadn't really noticed." Nora knows this is either her best strength or her tragic flaw—her desire to be liked by everyone and her subsequent ability to pretend as though she doesn't notice anyone else's flaws, even in their absence.

Sonja snorts. "Well, you will."

In the other room, Petra's voice is raised; she's yelling at some poor Schnitzelkönig employee. The look on Sonja's face says, *See?* "She yells at everyone."

Maybe this was a mistake. Nora feels her anxiety spike. "Does she yell at you?"

"Only once or twice. You'll be okay—don't touch her stuff, don't go in her room, clean up after yourself. She's an only child."

Nora nods, like this is a complete explanation, like she herself is not an only child who has never yelled at anyone. Ever.

Petra has finished with the Schnitzelkönig employee; they have probably already quit their job and left the building. She reenters the room, looking perfectly calm, and fixes her sights on Nora. "So," she says. "We have not had a chance to get to know one another."

She leaves the statement hanging, and Nora can't tell whether it was simply an observation or meant to initiate a conversation. She feels as though she's been cornered by a dangerous animal, a bear or something, and there's a rule she's forgetting about what behavior will get her out of the encounter alive. Play dead? Make loud noises? Run?

As absolutely absurd as any of these options would be in this situation, each one feels preferable to standing here making small talk with Petra. Her phone rings in her pocket—most likely her mother, sensing distress in her daughter's strange new world and calling to ask what it is. She peeks at the screen—sure enough.

"Do you need to answer that?" Petra looks amused. She knows, somehow, how she makes Nora feel. Possibly because she's doing it on purpose.

"Yeah. It's my mom," Nora says, her voice small. She feels like a child at a sleepover, her mother calling all the time to check in and make sure she's doing okay.

Petra's dry voice follows Nora as she slips into her bedroom to take the call, condescending and judgmental. "She is always on the phone with her mother."

Nora shuts the door behind her and sits on the bed, where her cat has fallen asleep. The call has gone to voice mail. She wonders what everyone would say if she moved home one week after moving away.

4

The food from yesterday seems to have multiplied; there's so much left-over turkey, they'll be eating it in soups and casseroles and sandwiches for the rest of their lives. Hilda pictures rolling around in it, making nests of it, stuffing pillows with it. Eternal turkey, punishment for bad timing.

The house is hushed, funeral quiet. It's been almost twenty-four hours and still no one has figured out what to say, so instead they make awkward small talk and exchange pitying glances. The old farmhouse is like a bank vault protected by a laser field, but the lasers are quips about the weather and sad, knowing looks. You can't get from the kitchen to the living room without tripping one.

Iver has fallen asleep in front of a football game in the living room, and Hank and Irene have gone into town to get milk. Marlen's taking a nap, too, but in his bed. Ole is off by himself somewhere, seldom seen or heard at family functions these days unless there's food on the table. It feels like forever ago that he and Nora were little and loud, constantly underfoot and always asking questions. Hilda misses that. Then again, she misses everything that happened prior to now. They hadn't known how lovely it had been to be bored, inconvenienced, irritated, sleep deprived. How lovely it had been to be alive and able to ignore death.

The side door swings open, cracking against the wall, loud as a gunshot, and Hilda jumps, flinging a drumstick against the refrigerator.

It's Hank. He doesn't take his boots off, even though it has recently snowed and the driveway is slushy. He leaves a melting gray-brown trail behind him as he clomps across the kitchen, not even glancing at Hilda. Irene appears at the door a second later, out of breath, wide eyed but still present enough to remove her boots.

"Hank," she hisses, casting an apologetic glance at Hilda, "you're making a mess."

He dismisses Irene with a wave of his hand, stumbling around the kitchen, opening cupboards, running his hands along the counters, looking for something.

"Hank?" Hilda retrieves the drumstick from the floor and deposits it in the garbage under the sink. A little less turkey for the freezer; she feels relieved. She swipes at the streak of grease on the fridge with a washcloth. "Is everything okay?"

He gives her a look so incredulous as to be disdainful, as though he can't comprehend how anyone could ask that question right now. At least it's not a pitying glance. Hilda looks to Irene, still hovering by the door. Her face is white.

"Irene? Are *you* okay?"

"Where is your radio? Do you not have a radio?"

Hilda jumps a second time, shocked at the volume of Hank's voice, the sharpness of his tone. Their personalities clash sometimes; he's a little brash, a little inconsiderate, but he's never yelled at her.

"No, I—I don't have one." She feels like she's supposed to explain herself, but she has no explanation, and Hank stares at her, like she's a bad person for not preserving antiquated technology, like she's just admitted to dumping bald eagle eggs in the garbage.

"I'm so sorry, Hilda," says Irene. "He's a bit concerned about something we heard on the way home . . ."

Hilda bristles at the apology. She hates it when her sister apologizes for Hank. "Do you have a radio app on your phone?"

Hank searches his pockets, comes up empty. "Irene!" he barks. "Where's my phone?"

Irene shrugs meekly and Hilda has to turn away. It's not her business, their marriage. She grabs her phone from its charger to distract herself and sees a slew of text messages waiting for her. None of them make any sense.

Do you think this is real?

Hi Hilda R U ok?

Are you seeing this???

Something is happening. Hank's anger that she doesn't have a radio doesn't stem from a love for radios, a desire for their preservation—something is happening, and he wants to know what it is. He's not raging; he's panicking. It should have been obvious, but everything's happening so quickly . . .

She puts the phone down. No, she is not seeing this, not yet, and there is something familiar in her that feels resistant to it, something that knows she doesn't want to know, just wants a few more minutes of ignorance.

"I don't know where you left it," Irene's saying. "Maybe still charging? In the bedroom?"

Hank shakes his head slightly, not like an answer, more like he's moving his brain around to get it going again, and Irene pulls her phone out of her purse. Her brow knits as she scrolls through her own barrage of strange text messages.

Yes, something is happening. Hilda feels like she's cresting the top of a roller coaster. She takes a breath and picks her phone up again. A text from Donna, the neighbor ten miles north: Do you think this is real? One from Sherry, seven miles east: You watching the news? Janet: Turn your TV on now. I can't believe this.

She puts the phone back down. It feels like people are clutching her shoulders, talking all at once. She hates this about smartphones. Before smartphones, if you were safe within the four walls of your home, people had to wait their turn to talk to you, or at least put in the effort to knock on your door. And there was phone etiquette back then too. You didn't just call people up and say, "Turn your TV on now." You said, "Hello, Hilda, how're you? I'm fine, thank you. What are the chances you're watching the news . . . ?" It was calmer. Even emergencies were calmer.

Hank looks like he's ready to run through a wall. "I don't know where my phone is! I don't have time to download an app! I should've stayed in the car!" Then: "TV!" And he's taking off for the living room, his wife and sister-in-law following the path of melting snow he leaves on the floor. Maybe Hank is overreacting. And Irene. And Donna and Sherry and Janet.

But no. Some part of her knows this, somehow, that he's right to run around her house shouting. It's not an inappropriate reaction to news like this.

News like this. She stares at the phone, trying to remember what the news is, exactly. It scratches at her brain like something she has forgotten instead of something she doesn't know yet. What a strange sensation, but not an unfamiliar one. This is how she felt at the doctor's office, too, the day they got the news about Marlen's cancer, right before the doctor opened his mouth. It was like she already knew what he was going to say, even the words she'd never heard before. Is it a trauma thing, to become a bit psychic?

Marlen stumbles from his bedroom, curious about all the yelling, but somehow Iver remains blissfully asleep in the center of the chaos, head back, mouth open.

On the television, the football game has been supplanted by images of the sky, bright and blue and normal—one shot has a city skyline beneath it; another, mountains; another, desert. A Breaking News banner scrolls across the bottom of the screen, the kind that should accompany action—something burning or exploding or being attacked.

Today, nothing but beautiful blue skies. *Breaking news: it is so nice outside.*

Hank turns the volume up as a woman appears on-screen. She's half newly traumatized deer in headlights, half professional never-fazed news anchor, her eyes wide, her voice strong. She has glossy brown hair and is wearing silver hoop earrings, which she plays with absently while waiting for some kind of cue. Her eyes dart to the left, and she nods as someone says something from off screen.

"We're going to be hearing from NASA shortly," says the woman. Everyone looks at one another anxiously. *NASA?* "Keep it locked here for live minute-by-minute coverage."

Hilda has forgotten about the pot of broth on the stove, the heap of shredded turkey on the cutting board next to piles of diced carrots and onions and celery. The bag of frozen peas melting on the counter. Her elderly father snoring at her elbow. The cancer, even. She reaches for Marlen, an automatic reflex usually met with a reciprocal reach, a hand already on her shoulder, anticipating her anxiety, only to find that he's sunk to the couch across the room. For some reason, this is the most alarming thing that has happened today.

The screen goes back to showing shot after shot of an oblivious world. Irene speaks tentatively. "On the radio earlier, I think they said there's been a gamma ray burst . . ."

"Blast," says Hank. "There was a gamma ray *blast.*"

"Burst," Irene says, quietly but firmly.

"Sure," says Hank, like it doesn't really matter. But everyone can see it does matter to him. He likes being right, but unlike Hilda, he isn't right often, because he isn't a very good listener. He sets his mouth into a line, and his eyebrows settle, perfectly parallel, on his forehead. He turns off the television. "I—you know what, I shouldn't have . . . this is probably not a big deal."

Marlen speaks for the first time. His voice is tired, like he's still half-asleep, but everyone's eager to hear what he has to say. Marlen loves logic. He's smart. He teaches high school and knows how to calm a room. "If that's what it is—a gamma ray burst?—we'll be okay."

Irene sneaks a sideways glance at her husband, smug at this confirmation that she was right, but he doesn't notice.

"Well, *that's* a relief," says Hank sarcastically. "Maybe you could let NASA know. 'Hey, NASA, *Marlen* here—I'm a small-town high school English teacher, and I just wanted to let you know that I know a lot about gamma ray blasts, and you really don't need to be throwing a fit . . .'"

Marlen smiles. "I mean, I don't know a *lot* about gamma ray bursts, but it's a topic I've researched a bit."

Marlen's a chronic researcher. His favorite pastime is picking a topic and studying it to death, until he's as close to an expert as one can get without going to school and taking classes. When Hilda first started dating him, pre-internet, he'd owned an entire set of encyclopedias and a large collection of secondhand textbooks for classes he never planned on taking. His high school students have diagnosed him with a few different things, and they're probably not wrong about at least three of them. Kids these days, with their TikTok psychology PhDs . . .

"All right, Mr. Encyclopedia," says Hank. "Hit us with it."

"Ahem," says Marlen, pushing pretend glasses up on his nose. "Okay, so a gamma ray burst is, essentially, what happens when two neutron stars collide or one blows up. Since it happens way out *there*"— he points out the window, and everyone looks where he's pointing, like there might be visible neutron stars colliding in the canola field—"it's actually an event that happened years ago, the effects of which just take a long time for us to know about—kind of neat, eh?"

No one seems to think it's neat. The fact that the colliding or blowing up has already happened seems to imply that their fate is somewhat sealed.

"These kinds of stars are generally too far away for us to know about, but when this happens, they emit a lot of energy. I wanna say . . . ten quadrillion times as much energy as the sun? I think that's the number. So basically the radiation would cook the atmosphere, destroying the ozone layer, which would allow the sun to hit us full force, and *that* would kill off the entire bottom of the food chain—"

"We're all feeling better about this by the minute," says Hank, but Irene places a hand on his arm to shush him.

Marlen raises his eyebrows. "*But*. I've got a couple of big *buts*—" He uses this line often in his English class; it always gets a laugh. It doesn't here, today. "That star—those stars, in the case of a collision—would have to be *very* close to us to have that effect. I'm pulling numbers out of *my* butt here, but I want to say it would have to be closer than fifty light-years away to do damage. And I don't think any of these kinds of stars are that close—the nearest is something like four hundred light-years away. It would also have to be pointed *at* us, I think. We'd have to be unrealistically unlucky on several unrealistic fronts. On top of all that, the ozone layer would do a fairly good job of protecting us from the blast, if it was head-on, and close enough—which, again, both so unlikely. It wouldn't be a mass extinction event by any stretch of the imagination, even the very worst-case scenario. All of this"—he motions at the television, at the phone in Hilda's hands—"is just hysteria."

"Oh," says Irene, eager to feel optimistic. "That's good."

Everyone settles for a moment; each person feels the relief and sudden exhaustion of a subsiding adrenaline rush.

But Hilda frowns. It still feels too familiar, like the night they found the lump. Marlen was too relaxed that night, and now she wonders whether it had been a show then and whether this is a show now. She's never thought of him as a liar or an actor; she's always thought of him as genuine, a what-you-see-is-what-you-get kind of person. What if that just means he's a very *good* actor, a very *good* liar? Maybe he's even fooling himself.

But there's something else. The familiarity isn't limited to Marlen. It's the scenes flashing across the screen, the mud on the rug, the look on Irene's face. The silver hoop earrings on the news anchor. Tripping a déjà vu wire in her brain even though she's never experienced anything like this before.

Marlen leans forward and turns the TV back on.

There's a young man on the screen now. He has owllike eyes, and he looks petrified, as though he has never given a public-facing speech in his life, like he's been plucked straight from his lab and shoved in front of the entire world.

"This morning NASA identified an incredibly rare double gamma ray burst just outside our solar system," he says, his voice trembling. "Gamma ray bursts are the brightest electromagnetic blasts known to occur in the universe and can be a result of the collapse of the largest types of stars or the collision of two neutron stars. Although this is not a new phenomenon, the occurrence of two such events so close together is almost unheard of, and we are working to understand what the effects will be on our planet and on humankind." As though he'd been forgetting to breathe during his speech, the scientist takes a gasping breath, followed by a greedy drink of water and then a few more little breaths that don't seem deep enough to do any good. He continues: "In the event of a single gamma ray burst, our atmosphere is likely thick enough to protect life on Earth from the blast, but at the cost of our ozone layer. In the event of a *double* burst . . ." The scientist swallows several more times; he looks incredibly guilty, as though he were in some way responsible for the explosion. "According to present calculations, the first blast could destroy the atmosphere, and the second blast could . . . affect . . . at least fifty percent of the globe, probab—er, possibly more. The estimated timeline would set the blast to hit our atmosphere sometime between December 27 and January 3. Precision is difficult at this time due to—"

Everyone looks at Marlen to assess how they're supposed to react, and they are alarmed to see all his confidence and calm reassurance has dissipated. He turns the TV off again, and everyone sits in reverential silence for the second time in as many days. It's one thing to learn that someone you love is dying, and it's another thing altogether to learn that *everyone* you love is dying, and you along with them. But, as it turns out, the silence following either revelation is about the same.

"Sounds like we're unrealistically unlucky on several unrealistic fronts," says Hank.

The back door opens; they hear footsteps creaking through the old farmhouse, and finally Ole stands in the doorway to the living room. He almost looks like he's going to walk out again without saying anything, but then he notices his aunt's face, streaked with tears. "What's going on?"

"The world is ending," says Hilda, her voice as small as a mouse squeak from somewhere in the walls. Immediately she shrinks with regret at having said something so alarmist to her nephew, but Ole just snorts. "Okay?" he says, glancing around the room, waiting for someone to acknowledge this as an overstatement. When no one does, he mutters, "Call me when lunch is ready," and retreats up the stairs, the creaking of his footsteps over their heads as loud as if he were still in the room.

They spend the afternoon on their phones and in front of the TV, sharing bits of information as it comes. More information is available every second—too much information for anyone to process in one sitting. Gathering it feels important, even though none of it is definitive or conclusive or helpful.

"This article says it could be much sooner than the twenty-seventh; they're just trying not to panic everybody," says Hilda. She's the most agitated person in the room—after all, she is a mother whose child is not with her. Worse, her child is not answering her frantic phone calls.

Maybe Nora's working. Maybe she's out with friends. Maybe she doesn't know the world is ending—though this seems impossible for someone who was born in the iPhone age. She basically downloads news updates directly into her brain.

"Says here it's *three* bursts, not just two," says Hank. He has calmed down considerably, but Hilda thinks it might be false bravado; he's picking up Marlen's slack.

Marlen, come to think of it, hasn't said a word in quite a while. She glances at him, worried, and he offers what's probably meant to be a comforting smile. There's a small tear on the sleeve of his T-shirt, a muscle twitching in his eyebrow. It's interesting, the little details that float through the haze of heavy news cycles, how the brain reaches for those light things when it can't handle the heavy stuff.

Iver wakes up. He's been out for hours. They tell him what's going on, and his reaction is similar to Ole's, though he at least pretends he's as concerned about the end of the world as the rest of them. "This is awful," he says, and waits the appropriate amount of time before he adds, "Have you all eaten already?"

5

The rainbow-haired teenagers are trying to teach Nora how to make latte art. It looks easy when they do it—between the two of them, they can achieve a latte bear, a latte stack of hearts, a latte sparrow, a latte fern, and a latte Freddie Mercury (the tall teenager, whose name is Millie, does this one, and she acts as though this niche skill has come quite naturally to her, like everyone should be able to make Freddie Mercury appear in lattes if they aren't total idiots).

Nora is only able to make an unappetizing latte glop that looks like a bird has just flown overhead . . .

The rainbow-haired teenagers are annoyed with her. Latte art is easy, they keep saying, like they think Nora is being purposely obtuse. The one named Millie has made three Freddie Mercurys just this morning, and they're starting to feel pointed.

"I give up," says Nora, after her eighth consecutive glop.

"You are not allowed to give up," says Millie, rolling her eyes. She whispers something in German to the other barista, and this feels pointed too.

Nora sighs and tamps fresh grounds into the portafilter. The other option in this work-abroad program was a cheese-making internship. She hadn't even entertained it, because making cheese sounded harder than making coffee. But now she sees she was probably wrong—surely making cheese is easier than this. Surely everything is easier than this.

The shop is busy today. This is the part of the job Nora likes—the people. Strangers, people with no context, still feel like such a novelty. Today there's a woman at the table by the window, the one where Nora and Jacob had their first meeting, hair and makeup done as though for a wedding, wearing sweatpants tucked into large, puffy boots. She's talking loudly on her phone, able to ignore the dirty looks from the other customers in a way that suggests she is very used to people giving her dirty looks and either doesn't understand the meaning of them or doesn't care. She would do well working with Millie.

At the table beside hers sit a couple of young men, the number-one source of dirty looks being cast in her direction. They have completely abandoned whatever conversation they'd come here to have and are solely focused on causing the woman to understand how disruptive she's being.

At the next table, a student on a laptop, dressed all in black, shockingly white hair, mile-long eyelashes. Seemingly oblivious that at the table across the room a guy has been looking at her about ten times as much as at the novel he brought, which is starting to seem like a prop; he might as well be holding it upside down. He has short, fluffy, curly hair and thick, fuzzy eyebrows that sit low over his eyes.

Next to his table, an older lady and a teenage boy. The only ones in the shop speaking English. She might be a guidance counselor, because she's asking him about his "plans," but his voice is so low Nora can't hear what he's saying back. Maybe they're an unexpected bank robber duo. Maybe they're planning a heist.

At the last table, a troubled-looking man who probably always looks troubled even when he isn't. He's sitting at a table, staring at the neon sign behind the counter like that's what's troubling him, but a minute ago it was the table in front of him, and before that it was something out the window. Trouble everywhere.

And then that trouble materializes. There's an extra-loud exclamation from the woman by the window. The rainbow-haired baristas shoot withering stares in her direction. They have very little tolerance for displays of emotion, noises above a certain volume, people who don't catch on to things that should be easy to catch on to.

But now the lady is talking to the men at the table next to hers, turning the screen of her phone so they can see it, and Nora watches something crawl through the room, from the men to the student to the prospective bank robbers to the troubled old man—information of some kind, from table to table, like a rapid plague.

The other baristas notice it too; they pull out their phones and start to scroll, but Nora's phone is in the back, inside her purse, turned off. She's on a limited international data plan and mostly doesn't use it when she's out of range of her apartment's Wi-Fi. It's been liberating, coming here and feeling freed from the constancy of phones—social media, ongoing text conversations, the obligation to return phone calls as soon as possible. She can pretend her ex isn't calling her because he can't, not because he doesn't want to.

But now she realizes she's isolated herself; she's floating alone in space, watching the people on Earth scurry around like ants, but she doesn't know why they're so upset.

Soon the back room door opens and Jacob appears. He's been working on the books in the office, one of his many part-time jobs at Begonia. He looks calm, but in a put-on way, like a kindergarten teacher trying to herd children through a zoo on a field trip, a person who has to appear to be okay, no matter what. "Everybody!" he says loudly. *"Alle!"* Like a few of his kindergartners have crawled into the lion's cage and he needs to extricate them without exciting the animals.

But the room is in a panic, and no one hears him. People grab their purses and jackets and head for the door. If Jacob had been about to ask them to leave, it's unnecessary now. The shop is empty.

He turns to the three behind the counter.

Millie has never appeared to be anything but disgusted, but right now she's just scared; she looks her age for once. There's a brief discussion, in German, and the baristas leave. Nora, finally, asks the question, though she's not sure she wants to know the answer.

"What's going on?"

Jacob turns to her, uncertain. "I don't really know . . . ," he begins. He seems to be sizing her up, trying to figure out how to tell her something, wondering if she can handle it.

She doesn't like this. This silent assessment feels similar to Petra's the other day, when she'd observed how often Nora talked to her mom on the phone. He's much kinder than Petra, of course, but it still speaks volumes to Nora about how easy she is to read, about how her naivete emanates from her like a visible aura, broadcasting to everyone that she's helpless. She's dependent. She's a child.

Which is not fair, because she's not any of these things. She just hasn't had a chance yet to prove it to anyone. Not even to herself.

"What's going on?" she asks again. She tries to stand up straighter.

"Ida wants me to close for the rest of the day."

"But why?"

"Because the world is . . ."

"Is what?"

"Well, it's probably not actually . . ."

"Not *what*?"

"They're *saying* the world is ending."

"That's not funny," she says, assuming this is a joke meant to soften the blow of the actual news.

"I don't think so either," he says. He looks like he might cry.

They stand silently in the empty coffee shop. She waits patiently for the punch line.

Jacob drives her home. As she climbs out of his car, a mustard-colored Corsa with a sticky passenger-side door, he wishes her luck.

This feels ominous. "You think I'm going to need luck?"

"Aren't we all?"

She still isn't sure what the extent of the situation is. She's been afraid to ask any more questions. It feels like a thing that should be processed in the relative privacy of her apartment.

"Good luck to you, too, then," she says.

"Thanks." He tries to smile at her. "Oh, and I'll be in touch, or Ida will, about if we're open tomorrow and whatnot."

"You don't think we will be?"

He looks at her, sizing her up again. "Maybe. I hope we will be."

When she closes her apartment door behind her, her phone connects to the Wi-Fi and begins to light up with text messages and notifications. Her mother's number appears on the screen, and she swipes it away. The Top Stories widget dings with articles from the BBC, the Canadian Press, CTV.

She looks all over for that punch line, but she can't find it.

The world, it would seem, is ending. And when she finally accepts this fact, she finds she's not overly surprised by it. She tries to pick up her cat; she needs a hug.

But the cat doesn't want a hug, so no hug is had.

Sonja is still in her bedroom, and she hasn't given any indication that she knows what's going on. Nora taps tentatively on the door before she's even thought about what to say. How do you share news like this? She feels flashes of conflicting emotions—horror, excitement, guilt, dread. Something is bubbling up inside her, and she worries that she's going to start laughing, that she won't be able to calm herself down. She recognizes it—hysteria.

"Come in?"

Now she can't imagine laughing. "Hey, Sonja."

"Hey, what's up?" Sonja smiles brightly, oblivious to the strange energy Nora brings with her into the room. Sonja is not a perceptive person. She calls herself an empath, but maybe this is what she wants to be more than what she is. She's hunched over her foot, painting strokes of fire engine red onto her toenail. She looks straight into Nora's face and somehow misses the terror, the apprehension, possibly even the frown.

"Uh . . ." Nora shakes her head. What's she supposed to say? *Hey, Sonja, FYI, the end is near?*

"Oh, *question*." Sonja caps the nail polish and sets it on her night table next to three coffee mugs, an empty cup, and a pill bottle. "Do you want to come with me to a house party tomorrow night? I met a guy at ALDI—we were in the produce aisle and got talking, and he invited me, and I said okay, but then I was like, maybe I shouldn't go alone to a guy's house who I met at *ALDI* . . ." She rolls her eyes and gives Nora a look like, *Isn't it so annoying to be so nonchalantly glamorous that men fall all over you while you're just trying to shop for carrots?*

Nora has never met a guy at ALDI, or any other grocery store, for that matter. She hadn't realized that was a possibility.

"So? Up for it?" Sonja's eyes are glittering; she has never met someone her age who hasn't been up for it, regardless of what 'it' was.

"Well—actually, Sonja . . . have you checked your phone lately?"

"Why? Is something wrong?"

Nora can only nod, and Sonja begins rummaging around in the covers, hunting for her phone, holding her freshly painted foot aloft in something like a yoga pose as she twists to each side. When she finds it, she scrolls and taps and types for an agonizing amount of time, her face oddly neutral. Then, without saying a word, she stands and marches out of the room, out of the apartment, Nora trailing curiously behind her.

It feels, for some reason, like she shouldn't call after Sonja, like how you're not supposed to wake a sleepwalker. Sonja descends the stairs quickly, gaining speed with each flight, but comes to an abrupt halt in the doorway of the apartment building, holding the heavy glass door open with one hand, peering tentatively out to the street.

Nora stops just behind her; she can see from here that Sonja's face is white, her hand on the door trembling, her body swaying slightly.

"You okay?"

Sonja doesn't seem to hear her.

"Just need some fresh air?"

No answer.

They're still too new to each other; Nora doesn't know if she should reach out and pat the girl's back, brace her against falling, give her a hug. She looks past Sonja into the street, which is strangely empty. Maybe this is why Sonja came downstairs, to see if the real world matches the surreal things she read on her screen.

It doesn't, Nora decides. It looks the same as always, just less busy—not like an apocalypse, more like a Sunday morning.

A man in a suit and dress shoes runs past, full speed, his feet clacking loudly on the sidewalk, and breaks the spell. Sonja flinches. She turns to look at Nora, and her eyes are large behind her thick black curtain bangs. "I can't . . ." She trails off and turns away again, watching the street for something that will confirm or refute her worst fears.

"I can't either," says Nora unhelpfully.

6

When Marlen was nine, he became a prophet.

He knew what prophets were only because of his best friend, whose aunt was a Pentecostal—and he only sort of understood what *those* were. That kid had all kinds of stories about his aunt—she spoke in tongues; she prophesied; she even claimed she could heal people (only sometimes, and only very small, particular ailments, and only during the summer, and only if her husband wasn't available, and so on; there were more stories that ended with explanations of why a certain person couldn't be healed than ones that ended with healings).

One day, at recess, the kid said to Marlen, "Apparently anyone can be a prophet."

And Marlen said, "Not me. I'm not a Pentecostal."

And the kid said, "I don't think that matters."

Marlen was intrigued. He might like to have this particular superpower, even if there were other, better superpowers more attractive to him, like flight or invisibility. But the best superpower was the one available to you. "How do we check?"

The kid thought about it for a moment and said, "I think you just say something and see if it comes true. If it comes true, you're a prophet. If it doesn't, you're a *false* prophet."

"What happens to false prophets?"

"They go to hell."

"What if I'm just not a prophet, but not a *false* prophet?"

The kid shook his head. "If you prophesy and it doesn't come true, you're a false prophet. You go to hell."

The stakes seemed high, but Marlen was too curious to let hell factor into his decision-making. *Besides,* he thought, *maybe God could forgive a nine-year-old for getting it wrong.* "So I just say something?"

"Anything, yeah."

"Like, *There will be five hundred chocolate bars at my desk when we go inside?*"

The kid shook his head again. "It has to be about someone else. You have to prophesy *over* someone. You can't prophesy *over* yourself. I don't think."

The exaggerated *over* evoked for Marlen frightening images of a grizzled old woman with long fingers stretching *over* him across the sky.

The friend said to Marlen, "Try prophesying over me."

"Okay," said Marlen, an adorable little boy at that point, with the biggest teeth in the grade three class. He held up his small hands, stretched them *over* his friend's head. "You're going to get hit in the head with a baseball."

The kid's eyes bugged out. "What? Why that? Why not something nice?"

Marlen closed his eyes halfway. "That's what popped into my head," he said gravely. "I didn't want to mess it up."

Two days later the prophesy was fulfilled.

(It wasn't a baseball—it was a football—but *still.* The boys were rattled.)

It had been one of those experiences for Marlen. Mystical, something that made him wonder—*was* he a prophet? Would that kid have been hit in the head with anything if Marlen hadn't said so? Was it going to happen regardless, or had he spoken it into being?

He forgot about this brief foray into the world of Pentecostalism for years, but he's thinking about it again today. Hilda doesn't know this, but Marlen knew he was going to die long before the doctor told them he was terminally ill, long before Hilda pushed him to get checked out. Not in a fortune-telly way, with the word *cancer* in his head and a clear vision of his family wearing black and crying in a church—it was subtler than that.

He knew he was going to die because he woke up one morning, about a year ago now, and had this thought: *I need to write my book.*

His book was something he'd been thinking about for almost as far back as he could remember, since he was twelve or thirteen and had discovered, thrillingly, that authors were normal people who just so happened to also be published by other normal people. A goal within his reach, something that would become a recurring daydream. Over the years he constructed the book in his head—or, rather, it constructed itself, and he observed it. Characters sprang into being, a plot began to unfold; it was like watching a bed of flowers grow from seed. Someday, he always thought to himself, he was going to write that book, and he was going to get it published and hold it in his hands. Other people were going to read it.

But, like most people with a lifelong aspiration, all he ever did was daydream about it. Writing a book in theory is easier than writing a book in actuality, especially when you have a job, a wife, a kid, other hobbies, friends . . . so his dream had become more and more far away and unreal, like it was a dream about being taller or marrying a famous actress, something that couldn't be accomplished simply by deciding one day to actually do it.

Until that morning when he woke up and thought, *I need to write my book.*

And the thought beneath that thought, which was really more of an impression, was, *And I need to hurry it up, because I don't have a lot of time.*

Maybe that was why he hadn't felt all that urgent about getting the lump checked out, why Hilda practically had to drag him there. He knew the cancer wasn't beatable.

So that, in and of itself, confirms Marlen's calling as a modern-day prophet. He's two for two: the kid with the Pentecostal aunt got beaned in the head with a ball, and he is going to die.

Ah—but there's more.

The book Marlen wrote—yes, he got to it right away, quietly work-ing on it at school in spares and lunch breaks, seventy thousand words in nine months—is about a gamma ray burst. He'd done the research, just as he told his family, but it had been with something specific in mind for once. He'd entertained the worst-case scenarios, pictured the sky turning so white-yellow that human eyes couldn't perceive it as any-thing but pitch black. He watched the calamity play out in his mind's eye—so vivid it gave him a headache—and wrote it down. In his novel the world ends in a violent blast, the result of two stars colliding way out in space, so far away as to feel impossibly inconsequential—like a girl batting her eyelashes in Tokyo and knocking down a building in Vancouver.

This was, incidentally, the first piece of the novel that came to him, as a teenager, before the setting, the characters, any of it—one violent explosion, as though the beginning of the book was born out of the end. He'd always thought this had to do with the fact that he was a teenage boy, and teenage boys like explosions. Now he understands that it has more to do with the fact that he's a prophet (kind of like the kid's Pentecostal aunt: not a prophet all the time, or even most of the time, but a prophet nonetheless).

The feeling of divine urgency led him to publish with a small local subsidy press, instead of trying to figure out how to get someone else to do it (he'd entertained this possibility for all of three minutes before realizing that the traditional publishing process is A Whole Thing, requiring years and years of query letters and literary agents and editing and self-promotion).

He had not let it slip to a single soul that he was writing this book; his plan was to upload the file, get the printed copies in the mail, and surprise Hilda. One last present for her, a tangible memento of him, while also achieving his lifelong dream, two massive birds with one substantial stone.

Hilda was in the book, and he hoped she didn't read too much into it that she died in the end. He was trying to make a point with this: simply, that everyone dies, that *his* death wasn't going to be special or particularly unfair. It was meant to be a tribute to their family, a commentary on grief, on love, on relationships when time is short. A love letter to a lot of people, but especially to his wife. In this way, he processed his own demise well before that day in the doctor's office, and in doing so he has processed the end of the world, accidentally, as well.

It had been quite the surreal experience, sitting in the living room surrounded by his family, watching his story come to life. He hasn't quite processed *that* yet.

But right now, his main problem is this: he has a stack of books arriving in the mail any day, and he can't imagine anyone's going to want to read them. It's a bit too soon, isn't it? It feels irreverent. For example, what if one of his friends, upon hearing of his cancer diagnosis, had come to him and said, "Marlen, what a coincidence! I actually wrote a book about you dying of cancer! Here's a copy. Read it before you go."

He wouldn't have liked that very much at all.

It feels like a riddle. *When do you do something if now is too soon but there is no later?*

7

Hank and Irene drop Iver off at his house in town before continuing on to theirs just north. The car is quiet after he gets out, no more small talk.

Hank doesn't want to talk, for once, but Irene doesn't want to sit in silence. Ole notices this from the back seat, the way his mother keeps asking how his father's feeling, what he's thinking, what he thinks other people are thinking and feeling, what he thinks will happen next. He notices how his father answers with grunts and shrugs.

For the first time Ole begins to feel uneasy. Is the world actually ending? What would that even look like? The end of the world would mean the end of *him*, of his consciousness, of his existence, but that doesn't feel right or possible. Maybe it means a continuation in another place or another state, but that feels absurd, too, frightening.

Ole closes his eyes and tries to imagine nothingness, but of course he can't, because even with his eyes closed he is present in this car, with these people, the smells and the sounds and even the red glow of the sun on his eyelids. It's not the event that scares him; it's the fact that he can't picture the part after it, and this fear is so vague and enormous that it makes him dizzy. It's like standing on a bridge over the Grand Canyon in the dark, knowing there is vast emptiness under you but not being able to see it. It occurs to him that there has already been a time where he didn't exist—most of the time in the history of the universe, actually. Why doesn't the thought of not having existed *before* bother him as much as the thought of not existing *after*? It's the same exact thing!

No, wait, the thought of not existing before is also very hard for his brain to chew on; he just hadn't thought of it until now. If brains could throw up, his would be frantically working to expel everything inside of it right now.

"Ole? Honey? You all right?" His mother is twisted in her seat, trying to catch his eye.

He shrugs and grunts, emulating his father. The only thing worse than finding out it's the end of the world is having to talk through your feelings about it with your mom. Still, guilt gnaws at him. He loves his mom. He doesn't want her to feel bad. He wishes there were a way to communicate telepathically with her so she'd know he's not mad; he's just freaked out about the Grand Canyon thing, but he doesn't want to say it out loud.

Irene turns forward again. She is fully aware that no one in this car wants to talk to her. But why is it more important for them to get what they want than for her to get what she wants?

"We only have two months left to talk to each other," she says in a low voice so Hank will hear but not Ole.

But Ole hears anyway, and from the back seat comes a quiet "Good."

He's not sure why he says this. He's not sure he had a choice; it just came out. He loves his mom; he hadn't meant it. He feels bad. He feels a lot of things, and he isn't sure what to do with any of it.

Both Ole and Irene turn their heads to their respective windows so their family won't see them cry.

8

Everyone left yesterday, and the parting was weird. Hilda felt irrationally clingy, almost angry, and when the door closed behind them, she'd opened it up again so she could watch them drive away. Then she'd gone inside and crawled into bed with all her clothes on, even her house slippers, and Nora's cat came and lay on her ankles. Normally Hilda would've shooed the cat off the bed, out of her bedroom, but right then it felt comforting to have it there, a stand-in for Nora, who has not yet answered her phone.

She frowned down at the cat, suddenly remembering a promise her daughter made to her a few months ago that the cat would go to stay with a friend when Nora left for Berlin. So much for that.

(And in that moment, Hilda felt oddly thankful.)

Now she's sitting in the kitchen, thinking about all of it, about the apocalypse, about people leaving when there's limited time left to be with them, about how feelings that aren't anger feel exactly like anger. Marlen appears in the doorway, hovering there like he's unsure about whether he wants to fully enter the room or not. This is how he moves through the house these days, and at first it made Hilda sad, but now she has decided that she just hates it. She wants him to *commit*. She wants him to do what he used to do—enter a room singing, wrapping his arms around her, kissing her neck, telling her some weird piece of trivia he encountered that day, a fact about trees or oceans or an extinct species she's never heard of.

"Come in and sit," she says, more brusquely than she means to. He looks wounded, and she hates that too.

"I was thinking I might go to bed . . ."

She glances at the clock. "It's not even eight yet."

"Well, you know, Hildy. I've been so tired lately."

His face is gaunt and slack and gray. "Right. Sorry." She wants to find the compassion she'd had just last week. It had burst out of her then. She'd been a garden of compassion, blooming at the sight of him, at the thought of him, everything in her reaching for him like he was the sun in the sky. But now he's like the kitchen that needs painting, and she can't shake the pointlessness of painting a kitchen that's going to be obliterated, and she's annoyed that the kitchen still thinks it *needs* painting. She is no longer a garden; she's a resentful old farmwife now, a bed of weeds. And she's going back and forth between feeling bad about it and justifying it—after all, she's dying, too, now. Where's his compassion for *her*? Doesn't she need some moral support now, the stuff she'd shown him in his first hours and days processing the end of his life?

"Okay," she says, "well, I'll come, too, in a bit. I'm going to try calling Nora again." At the mention of Nora's name, the cat jumps up onto the table. Hilda shoos her off.

Marlen sighs, and his face seems to grow even longer. "Have you tried calling her boss?"

"Yes, yes, of course. She was really rude, said she wasn't sure why she'd know where her employees are when they're not at work."

"We should call her roommates."

Hilda stares at him. "I *have* called them. Multiple times each."

"They're not answering either?"

"No. I keep getting the one girl's answering machine, and the other girl doesn't have one; it just rings. Also, I'm fairly certain I told you all this already—"

"Can't we book a flight for her ourselves? Or go to her?"

"I told you this too—I've been *trying*. All of the airlines' websites are down." Hilda takes a breath. It's not right to be so frustrated with him; he's in a fog these days. He forgets things as she's saying them, it's not his fault. "If I know my girl, she's trying to book her own flights, trying to figure everything out on her own before she talks to us, and she's probably telling her roommates not to take our calls either. She reminds me of *someone* . . ."

Marlen sighs again—though, on second thought, Hilda isn't sure if it's a sigh or just a labored breath. "Are you still upset that I wouldn't let you tell her about my cancer?"

"No."

"Really." He leans forward, trying to get a closer look at her face. "I don't believe you."

Hilda flushes. She's always loved this about him, that he calls her bluff when she acts like she doesn't care about something or isn't upset. He gives her that look when she starts to shut down, and she can't help but open up again. She's glad that's still here, that he's still perceptive. "I'm not *upset*," she says. "I just don't understand why the two of you think it's your job to save everyone else's feelings."

"That's not why—"

"Yes, it is, Marlen. You didn't want to tell her you had cancer over the phone because you wanted to be there to control her reaction. And she doesn't want to talk to *us* right now for the exact same reason."

Marlen's quiet for a moment. "Well, if that *is* what we're doing, is it so bad—"

"Yes, actually. Because the people around you would like a little *autonomy*, Marlen. Nora would probably like to be treated like an adult, and I know *I* would like my daughter to answer her phone when I call her, and I want her to give it to me straight even if all she has to say is, 'Mom, I'm stuck here, and I don't think I'll ever see you again,' and if that is what she says, well . . ."—Hilda's mouth wobbles, and red splotches appear suddenly around her eyes—"then I will head straight to the ocean and start swimming. As it is, I just feel *so*—why are you looking at me like that?"

He's smirking a little, but it's a Marlen smirk, not irritating or condescending. "You think she's not calling home because she's like me. I think it's because she's like you."

"Me?"

"Yeah. I don't think she's trying to control other people's emotions. I think she's just growing up into a strong and independent woman. Like her mom."

The doorbell rings, and Hilda presses her fingers to her temples. She takes a deep breath, and an enormous smile appears on her face, just like that—her ability to instantaneously transform is a skill that has always startled and amazed Marlen and given him the oddest sensation that he is married to a robot whose facial expressions are controlled by buttons just beneath the skin, in that space right above the ears.

"I wonder who that could be!" Her voice is bright and just a little tight; she's only slightly breathless. She's incredible; she should win an Oscar. She rushes to the door and opens it.

He hears a quiet, muffled exchange, and Hilda comes back carrying a large box.

He raises his eyebrows. "What's that?"

"Don't know—it's heavy. And it's got your name on it." She drops it on the table; it lands with a weighty *thud*.

Right. He had hoped it might arrive when she was out.

"You going to open it?"

He shakes his head. "No. Not now."

Curiosity flickers across her face.

"It's textbooks," he says. "I ordered them for school. Who knows, now, if I'll even need them." He tries to look sad, like opening this box and looking at these textbooks would just be too hard right now.

Sometimes he's a good actor too.

9

Nora gazes out the window at chimneys and rooftops. What she wouldn't give for the crusty rainbow-haired teenagers to flaunt their Freddie Mercurys in front of her right now. Instead, she's sitting in her kitchen, staring at the text she got from Jacob early this morning.

> Hey Nora. This is Jacob from Begonia. Ida says we're going to stay closed for a few days while we see what's going on. She says to let you know that if you need to/are able to fly home, please make that your priority. Good luck; let us know if you need ANYTHING.

Berlin is in emergency mode; Nora feels it more than sees it. No one is out in the streets yet, screaming or rioting, but every single person is doing these things in their minds, and it's palpable.

When she first read the news, she expected to look out the window and see fires, violent crime, screaming children. Maybe that's what Sonja had been expecting, too, when she rushed down the stairs and opened the door. But there was just this eerie silence, and this was worse than all those things. They'd come back into the apartment and Sonja had immediately gone to work painting her other toenails like nothing had happened, bringing that eerie silence into their flat.

Nora's mother's phone calls have begun to increase in frequency—at first they came every twenty minutes, then every ten, then every two.

Now they come repeatedly, with no breaks in between, and Nora can't answer them, though she desperately wants to. If her mother's voice had been merely comforting before, it's necessary now. It's the only sound she wants to hear. She needs to know her parents are okay, they are safe, they have a plan.

They *will* have a plan.

But isn't this part of becoming an adult and moving away from home? Hearing big news and deciding for yourself how you're going to process it and what you're going to do about it? Nora wants a chance to prove—not to Petra, not to Jacob, to herself—that she's not a child, that she's not dependent or weak. This is going to be her *only* chance. Ever.

The first problem—and possibly the only one that matters—presents itself almost immediately. Governments begin advising people to return home as soon as possible and to avoid unessential travel, leaving billions of individuals to decide what "essential travel" is at the end of the world. These billions of individuals, in turn, decide that being where they want to be is essential. For many of them, this isn't a place they can get to by car or airplane, but the place you can fly to is at least something tangible, unlike the place you wish you were emotionally or romantically or relationally or spiritually or whatever, so everyone immediately begins booking flights.

Nora pulls up an airline website to book flights home only to discover that it crashes every time she clicks the "Dates" button.

She texts Jacob back.

Thanks Jacob. Let me know if you need anything too, k?

She regrets it immediately. As if she could help anyone. She can't even help herself.

Time is weird when you're running out of it. It passes in clumps, like clods of mud falling off the wheel wells of a car—hanging on, then suddenly letting go. One minute seems to last an eternity, then four hours are gone—and it feels like a tragic loss every time, considering how few of them are left in general.

Sonja emerges from her bedroom sometime after the sun rises on what Nora thinks must be the second day, but which feels like the fortieth, a look on her face that clearly says, *I need us to pretend like nothing is wrong.*

So, because Nora is a bit of a people pleaser, they do.

More clumps of time fall off, and finally Petra comes home from wherever she's been. Nora's relieved to see her. She's been continually refreshing the airline websites, one after another, over and over, because that's all she can think to do, and Sonja won't even acknowledge that things have gotten very, very weird. So here, at last, is someone to talk to, someone who will acknowledge the gravity of the situation. She can even yell about it, for all Nora cares; that might feel good.

"Hey, Petra."

"Hey." Petra has a woolen blazer slung over her arm and a back-pack on the other shoulder; she looks tired but not bothered, not like someone who has just found out the world is ending. She bends down to pet Nora's cat, which stands perfectly still for her, staring adorably up into her face. This nonchalance feels wrong.

"How're you doing?"

"Fine."

"And, um . . ."

Petra turns and raises her eyebrows, waiting.

"I'm assuming you've seen the news?"

Petra gives one quick nod but doesn't speak. She looks like she's still waiting for something.

"Are you . . . okay?"

Petra nods again. "Oh yes. I find it fascinating, honestly," she says, setting the backpack down.

Sonja peeks out of her bedroom. "Hi, Petra."

"Hey."

"Are you okay?"

Now Petra looks suspicious, like she thinks her roommates might know something she doesn't. She studies Sonja, then Nora, and picks up her backpack once again. "Am I not supposed to be okay?"

Sonja opens her door the rest of the way and leans on the frame. "No, I just thought that, given the news—"

"*Yes*, the news. Do you not find it fascinating?" There's that ridiculously out-of-place word again. Petra clocks their disbelief. "What? It is not as if I thought I would live forever, or that the world would last forever, and this is a very interesting way for it all to end."

Sonja looks stricken, as though Petra has slapped her across the face, but Petra doesn't seem to notice; she crosses to her bedroom and tosses her backpack inside. They hear it land softly on her bed, and she tosses her blazer in after it. She moves to the kitchen sink and washes her hands, as she always does before touching anything when she enters the apartment. She talks as she moves, her voice a grating monotone. "My friends and I cannot stop talking about it." She wipes her hands, then clutches the towel for a moment, staring around the kitchen like she's trying to remember what she had been about to do. "I do not think people grasp the rarity of this. The odds of an event of this magnitude happening during our lifetime . . ." She finds an apple in the fridge and studies it. Apparently it doesn't meet her standards; she puts it back and grabs another. "I cannot help but feel . . . special." It's like she's confused about the meanings of some very specific words. *Special. Fascinating. Interesting.* "An event like this will happen once in all of human history, and here we are to witness it. It is going to be . . ." She waves the acceptable apple in the air; she looks like a high-society lady at a cocktail party, trying to describe an opera or a symphony instead of a catastrophe, a fancy glass in her hand instead of an apple. "Beautiful, actually. Did you know that at the very end the air will turn to plasma? Our lungs will not know what to do with it. We will all, collectively, hold our breath, as a planet, as though waiting to see what comes next . . ."

Nora sneaks a glance at Sonja, who looks like she's going to faint. She's gone from ignoring the situation altogether to being told that she is going to suffocate along with the entire human race before being fried to death.

Petra bites into her apple and leaves the room without another word; the sound of her teeth piercing into the crisp flesh hangs in the air until it's replaced by the soft click of Petra's bedroom door.

Sonja swallows hard, her eyes enormous. She lowers her voice to a whisper. "Her whole family is like that. I met them when she moved in. Weird vibes."

Nora can't stop thinking about the plasma thing. It's a hideous mental image, not beautiful, not poetic like Petra has deemed it to be. The whole planet, the children and all the pets, everyone unable to breathe at the same time?

"Heyyyy, hey, hey, hey." Sonja is patting her shoulder now, playing the role of the empath. "Don't cry. We're both going to get home, and it's all going to be okay."

Nora's phone lights up with a text from her mother.

Nora, please call your father. He is about to blow a gasket. Jeg elsker deg.

She smiles, hearing her mother's voice in her head, her signature slip into Norwegian to say *I love you.* It's not that she doesn't want to call them—she wishes they understood.

She swipes at her eyes and clicks one of twenty open tabs on her laptop. *One seat. One way. Berlin to Saskatoon. Flexible dates. Search.*

Wonder of wonders: there it is.

Heart pounding, she punches in her credit card numbers, double-checks the date, and presses the purchase button. Now she can call her parents, tell them, yes, I've seen the news, yes, I'm hearing that it's probably really bad, but we will be together in two weeks and twenty hours, and we can see what happens from the (fingers crossed) safety of our creaky old farmhouse.

Maybe they'll be impressed by the way she's taken charge, solved the problem on her own. Maybe they'll even feel relieved that they don't have to do anything for once.

But as she picks up the phone, her email pings with a new message. She reads the first few words with a pit in her stomach:

> We're sorry, there has been an error completing your transaction. Please contact your credit card company . . .

Perhaps her pessimism is the reason she doesn't feel surprised or disappointed by this.

Sonja raises an eyebrow. "You okay?"

But Nora knows Sonja doesn't want to talk about the end of the world, so she smiles and says she's fine. She focuses on a crack in the wall that runs from the corner of the window up to the ceiling and wills herself not to cry again.

Special! Fascinating! Interesting!
Beautiful, actually!

10

Sometimes Iver is lonely, and sometimes he is just alone. Same as how he sometimes feels elderly, and sometimes he just feels older. Oldish. Old, as a matter of fact, but not in a way that makes him feel bad. Same realities, different emotional impacts, and he doesn't know what makes the difference from one day to the next, why one day he'll wake up and grief will wash over him and drown him in his bed, and the next day he'll wake up in the same empty room and understand that this is just how it is now. He thinks of his late wife. She always used to repeat that quote about containing multitudes, and he thinks, *I contain multitudes, too, but only sometimes. And sometimes I'm as empty and echoey as a Quonset.*

Today is an empty day. He is aware that there is no one with him in his old, dirty house, that he'll eat every meal alone and speak to no one if he doesn't make the effort to venture out, to call his friend Arnold to meet him for coffee, but he's not bothered by it at all. These days are nice, just the fact that they exist.

When you lose someone you love so much, you go through a time so low and terrible you think you'll never feel neutral ever again, but here he is. Look at him go! Neutral as beige. He regards his wife's reading chair with the crocheted blanket thrown over the back, the unfinished novel on the seat, untouched for years, with an almost detached appreciation for what they had, acknowledging that this is what they have now. He notes his son's child-size baseball hat still hanging on a hook by the door, an important symbol but not a dagger to the heart, thinks of the Thanksgiving dinner with his daughters and their beautiful families without wishing they'd invite him over more often. Knows that the world will end in a matter of months without feeling shaken.

He's known for a while now that the end is near, one way or the other. Might as well end now, before he ends up in a home or loses what's left of his vision. Might as well fry to death; that's fine.

What a gift, one he doesn't take for granted, to be able to interact with reality without being hurt by it. He pours himself a cup of coffee and drinks without waiting for it to cool. It doesn't burn his tongue, but it tastes terrible; his coffeepot has needed cleaning for years now. He dumps it down the sink and heads for the front entryway, stubbing his toe on the doorframe on his way out of the kitchen. It doesn't hurt at all.

He will go get himself a coffee that doesn't taste like fertilizer water.

The Pot Hole is the town's only coffee shop. Its name is an homage to coffeepots and terrible roads, and it's owned by a sweet silver-haired fiftysomething-year-old woman named Alfie, who for sure did not consider that this was a name more appropriate for a cannabis dispensary than a café. Alfie also owns the trading post across the street and runs the book club at the "library" that takes up one wall at the senior citizens center. She sometimes works at the grocery store when the owner has to go into the city for doctors' appointments, and she is responsible for every single baby and wedding shower and funeral luncheon that gets thrown in the tiny Lutheran church where she also serves as piano accompanist and even preaches the odd sermon. She is never grudging about her millions of jobs, but she will look sideways at people who say they're busy when she knows perfectly well that sometimes they have a spare moment to sit and read a book.

(She could never.)

And yet, even in the midst of the hustle and bustle of being Alfie, the one-woman town council / preacher / welcoming committee / librarian / entrepreneur / mistress of ceremonies / whatever else she gets up to, she has always had time to make Iver feel like he is one of her top priorities. She makes him feel as though, of all the people she bakes for and plans for and takes care of and knows, he is her favorite. And it's a long list to be at the top of.

So on a day like today, when he feels nothing, when the coffee is bad, when the house is empty, she can be counted on to make him feel—not just something, but something nice.

The Pot Hole shares a building with the gas station; it's tucked into the back corner behind the shelves of chips. There's a counter, the shop's name carefully painted on a board above it in dusty rose. On the counter are two thermal carafes and a stack of plastic cups, a basket of cup sleeves and cup lids, and a jar where you put your loonie after you pour your own coffee. Sometimes there's a little thermos with cream in it; sometimes there's a box of sugar cubes, occasionally a box of free cookies.

The gas station opens at 6:00 a.m., the Pot Hole at 9:00. Iver is there at 9:01—and the door is locked. The shop is dark. The street is quiet, like a high school hallway in the summer, Iver, the lonely janitor, wandering the liminal space with a bucket and a mop.

The feelings—or rather, the nonfeelings—of nothingness and neutrality are gone (if something can go that was not present in the first place). His toe throbs; his tongue feels raw where he burned it on his coffee; the end of the world feels like the awful thing that it is. Alfie has abandoned her post, and Iver had not gotten the chance to say goodbye or, more importantly, *Thank you*. He stands in front of the door like it has been slammed in his face, his mouth opening and closing in half-spoken objections.

"Iver!"

A thrill of hope, like in the Christmas carol. He turns, and there she is, beaming at him, like *he* is the one whose presence is so important.

Alfie.

Late, for the first time in her coffee shop career.

"Looks like Craig isn't coming in to work today," she says, looking at her bare wrist, "and I'm late, aren't I?"

"I don't think so!" he says. "You're never late. Always right on time."

"How are you doing, Iver?" She has a box in her arms of all her coffee things, and she sets it on the ground so she can access the great ring of keys in her purse. There are more keys on that ring than there are buildings in this village.

"Wonderful, under the circumstances," he says, because he feels like he's supposed to acknowledge them, the circumstances.

"Well, what are you doing under those?" she asks cheerfully, patting him on the shoulder.

He follows her into the coffee shop and tries to help with the various tasks involved in setting everything up for the day before pouring himself a coffee and stuffing a five-dollar bill into the money cup.

"Iver," she scolds him, "you're going to go broke if you always tip five hundred percent."

"I only tip that much for very good service."

"Well, thank you. That's kind." She's fiddling with a coffee carafe that doesn't want to open.

He lowers himself into a nearby chair and sighs contentedly. The coffee is warm and tastes nostalgic. The store smells like gasoline and Little Trees air fresheners. Everything is right in the world. Alfie reminds him of the woman from an Emily Dickinson poem his wife had loved so much, who feels that if she could keep only one heart from breaking, then her life will not have been in vain. He would never say this out loud, of course. She would get emotional, and that would be awful—he wouldn't know what to do with it, and he could never come in here again—but he thinks it quietly in her direction. What a gift, one he doesn't take for granted, the ability to interact with reality and actually take pleasure in it.

11

A text from Jacob:

Mama I think I'm having a heart attack.

Nora stares at it for a minute, perplexed. Is it hyperbole? A legiti-
mate request for help? Why had he called her "Mama"? Is it a joke? A
slangy way German guys refer to women?
Then:

Sorry!! Wrong number!!!

She starts to reply that it's fine, but stops. His texting her instead
of his mom wouldn't negate the fact that he was having a heart attack.
If he had been serious about that.

It's all good. You okay though?

Oh ya! All good.

She waits for him to say it was a joke, but, as on the day they found
out the world was ending, there is no punch line.

Okay. Because you just said you were having a heart attack.

Haha ya.

Five minutes go by, and she finds herself worrying like a mother whose child has stayed out past curfew. Petra strolls through to get an apple and stops to assess the situation—Nora's not sure how she can even tell there *is* a situation, but, somehow, she can.

"What is wrong?" she asks.

"Nothing."

"Something is wrong." Petra stands there, looking unimpressed and impatient, as though Nora's unwillingness to open up to her is wasting her time. "What is it?"

"My friend's just not feeling well. It's nothing."

"Oh." Petra appears to have wanted something worse than this to be happening to Nora. She lingers, studying the walls of the apartment critically. She has been around a lot more since classes were canceled, and Nora isn't sure what to do with her. She likes to talk about black holes, and she has favorite physicists, and she refers to biochemistry as a "gut class." She can ramble for hours—literally, hours—about the laws and theories and rules that govern time and space. Still, Nora isn't always confident that Petra is right about half the things she spouts off. It's not that she's not smart, Nora thinks. She's very, very smart. It's that she's not yet as smart as *she* thinks she is. She probably will be one day.

Would've been.

Petra's attention drifts out of the room, and she wanders after it; Nora feels herself relax, as though she's just been cornered by a caracal who decided it wasn't hungry after all. She looks back at the screen. No new messages.

Sorry, just confirming: are you okay?

Then, to her horror, or surprise, or amazement, or excitement, her phone lights up—not a text, but a phone call. From Jacob.

She recoils, staring at it like it presents some kind of immediate danger; then, when it does nothing but ring, she gingerly presses the answer button.

"Hello . . . ?"

"Nora. Hi."

He sounds breathless. Maybe he *is* having a heart attack? But then—should he not be calling 911 instead of her? Or the German equivalent of 911? Wait—what *is* the German equivalent of 911? This thought startles her. How is she in a foreign country and hasn't thought to find out what number she's supposed to call in an emergency? "Is your . . . ?" It feels like such a personal thing, to ask him about his heart. "Are you okay?"

There's lots of breathing going on over there. That's probably a good thing. Certainly it's better than no breathing. He gives a little gasp before answering. "Actually, Nora, I'm not feeling super great. And I can't get anyone on the phone. My mother's line is busy, and 112 seems to be unattended or something—it just rings and no one answers . . ." The thought of this silences him momentarily, and when he speaks again his voice sounds strange, like he's sucked just a tiny bit of helium from a balloon. "I'm sorry if it's weird that I called you; I'm . . . kind of freaking out. I'm not thinking straight."

A panic attack? Maybe? Is it patronizing to ask him if that's what it is?

"Do you think it might be a panic attack?"

He's quiet, and she worries she's offended him. "I don't think so?" Then: "Actually, I don't know. I've never had one. What do those feel like?"

"Pretty much like a heart attack."

"You've had both?"

"Um, no—"

"Sorry, dumb joke. How do you tell the difference?"

She doesn't have a good answer. She's had exactly one panic attack, quite recently, after her breakup, before leaving for Berlin. She'd suffered through it alone in her bedroom, and, like him, she'd thought she was dying the whole time. The only way she'd known it wasn't a heart attack was that it hadn't killed her—which is not an especially helpful marker until after everything's over. What good would it do him now? "If it doesn't kill you, you're fine"? Probably not.

"If it doesn't kill you, it's not a heart attack." Her mouth didn't get the memo that this thought had been vetoed.

But he laughs weakly. "Thanks."

"Sorry, I shouldn't have said that. Just thinking, though—it would make total sense for you to be having a panic attack right now. You're going through a fairly stressful time—"

"What, the end of humanity?"

"Yeah, that. And I think panic attacks in people our age are more common than heart attacks. Especially during apocalypses. I've actually never heard of someone our age having a heart attack during an apocalypse." Though she has no control over it, she knows exactly where she inherited this incessant, nattery joking from, because she grew up being subjected to it any time life got a little thorny—the last time being the night her boyfriend dumped her.

"It's for the best. I always thought he sounded like a frog." That's what her father said from the doorway of her bedroom as she sat sobbing uncontrollably on the floor in front of her bed. "That's probably why he broke up with you over text message instead of over the phone."

"Marlen!" Her mother kept admonishing him like that, and he just kept right on joking. If Nora can't get it under control now, she muses, she's going to be worse than her father in just a few years . . . *Oh, right, the world's ending! Never mind!*

"You're probably right." He doesn't sound much better, but she thinks she hears less helium in his voice, maybe even a small smile. He either isn't annoyed, or he's sweet enough not to show it, even when he thinks he's dying.

"I googled it, when it happened to me," she says, attempting to be serious, helpful. She tries to remember the things she read on the internet.

"Yeah? Did you find out how to make it stop?"

"Mmm . . . I think it said not to try to make it stop? Just let it happen. Let yourself move through it. Try to notice things around you to ground yourself, like smells and sounds. And . . ." What else? "It said you're not supposed to tell a person who's having a panic attack that they need to calm down."

"So, what, then? You're supposed to tell me to freak out?"

"I don't think so."

"I'm joking."

"Oh. Ha . . ." She feels guilty for laughing; she feels guilty for not laughing. It's such a strange thing, to be talking him through such a personal experience. Strange, but also natural. "Um, so . . . what can I do for you? Right now?"

He's quiet for a moment. "Well. If it's not a heart attack, then it might just be nice to not be alone. Would you happen to be free at the moment?"

"Right now?"

"We could schedule another panic attack for next week if that's better?"

"Right. Right right right. Yes, now. I don't know why I said—I'm not busy." This is almost an overstatement. She's sitting in her kitchen uselessly, obsessively dialing the credit card company's 1-800 number over and over and despairing—everyone in the world is probably calling this number right now, when it's likely the people who work there have panicked and gone home. "Where are you?"

"Begonia. I came to check on things for Ida and ended up in my car in front, and this thing just hit me. I texted my mother . . . you . . . and here we are. It's pretty embarrassing."

It makes sense: he'd gone to one of the most familiar places in his world, the coffee shop he'd worked at since he was a young teenager, and maybe for the first time the reality of what was happening had really hit him. Of *course* he'd had a panic attack.

"I don't think it's embarrassing," she says. "I get it. I'll be right there. I'll walk to you. It'll take me five minutes."

***

When she arrives at his car, he's sitting in the driver's seat with his eyes closed. She taps on the passenger window, and he startles, but his face settles into a relieved smile when he sees her. She wonders if he feels that vague familiarity, the sense that they are safe places for each other even if this hasn't been proved in any substantial way thus far. She can't stop wondering what that is, whether she's imagining it, but, imagined or not and whatever it is, she's glad for it.

He leans across and pushes the door open, releasing a gentle breeze of soft, folky music. She sits and shuts the door after her so no more will escape.

"How are you doing?" she asks cautiously.

"I'm feeling a bit better," he says. "I googled a bit, like you said, and I think just knowing what it was helped. Found some breathing exercises. Now I'm just drained."

"How did people cope with mental health crises before Internet Times?"

"Right? You'd be at the library, mid panic attack, asking the librarian to help you figure out if you were dying or just having a breakdown."

"And the only thing you'd have had to help you figure it out would be a row of Encyclopedia Britannicas written before they invented panic attacks."

He laughs. "There has to be a sweet spot between 'no information available' and 'every possible worst-case scenario at my fingertips' . . ."

"It must have existed somewhere in the early thousands."

"Hey"—he lets out a long breath, still silently working through the exercises he found on the internet—"do you like ice cream? There's a shop around the corner."

"You're up for it?"

"Yeah. I think so."

"Let's do it." She's not sure if it counts as a date for a man to invite you to his panic attack and then tack ice cream onto the end of it, but she tells herself it does.

✳

It might count as a date, but it turns out to be the worst possible idea.

The ice-cream shop is closed. Of course it is.

There's a sign on the door that Jacob has to translate for Nora. "Best wishes everyone. Hug your loved ones tight. See you in heaven."

He chokes on the last words. "I think," he announces with an air of exhausted resignation, "I am going to be sick."

And he is, right in the gutter, while Nora stands nearby, wondering what he would like her to do. Watching someone throw up feels much more intimate than talking someone through a panic attack, though she feels, objectively, that these should be switched, or at least equal. They're both insides-on-the-outside events.

They walk back to his car in silence, and when they arrive there, he leans against it. "I'm so sorry," he says. "In this moment, I'm feeling kind of relieved the world's ending soon, so I won't have to relive this afternoon as I try to fall asleep for years to come."

"Don't be embarrassed, if that's what you mean."

He laughs weakly. "Oh, I'm not embarrassed. I *aspire* to embarrassment. If embarrassment had a basement, and then a dungeon underneath that, and then a trapdoor to a secret bomb shelter fifty feet below that, you will find me in the second secret bomb shelter fifty feet below *that*."

"And I'll knock on all the doors and say, 'Let me in! You don't have to be embarrassed for being human!'"

He looks into her eyes for the first time since he puked on the street. "Well," he says. "Thank you. Again."

"It's weird," she says.

"What, me? Spewing my guts everywhere?"

"No! The ice-cream shop being closed! The world ending! 'See you in heaven!' It's all so weird. Disorienting."

"It is."

"So . . ." She shrugs. She thinks of Sonja painting her toenails. "Let's just pretend it's not happening. Let's pretend the ice-cream shop is closed for a holiday. Let's pretend it's all going to be okay." She feels ridiculous saying all of this, because she doesn't actually think it's possible. She wants him to feel better so badly she's speaking out of desperation, and she's worried he can tell.

"I think that's called denial."

"No, it's called optimism."

"No, optimism is when it could go either way and you try to believe it's going to go the good way. Denial is when it's going to go the bad way, for sure, and you pretend it's going to go the good way."

"Who says it can't go either way?"

He doesn't dignify this with a response, but it makes him smile. He walks around to the driver's-side door and gestures for her to get in the car too. "Here, I'll drive you back to your place," he says. "I think I just need to go home and crash."

"Sure. Okay. Thanks."

As they buckle their seat belts, he peers at her out of the corner of his eye. "You want to hang out again sometime? If I promise to be more optimistic?"

"Sure."

She's such a hypocrite; she hasn't felt a shred of optimism herself in days. But right now the world—or this car, at least—feels full of it. She couldn't ignore it if she tried.

12

There have always been cougars in Saskatchewan, but they're not a cause for concern. That's what they told Irene's mother when she called to report the cougar she'd seen out her kitchen window, stalking her children.

Irene and Hilda had been playing in the front yard, running through the sprinklers in their matching swimsuits, and suddenly their mother was hanging out the window, red faced and hysterical, alternately screaming gibberish at something behind them and then at her girls. *Come in the house right now! Baaaaaahhhhhhh! Baaaaaahhhhh! Get in here! Shooooooooooo! Hilda! Irene!*

She wanted the conservation officer to come and kill the cougar, but he wouldn't. He said they should get a dog, keep an eye out, not let the kids wander too far. Irene had never seen her mother so angry. This was not a solution! This was irresponsible! The blood of the children would be on that conservation officer's hands!

An unnerving thing for a five-year-old to hear her mother say.

Irene lived the rest of her childhood under the specter of cougars, under the impression that cougars lined the boundaries of her yard, that cougar eyes watched her every move.

When Irene was nine, she was invited to a birthday party at a friend's nearby farm. The friend's mother was *not* afraid of cougars. Maybe she was blissfully unaware of them; maybe she had never seen one in person; maybe she didn't realize how large their paws were, how easily they could kill a kid. In any case, when Irene arrived at the party, the first order of business was a game of hide-and-seek, with no boundaries or borders. The kids were told they could hide anywhere, in the wheat field, in the old doorless barns, in the Caragana shelterbelts, all the places Irene had been warned that cougars like to hide too. It was exhilarating to be doing something so expressly forbidden at home. The threat of cougars felt nonexistent—if the adult in charge was not worried, why should Irene be?

As her friend counted to one hundred, she made a beeline for the Caraganas and crawled into a little clearing between the rows, sure that she was invisible. She could hear the faraway shouts of her friends being discovered and curled into a tight ball, pleased with herself. At that point in her life, there was no greater joy than to win at hide-and-seek.

But then there was a rustle in the bushes, and suddenly she was the opposite of invisible. She felt cougar eyes on the back of her neck. She pictured the massive cat from that day in her yard; she thought of her mother's fear, the children's blood on the conservation officer's hands, a phrase that didn't fully make sense to her but sparked a terrible mental image.

She immediately started crying and shaking and worrying that when her mother found out she was dead, she was going to be angry with her for playing so far from safety.

To this day, that moment, alone in the Caraganas, is what Irene thinks of when she thinks of fear. She has never since felt fear so visceral, so physical, so all-consuming.

Until now.

At first the news had been . . . surprising. Not shocking or terrifying, just numbing, like a shot of novocaine at the dentist. A sharp pain and then no pain, just a funny feeling that there should be pain, and a lot of it.

But apparently that wore off while she was sleeping, because when she woke this morning, she was alone in the Caraganas again, a little girl, cougar eyes on the back of her neck. And this time, she has a hus-band and a son, and she can't protect them, so this fear is worse.

Hank is not beside her in the bed; he's probably out puttering in the yard already, even though it's not even seven thirty. She slips her feet into her knit slippers and wanders into the empty kitchen, shivering. It feels strange to be so afraid first thing in the morning, before anything has even happened. Fear is usually an end-of-the-day thing, intensified by long shadows and the accumulation of dark thoughts and ideas, collected while the sun was up, suddenly taking on new meaning.

She tries to distract herself. She checks the weather app. She checks the fridge to make sure there are enough eggs for breakfast. She checks the thermostat, the temperature of the freezer, the back door to see if it needs oil for the squeaking. She checks the mailbox.

There's a flyer for a grocery store an hour away, a phone bill, and one envelope with no return address simply marked "Resident."

Curious, she tears it open. It's a typewritten letter. No name at the bottom, nothing to identify the sender.

Resident, it says again at the top of the page. Such an oddly formal greeting.

I am sure you've heard the news by now, of a cosmic event and the subsequent annihilation of the human race. *DO NOT BELIEVE IT.* It is an elaborate hoax—if not a purposeful one, then at the very least it is a colossal mis-take. None of this is real, none of this is possible, and none of this is logical. The chances of an event like this having such a deleterious effect on our planet are not just slim to none—they are none.

I am sure we will begin to see more terrify-ing things in the days ahead—the media will

shut down, the transportation industry will
shutter, food supplies will be scarce. None
of this has anything to do with outer space;
it will be the result of human fear and nothing more.

What can you do? You can take the simplest
course of action imaginable: Stay calm. Wait.
Encourage those around you not to panic. Help
them not to buy into the fear. Have common
sense. **January will come and we will be fine.**

Log on to www.januarywillcome.org for more
information and to print off copies of this
letter to distribute in your neighborhood.
It's available in five languages. If we can
calm the fears of the people, we can avoid
much pain and catastrophe.

Irene's heart has slowed; there is a warmth flowing through her, a
delicious calm, like a drug.

She thinks of the Caraganas, of the fear. One would think that level
of fear could be the result only of a real, present danger. But that day the
rustle in the bushes had been a *squirrel*. Neither Irene nor her mother
had ever seen another cougar again. All that fear, all those boundaries
and borders and cautions and threats to the conservation officer . . .
for nothing.

Through the window, she looks up at the sky, and then out across
the yard to where Hank is working on his truck. Maybe there are cougars out there. Maybe there are stars exploding in deep space.

But maybe neither of them is a thing Irene has to worry about.

13

"We are going to get tattoos." Petra stares steadily at Nora, and Nora realizes it's not only a statement but also an invitation, maybe a challenge.

"Tattoos?" Nora must have misheard. She's exhausted, but since she first heard the news about the end of the world, sleep has felt dangerous; if she's unconscious, she can't watch the sky or news, and watching feels important even if it's useless. Some annoying survival instinct that isn't going to do anything but make the rest of her life miserable.

Jacob has not texted again, has not called. She's watching for that, too, and maybe this is also a survival instinct, on some level.

"Yes. Are you coming?"

"To get a tattoo?"

"Yes." Petra is wearing her jacket, standing by the front door. She's giving the least amount of notice possible.

"Wh—" Nora doesn't even know what question to ask first. *Where?* or *Why?* or *What are they thinking?* The world is ending. Have they forgotten the world is ending?

"Petra has a friend who'll do it for free," says Sonja. She seems happy, almost her old self. She has either slipped further into denial or she's acting. "I'm getting an infinity symbol on my wrist."

"I am getting an hourglass," says Petra. Forever Sonja's antithesis, she looks like she would rather go for a root canal than get a tattoo, even though she's the one leading the charge. "Here." She touches the back of her arm.

"But *why?*" Nora is sure she's missing some key piece of information.

"To represent the constant passing of time," says Petra. "And the idea that maybe when it is all over, everything will be flipped upside down and we will live it again in reverse."

"No, I mean—" Nora pauses. *What?* She redirects her questions to Sonja. "Shouldn't you be trying to get home to your family? Looking for flights?"

Sonja shrugs defensively. "I will. I have been. I need a break. For my mental health. You do too—come with us."

"But . . . tattoos? *Now?*" She doesn't say it out loud, but she's also thinking, *Mental health? Now?* You go through life thinking health—mental and otherwise—is one of the biggest, most important things, but when you get down to those last days, it doesn't feel like it should make the priority list. Nora's not sure the list has more than one or two things on it.

(Tattoos are absolutely *not* on the list.)

But then she thinks about Jacob's panic attack the other day. She certainly thinks *his* mental health is still important. It's easier to want good things for other people while thinking you could do without them.

Jacob. She wonders where he is, why he hasn't called. She wonders whether this is one of the things that shouldn't be on her list of priorities. She should try to scratch it off.

Petra opens the door. "Yes. Something permanent in a time of particular impermanence. You might find it meaningful. Therapeutic. Or just . . ."—she flicks her wrist—"something fun to do." Petra says this as though she has never had fun on purpose but can imagine that being something in which *other* people might be interested.

Nora doesn't want to go with these women. She wants to throw in the towel, admit defeat, and call her mom. She is exactly as helpless as she appears to be, exactly as childish. It might be nice to lean into it, like falling into a soft bed at the end of a long day. Who cares what Petra thinks of her?

But it's not just Petra. She remembers the look on Jacob's face on the day of the big news, the hesitance to tell her, like he knew she wouldn't be able to handle it. Why had that bothered her so much? Maybe because her high school boyfriend had looked at her that way. Maybe because everyone always looked at her that way.

Getting a tattoo to prove to people that you're not a child: Childish? Definitely.

Nora doesn't care. It seems to be a common enough reason for other people.

"Are you coming?" Petra taps her foot impatiently.

Nora tries to look disinterested. "Sure."

✳

When Petra said she had a friend who would do it for free, what she actually meant was that she had a friend whose tattoo artist had offered to finish his arm sleeve for free. Petra had overheard the conversation and somehow shoehorned herself in on the deal—it was likely she'd simply informed the friend and the tattoo artist that this was happening, and everyone involved suddenly felt they had no other option. To make things even more uncomfortable, upon their arrival at the studio, it's immediately apparent that Sonja and Nora are surprise guests.

But it's the end of the world! Today this works in their favor. Money, despite being something Nora needs desperately if she ever wants to see her family again, has already become pretty much useless to the tattoo artist, a middle-aged green-haired tie-dye-suit-wearing man named Yannick, who has enough to live on even if he's never paid again (provided the world really does end in a couple of months) and nothing better to do than what he has been doing his whole life. It's gratifying to know that his art is so important to people that they would spend their last days getting it memorialized on their bodies, he tells them. Better than money, he says. He doesn't seem to realize that none of the women in front of him have the faintest idea who he is or what his art looks like.

Petra wants to go first.

She stands in front of the full-length mirror while Yannick sketches a freehand hourglass onto her triceps with a green Sharpie.

"What do you think of this?" he asks. His accent is thick, not German—French, maybe?

"Yeah," she says, sounding, as usual, unimpressed. "It is fine."

"It looks really good," says Nora, who for some reason feels the need to protect Yannick's pride from Petra's biting indifference.

But Yannick's pride is unaffected either way. You don't go around in a tie-dye suit if you care what young women think of you.

Petra lies on her stomach on a gurney-type bed, as though she's going to be examined by a doctor, her arm awkwardly splayed out to the side like a broken wing, and Yannick selects inks and tools and rubber gloves from his workstation.

Nora feels queasy.

She and Sonja sit on uncomfortable barstools against the wall, close enough that they could reach out and touch Petra, close enough that Nora feels the steady *zzzzz* of the tattoo gun in her molars. She pulls out her phone and dials the credit card company's 1-800 number.

Yannick bends over Petra's arm, his face set in concentration. He's not like a hairdresser who wants to hear his client's problems while he works, or if he is, he's not making it immediately apparent. Petra rolls her eyes up to meet Nora's. "Calling your mother, Nora?"

Nora tries to hold perfectly still, to keep her expression neutral. "No."

"Oh?" She sounds surprised.

"I'm *trying* to call my credit card company," says Nora. "Can't get through."

Nora feels as though she's won a tiny victory, though she's not sure Petra is aware of it. She wants Petra to be aware of it.

But Petra has moved on already. "What are you getting?"

"Hmm?"

"Your tattoo. What are you getting?"

Sonja touches her wrist. "*I'm* getting an infinity symbol," she says softly, forgetting that she has already said this. She's been much quieter since they arrived at the parlor, as though the idea of a tattoo was more exciting before there was Yannick and his suit and his gun and his uncomfortable-looking gurney bed.

"Why did you pick that?" Nora asks, trying to be a comforting presence in the room.

Sonja looks lost. "I don't know . . . ," she says at last.

"It is ironic," Petra interjects. "It is perfect."

"Why is it ironic?" Sonja, who had probably chosen the idea off Pinterest, looks worried now.

"You know," says Petra. "It means endless. Boundless. *Infinite.* And you are about to die. It is funny."

"I need to go to the bathroom," says Sonja. Yannick points to a door, and Sonja flees.

Funny. Ironic. Perfect. And Nora had thought *beautiful* was the most inaccurate description of the end of the world.

"What are you getting?" Petra asks again.

Nora doesn't want to get anything, but it feels like it would be a personal affront to Yannick and his art to back out now, not to mention she'd fail this silent test of Petra's.

"I don't know. A cat." She hadn't known she was going to say it until it came out of her mouth. Sure. A cat. Her cat, who liked her sometimes and not others, but whom she'd cared about enough, apparently, to cart all the way to Berlin.

"Where?"

She wants to ask where the least painful spot to get a tattoo would be, but now realizes she cares about Yannick's opinion of her. The tables have turned. Not that they were ever the other way around. "My . . . arm? Here." She touches her inner arm, where her cat will live for the next few months.

"That spot is less painful than some," mumbles Yannick, as though he could tell by looking at Nora that this would matter to her. Her face burns with humiliation. Is there a glowing neon sign on her forehead that says, *I'm a baby, please treat me like a baby*?

Nora dials the credit card company's number and holds her phone up to her ear. It rings but that's all. The ringing is starting to feel like it's coming from inside her head rather than from the phone, as if she's been going to loud concerts and house parties and working on construction sites without hearing protection, and then it clicks in Nora's ear, her cue to redial. She taps in the numbers and the ringing starts again.

14

After the package arrived, Marlen immediately hid it in his side of the closet, and he hasn't touched it since. He wants to be alone when he opens it, but this is proving incredibly difficult.

It's Saturday morning; he's sitting in the living room, waiting for an opportunity. He keeps missing the opportunities, napping through them. Hilda keeps sneaking out of the house to run errands or go for walks, trying so hard not to wake him as she tiptoes out and softly shuts the door behind her. It's happening so often it's starting to feel like she knows, like she's being conniving rather than courteous.

He hears her coming down the stairs, and when she arrives in the doorway, she's got her purse over her shoulder. This is promising.

She has her phone in hand; for days she's carried it around in a daze, repeatedly hitting redial. In the event that Nora ever does answer, Hilda might just hang up and hit redial. It's muscle memory by now. Marlen thinks he could replace the phone with the TV remote and she wouldn't even notice.

"I'm going out," she says, and he thinks, *Ah, good, I can open the package.* But then she asks him to join her.

He nods slowly. "Sure."

She notices his hesitation. "Actually, never mind. I didn't mean to interrupt whatever you're doing here . . ." She tries not to make a point of looking around the room, highlighting the absence of a book to read, a stack of papers to grade, anything that would constitute "whatever you're doing."

"No, Hilda. I'm not busy. What were you wanting to do?"

His voice is crisp. They've been like this for days, not fighting but just out of sync, like their marriage is a three-legged race and the news—all the news, the cancer, the end of the world—has knocked them off pace. They can't recover. They can't communicate. He takes a step when she's pausing to regroup; then they both start up with the wrong foot; then one of them is falling over. It would be comical if it weren't so frustrating.

"I was just going to the Pot Hole. Wanted to check in on Alfie. Thought you might . . ."

He softens. He can see that she's trying. He should try too.

"I'd love to."

He stands and reaches for her hand—that's one of the tricks of three-legged races, isn't it? Holding hands. Physical connection that leads to mental connection. Not trying to move independently of your partner.

Hilda loves Alfie. She knows that Alfie lives alone, has no family in the area, or maybe in any area, and probably found out about the end of the world while eating a solitary Thanksgiving Monday lunch off a TV tray in the ramshackle trailer where she lives with her dog. Someone needs to check on the woman who's always checking on everyone else.

She parks in front of the Pot Hole, and Marlen starts to climb carefully out of the passenger seat, looking pained, nursing his right leg a bit. She should've let him stay home. He wasn't avoiding time with her; he just needed to rest. She was trying to run while he regrouped.

The seating in the Pot Hole is limited and eclectic: a repurposed teacher's desk from the old one-room schoolhouse on the outskirts of town, with two mismatched but complementary chairs covered in floral vinyl, straight out of seventies-era dining rooms. A bar fashioned out of barnwood planks—one of the barstools is an old barbershop chair. There's only one proper table with four matching wooden chairs. The furniture is an homage to the Pot Hole's owner, gifted by some of the people whose lives she has been part of over her years in this village, and the seats are generally always full.

But not today. Today it's just Marlen and Hilda and—

"Marlen? Marlen! What's wrong?" He has stopped right in the doorway and seems to be trying to turn around, but the heavy door is already closing on her, the handle digging into her back. "Marlen!" Her voice is muffled by his chest.

He's facing her now, making a shushing noise and whispering something under his breath that sounds like, "Goat! Goat! Goat!"

"Hi!" The voice behind him is familiar, and all at once Hilda understands. *Ah. Go out.* Not *Goat.* And she wishes she had gone out, or that he had seen a goat, either one. As it is, they're caught, and the thing Marlen had seen was not a goat, but Nora's ex-boyfriend. Derek. They turn in the direction of the voice, plastering smiles across their faces.

"Derek!" Her voice is warm, and she registers her husband's displeasure at this. He thinks she's betraying their family by speaking kindly to this kid. "Well!" She doesn't know what else to say. *We've missed you? Long time, no see? What have you been up to?*

All things that feel inappropriate for this situation. They *have* missed him, but his absence is a result of him having dumped their daughter. It *hasn't* been that long; that's why this is so awkward. And they do not, under any circumstances, want to hear what he's been up to.

Besides, they can see that for themselves.

"*Well!*" says Hilda again. "Isn't it so nice to see you! And—" She's mortified to see her hand move out in front of her, as if controlled by someone else, pointing accusingly across the gas station at the girl waiting at the table for Derek. Hilda has forgotten the girl's name, but she was a grade or two—or possibly even *three!*—under Nora and Derek. She's young! She looks so young! What is he thinking, going around with someone that . . . *young?* Nora had mentioned the suspicious timing of a new girlfriend, suggesting the likelihood of, if not outright unfaithfulness, at the very least a wandering eye, but she hadn't mentioned that the other woman was . . . a child.

"That's Soph," says Derek. She waves, smiles. They're both so oblivious to the mortification of Derek's once-future in-laws (for Hilda can't help but think of herself this way even though she knows she shouldn't). "She went to school with me and Nora."

Hilda tries very hard to remember what it was like to be nineteen. Wouldn't she, at that age, have thought it was awkward to be on a date and run into the parents of the girl you'd dated for a couple of years and then dumped unceremoniously by text message?

Then again, if you were the kind of person to dump your girlfriend via text . . . the answer's in the question, isn't it?

"Right," Hilda manages. "I remember . . . Soph."

Marlen frowns suspiciously at all of them—at Hilda, at Derek, at Soph—and grunts. He has nothing more graceful than this to offer, and Hilda can't blame him. He's not typically a grudge holder, but they have decided as a family unit to hate Derek forever.

"Well!" says Hilda for the third time. She hopes this will be the last one. "We were just going to grab some coffee. So nice to run into you! And Soph!"

Thankfully Derek doesn't linger. He goes back to Soph while Hilda and Marlen pour themselves a couple of coffees. Marlen drops his change noisily in the jar, like he hopes the sound will scare off the offensive youths.

It doesn't.

It's a rule that people you greatly dislike can do the most banal things and drive you as mad as if they were behaving in egregiously hostile ways, and this is the case here too: Derek and Soph have taken the good table, leaving Marlen and Hilda to sit at the next best option, the teacher's desk. Marlen leaves the spot behind the desk for Hilda, so she has a place to put her legs, and he has to sit awkwardly with both of his legs to one side like he's a lady in a dress, riding a horse. His chair squeals when he shifts his weight. He hopes Derek will notice how uncomfortable he is and feel bad. He glowers at the good table, whose inhabitants are still oblivious to his displeasure. "Why is anyone *dating* anyone right now?" he grumbles. "What's the point?"

"We're on a date at the moment," Hilda points out quietly, trying to guide him, by example, to the right volume.

"That's different."

"How?"

"Well. We're in a *real* relationship."

Hilda pats her husband's hand. "Yes, we are. And Nora's okay. If you ask me, she dodged a bullet there."

Marlen has noticed himself doing old-mannish things lately. Creaking and popping and hating popular music and making harrumph noises when he agrees with Hilda but doesn't want her to know.

"Harrumph."

A truck pulls in at the fuel pumps; a bell dings to let the gas station worker know he has a customer. Marlen looks around. "Craig's not here today."

Derek mistakenly thinks Marlen is addressing him. "It doesn't look like anyone's working today."

Marlen ignores this and leans back toward his wife. "Guess the gas is on the house."

It seems to occur to everyone in the room at the same time, though no one vocalizes it, that Craig might never be back, that he might have left town to be with family or simply stopped coming in to work because it doesn't feel worth it to him anymore. There's a moment of horrified silence.

Hilda is also thinking of Alfie. What if she doesn't come back either? This is an unbearable thought. It feels connected to her inability to get hold of Nora—like life is a side-scroll video game, and every motion that propels things forward creates less space for the possibility of their reunion. Alfie's absence, and the subsequent end of the Pot Hole, would move it all along much too quickly. But she's been here recently—the coffee is still warm. And it would feel out of character for Alfie to give up so quickly.

Marlen shifts in his chair again, and again it squeals at him. He scowls. His face has thinned out, Hilda notices, and he shaved this morning. The combination makes him look younger and older, all at once, like he's melting into the future and the past at the same time.

The couple behind him is laughing at something.

"Isn't it weird," he says loudly, "how quickly you get used to dying?"

Hilda glares at him.

"What? Am I not allowed to talk about it? We're all dying here." He might as well be yelling at the kids behind him. But he can't help himself; he feels like they're laughing at a funeral. His funeral. His wife's funeral. His daughter's funeral.

"You're not used to it; you're just in shock." She gives him a look that says, *Stop being an idiot.*

He shakes his head and reciprocates with a look that says, *I will stop being an idiot when I feel good and ready.* "Nah, I feel like I'm used to it."

The couple stands, taking their cups with them. Derek gives a two-finger farmer wave on his way past the teacher's desk. "See you," he says politely. The door shuts behind them, and Marlen has the decency to look ashamed of himself.

"What was that?"

"What was what?"

"You were acting like *Hank.*"

Marlen inhales sharply. "Ouch." He takes a sip of his coffee. "But also: you're right. And I'm sorry."

"It's okay. I get it, I think." She examines a jug of No Name liquid charcoal starter on the shelf behind him. "Also, I don't know if you meant it, but it's been *one week.* You are not used to the idea of dying."

"It's been more than a week for me," he reminds her, and she flushes with embarrassment. He doesn't tell her how much longer than a week it's been for him. She would think he was losing his mind, and neither of them needs that on top of everything else. "But—everyone gets used to the idea of dying as a kid, when they first find out that everyone dies. This isn't a new thing for any of us. It's just, the date got moved up, and we know when it is now. It's an adjustment, but it's not 'if' to 'when.' It's . . . 'someday' to 'soon,' and 'we don't know when' to . . . 'December 27.'"

Hilda sighs. He's being ridiculous. Kids don't get used to the idea of dying. They don't think about it. They learn to ignore it. That's not the same thing.

The bell over the door jingles, announcing Alfie's blessed arrival. She's carrying a box and looking even more scattered than usual, but her face is still calm and kind, and she brightens at the sight of them. She has the ability to make anyone feel like they're important to her, but Hilda has always secretly believed that she might actually be Alfie's favorite.

"Hilda! Marlen! How are you guys?"

Hilda relaxes into a grin. "Just fine," she says brightly.

"Well, *that's* weird," says Alfie with her usual soft sarcasm. "The rest of the town's prepping for the end of the world." She hefts a full carafe onto the counter and checks the cream and sugar. "Then again," she mumbles over her shoulder, "prepping's not gonna do anyone any good. Everyone would be much better off doing what you two are doing."

Hilda looks at Marlen. "What *we're* doing?" Bickering? Holding a grudge against a nineteen-year-old? Obsessively redialing the phone?

"Sitting down. Having coffee."

Marlen looks amused. "Hmm. Hear that, honey? Apparently we look very calm and sane and sweet to the onlooker."

"Calm and sweet, at least," says Alfie, winking at Hilda.

"Would you like to join us?"

"Oh, thank you, I can't," says Alfie. "I'm very busy."

"I thought you said everyone should be doing this." Marlen gestures at the cups in front of him and Hilda.

"*They* should!" says Alfie. "I don't have time. Things'll fall apart!"

Somehow Alfie manages to say this without a trace of bitterness or resentment.

15

Ole is cleaning his bedroom. Folding his underwear, hanging up his T-shirts, lining up the action figures on his shelf (which haven't been touched in years and have acquired thick little dust hats).

This might seem counterintuitive, to find out that your bedroom is about to go up in flames and think, *I should organize this*, but it feels important to him. He needs to acknowledge his possessions, the things he has accumulated in his time in this bedroom. A way of saying good-bye to his quick life.

Besides, his parents are moving around the main floor like a tornado, having a historic fight, and he, man of zero desire to be emotional or near emotional people, wants nothing to do with it. So he will stay in his bedroom, and he will clean it until the yelling stops. If it gets clean before the yelling stops, he will mess it up and start over.

They're fighting about the Letter. It arrived soon after the news about the world blowing up. The Letter says it's all a hoax and there's no reason to be afraid. Ole's mother pulled it out at supper the other day—yesterday? Two days ago? Time has no meaning right now, especially since school's been put on pause—and read it to them, her voice calm. When she finished, she looked up at them and smiled and gave a sigh of relief and said, "I looked up this website, and there are *real* scientists on there, and *they* say—"

"Irene."

Ole and his mother both flinched at the volume of his father's voice. Ole noticed his mother's hands begin to tremble. She set the paper down and hid them under the table.

"What are you doing?" Ole's father lowered his voice, but his jaw was set and his eyes were hard.

Her shoulders flinched. "Reading this letter . . ."

"Why? This letter is nonsense."

She was silent for a moment, then: "The website has articles written by *real scientists* about exactly why—"

"Irene!" Ole's father stood up so fast his chair fell backward and slammed against the ground. It seemed like such an overreaction. Ole felt his face grow hot, an alarming pressure building behind his eyes. "Stop this," his father said. He looked like he was going to say a lot of other things, but all that came was, "This is not helpful." Then he righted his chair and sat on it, wiped his hands on a napkin, and dropped it on his plate, right on top of his half-finished shepherd's pie. "What's for dessert?"

Ole's mother left the table, came back with a Pyrex dish containing the dessert, and slammed it down in front of him.

"Death by chocolate," she said evenly.

A retort. *Death by chocolate, yes. Death by gamma ray, no.*

They ate it in silence; then Ole's father left the room without saying anything else.

Ole wishes the silence had continued; it was awful, but it was better than the fighting.

Ole's bedroom has never been this clean.

16

"We are going skydiving," Petra says. Not a question, but not a challenge either. This time it's a demand.

"Have fun," says Nora.

"You are coming with us," says Petra. At the door Sonja bounces nervously on the balls of her feet.

"No, I'm not," says Nora.

"You are about to die," says Petra, "and you have experienced practically nothing in your life. Why would you say no to this opportunity?"

"Skydiving doesn't"—Nora is feeling facetious; she tries on Petra's German accent—"*speak* to me." She sounds more like she's doing a mocking imitation of Yannick.

"*I* speak to you," says Petra dully. "I say come skydiving with us."

Nora looks at the two of them, waiting for her by the door. Why is Petra so insistent on her presence? Is she really this determined to prove to Nora that she's superior? Or is she altruistic, invested in Nora's growth?

"Why do you want me to come so badly?"

Petra glares at her. "Because Jori refuses to take us unless we can fill a plane; 179 euros per person."

"Oh. Well, I'm out for sure then. I don't have any money. I still can't reach my credit card company."

"I will pay for you."

"Just pay for my seat and I'll stay home."

At this Petra seems to turn to stone. She is not going to argue anymore, but she hasn't given up. She stands, fixed to the floor, her face cold and calm. Sonja and Nora stare at each other, perplexed. She's like a sorceress using some kind of silent magic.

"Fine." Nora is surprised to hear herself say it. Apparently Petra was right: they are going skydiving.

❋

As the little plane ascends, Nora thinks about Derek.

When they first broke up, he crossed her mind every five minutes. He was a phantom limb, sometimes itching, sometimes burning and bleeding. Sometimes she wanted to fix it, get him back; sometimes she just wanted him to know how much he'd hurt her. It didn't help that they lived in the same small town, used the same bank and grocery store, had all the same friends. A phantom limb minus the phantom part, a lot of the time. A severed arm across the table, once a part of her, now disconnected but still *right there*. Sometimes even attached to someone else's body. Surreal.

The airplane ride from Saskatoon to Toronto had been like breaking up again. A re-severing, a physical manifestation of something that had, to this point, been mostly emotional distancing. Her flight left at 6:15 a.m., and she stared out the window into the darkness and allowed herself to be melodramatic, imagining him back on the ground, looking up at the sky, both parties regretting everything.

The afternoon flight from Toronto to Paris, in contrast, was absolutely beautiful. Healing. The sun was out. She could feel the chasm between them widening, but it was healthy and right; she felt like she was growing up.

There had been a seven-hour layover in Paris during which Nora was too afraid to leave the airport—this was her first time traveling internationally, her first time traveling solo, period, and she worried she'd miss a train or misjudge how much time she needed and become stranded there. But the Paris airport, to someone who has never been anywhere, is an experience in and of itself, and Nora had almost been able to forget him altogether for those hours. She had grieved, she had left, and she had forgotten.

So far, so good.

Paris to Berlin. Less than two hours, full of glorious, anxious apprehension—looking ahead instead of behind! *How to move on in three easy flights!* The phantom limb thing, she mused, was a metaphor that revealed how silly she'd been. She had two perfectly good arms. What did she need an extra one for?

But now she's learning another lesson: you can make progress, exponential progress, become a new thing altogether, and that progress can be completely undone and mean absolutely nothing in less time than it takes you to notice what's happening. She'd been under the impression that once you'd grasped and understood and implemented something, that was it. But progress is just upward motion, and just because you've risen to an altitude of 14,000 feet, that doesn't mean gravity has forgotten you. Nora knows this especially well right now. Gravity has not forgotten her; it's jealous for her, it adores her. It's waiting for her just outside the plane, like an anxious date.

As the plane climbs, Nora's heart seems to crack open again, right along the old break. She wishes Derek were here, witnessing her, looking impressed. She would show him her tattoo, introduce him to Petra and pretend theirs is an actual friendship in which she enjoys herself. Like, *Oh yes, I can hang with this kind of person; I can hold my own here.* As the thoughts crash around in her head, she can't help but notice that her motives are less "I loved him and I want him back" and more "I want to show him that I'm not as young and helpless as he thinks I am."

She looks out the window at the patchwork land, their shadow flying on the ground beneath them. Jori, Petra's friend, had singled Nora out as she took her seat in the orange-and-blue Cessna alongside a small group of other people Petra had presumably ordered aboard.

"We usually have you sign a waiver," he said, his eyes mischievous, one of those people who thinks anxiety is silly. "But what to do if you break both legs on landing? Are you suing me?" Then he laughed like a hyena, and Nora tried to look unbothered. She knew she hadn't succeeded by the way he laughed even harder.

*

As Nora rushes toward the ground, she thinks about Jacob. There's a clarity that comes with falling that tends to elude a person in a crowded Cessna, so her thoughts unspool easily and efficiently.

She hopes he's doing okay.

She wishes he would text her.

She wonders why she's leaving that particular ball in his court.

And that's it.

There is far, far less time to think about Jacob on the way down than there had been to think about Derek on the way up.

The free fall takes all of sixty seconds, and then her thoughts shift to Jori's comments, waivers and broken legs, and Petra's comments, how her life is almost over and she hasn't done anything, and then she's pulling up her legs like she'd been instructed earlier, landing in the grass, feeling the reverberation up her spine, and, just like that, it's done.

Her first thought is, *Okay, I'm safe now.* And then she laughs and laughs and can't stop laughing, and Jori, who had jumped tandem with her, grins proudly, as though he has told the joke that has elicited this reaction.

Before they get on the shuttle back into Berlin, she's given a photograph of herself, taken at some point during the free fall. Her face is flushed, but she looks calm, and she remembers feeling calm, like skydiving is a thing she has done a million times and which doesn't faze her anymore. Petra raises her eyebrows at it but has nothing to say. Sonja is green and silent, holding a barf bag below her chin.

Nora takes a picture of the photograph with her phone. With the clarity of a person falling from 14,000 feet, she decides that when she gets back to the apartment and in the range of her Wi-Fi, she'll send it to Jacob.

But when she gets there, for reasons not completely clear to her—pride? Loneliness? Insecurity?—she sends it to Derek instead.

17

Marlen finally has a moment to himself.

The box of books is inconspicuous. In many of his daydreams about being a published author, he'd imagined receiving a box with an obnoxious publishing house logo on the side, maybe his picture on there too. He's never been really clear on how these things worked. He'd imagined the mail carrier looking impressed and wanting to wait while he opened the box, and he'd imagined Hilda standing there, beaming with pride, taking his picture.

But it's just him, in his bedroom, with a nondescript brown cardboard box that looks a little beat up, like the mail carrier had punched it a few times, maybe kicked it up the sidewalk to their front door for no reason other than to show disrespect to the contents.

This is fine.

He peels off the tape and pulls back the cardboard flaps. There's a typed letter laid flat on top of the contents:

> Marlen,
> Thank you for publishing with Living Skies Press! We hope you are happy with the finished product and look forward to working with you again.
> Marcelle
> President, Living Skies Press

Marlen smiles. This was a letter written before the News. Normal.

"Thanks, Marcelle," he says to the paper, since it's his only witness. "I would've liked to work with you again too."

He pulls out a copy of his book. Here it is, the moment he has waited for his whole life. It feels strange, not as unreal and exciting as he'd dreamed it would be—but maybe that's just how it is when you're a prophet. Maybe nothing ever feels new and exciting.

It does feel wonderful in his hands, though. The cover is simple but eye-catching. He'd spent five straight lunch hours trying to get it right, then given up and hired a freelance designer from the internet who got it the way he wanted in less than thirty minutes.

I want deep space, he'd typed in the chat bar, and in the background, two tiny stars just a little brighter than the rest. Maybe they could look like they're starting to explode? Title across the top, my name across the bottom in huge sci-fi letters, like I'm a big deal.

The designer had typed back, Are you a big deal? 😶

He'd started to reply that he wasn't, but then he changed his mind.

To the people who are going to read this book, yes.

The designer had done a beautiful job.

He flips to the first page. Copyright information, his name, the year. For some reason this is more exciting than the book cover. It lends that sense of officiality. It says, *These are my words! Legally!*

He holds the feeling for a moment, allowing himself some vanity.

He turns another page. *Chapter One.*

That looks nice.

And there are his words, in ink.

There will come a point at the very end of it all when no one will be able to deny what is happening. No one will say, *The earth is not on fire*, or *I'm not melting.* These will be incontrovertible facts, and in that one gorgeous, horrifying moment, the only one like it in all of human history, wars will cease, the food chain will level, the wealth gap will slam shut. Everyone will be on the same page about everything. It could be an incredibly unifying experience for humankind if it were not also so obliterating.

For now, it's ignorable, like an ant rushing along a sidewalk. For now, a person can turn the TV off and put their phone down, make a pot of coffee, look out the window at the sky, blue as a freezie pop, and think, *Everything is normal and nothing is melting.*

He's not sure how true these words are now that he's living them. It's one thing to imagine how you might feel in a situation, and another thing to live it. Obviously. This is why they tell writers to write what they know. Marlen had ignored the rule, thinking it wouldn't matter, because even though this isn't his lived experience, it's not anyone else's, either, so who's going to say he got it wrong?

Turns out, *he* is.

Ignorable? That had been the wrong word. It's not ignorable, it's invisible, and the two are almost opposites, though Marlen has never realized this before. It's hard to ignore a threat; everyone knows this. An *invisible* threat? Something you can't see but which you know is looming and about to strike? Much, much worse.

It's okay. This book doesn't need to be perfect. It can be wholly and completely true without being inerrant.

He shuts the book, peers into the box at the twenty-four other copies waiting expectantly to be read. He wishes Nora were here to share this moment with him. She likes reading; she would be proud of him.

He sighs. He tries not to make Hilda more worried than she already is about their daughter not making it home, but he thinks he might be more worried than anyone. More angry about how helpless he is. The number of times he's refreshed the airline pages, the number of daydreams he's had about showing up on her door-step in Berlin . . .

Though in his book, this book he's holding in his hands, the book that has been right about almost everything else, they're together at the end. Nora makes it home.

And Marlen is a prophet.

18

They have school today, first time since the announcement.

The school's been closed for a week, not to protect anyone, or because people haven't been physically able to be there. There was just a silent agreement among the adults that they needed a few days. At the time, that had seemed wise. Now it feels shortsighted. A few days to process the end of civilization? It's like having your legs chopped off and being told by your basketball coach that you can sit out the first fifteen minutes of practice to get the bleeding under control. Being handed a Band-Aid. Many of the city schools are still closed, probably for good. Things just happen differently in cities than they do here, even apocalypses.

When Ole comes down the stairs for breakfast, his parents are at the table, looking stiff and sad. His father offers a pitiful, vaguely apologetic smile but doesn't say anything. His mother leaps to her feet, moving and talking too quickly, overcompensating for her husband's stillness. "Sit, Ole, have some breakfast. Do you want some cereal? Toast? What can I get you?" She's poised in the middle of the kitchen like a tiger, ready to spring in whichever direction he sends her.

"I'm good," he mumbles. He's hungry, though. He'd love some toast. Her homemade bread, hot from the toaster, covered in melting peanut butter . . . that's what he wants, but the air in this room is so thick; he doesn't want to speak into it.

"Oh, please sit down, Ole," she pleads. "You never sit with us anymore."

This feels unfair. He would sit with them if they could guarantee they wouldn't start screaming at each other, if it were actually nice to sit with them. He's not the one starting the fights, stretching them out so they last all day. "I gotta go," he says.

"Sit *down*," Hank growls, surprising all three of them. "You don't get to just sulk around. Sit down and eat."

Ole hesitates. His father's anger is stupid. His *father* is the one sulking around, picking fights. Ole's just trying to stay out of the way.

"SIT. DOWN." Neither Hank nor Ole moves a muscle as Hank shouts the words, but Irene jumps. They've never been a family that yelled at each other. Why did they have to become one now? At the very end?

Ole isn't a confrontational kid, not like his dad. His anger simmers—it doesn't boil or explode—so he sits. But it feels harder than usual just to sit. It feels like something else needs to happen, like he's holding his breath and he needs to exhale. "Chill out, Dad," he says. He barely speaks the words; they slip out like a sigh. It's not the most inflammatory thing he could've said by any stretch; he's heard his friends say much worse to their parents without consequence or escalation. But the words themselves don't matter; it's the fact that he's gone to a new place.

His father sits back in his chair, his jaw twitching. He wants to yell again; Ole can see that. Or—cry. That would be way worse. Ole looks down at the table, where magical peanut butter toast has suddenly appeared. He looks up; his mother is just standing there, staring at the two of them, mortified, the jar of peanut butter in one hand, a butter knife in the other. She looks like she might cry too. He can't imagine a more awful nightmare, sitting here in front of two bawling parents. That would be way worse than sitting here in front of two fighting ones.

Not very long ago, they were one of those very strange families that got along all the time. Just three mild-mannered people who didn't rub up against each other, frictionless. He sees now that it has left them completely unprepared to deal with conflict. No one knows what to do.

In the basement, the washing machine beeps, signaling the end of a load.

"I'll get that," Hank says, his voice so taut it's scary. He stands, his chair screeching as it skids across the hardwood floor, and he storms out the way Ole used to when he was much younger and had childish temper tantrums, slamming the basement door behind him. But this is different, because when Ole stormed out, he knew that he still loved his family. He had control. He was leaving, not being left.

In the basement, they hear the washing machine door slam shut, echoing the basement door. Ole pictures his father down there, raging against the washing machine, hanging shirts to dry on the wire clothes-horse, his large hands trembling. His mother looks as though she feels sorry for it; to this point it has been nothing but quiet and helpful.

It was all already too much; now it's more than that, the part that comes after the boiling point, where the water starts to disappear. He gets up, too, takes the toast, a pathetic signal to his mother, like a flare from a sinking ship, that he loves her, and walks out the front door. He's decided something: he's going to get on the school bus one last time. But he is not going to school, and he is not coming home.

19

"We are going to Berghain."

The *we* has shrunk to include only Nora and Petra; Sonja left this morning, having found a flight to the States. Her goodbye had been dramatic and insincere; she was visibly relieved to leave this apartment, as though this was where the end of the world was going to be localized and America was a safe haven. (Or maybe she was just relieved to leave Petra.)

Petra is packed and ready to go home to Hamburg, but she won't leave. Her bags sit by the door, waiting. She skulks around the house, perching on furniture, peering at Nora with an air of superiority, curiosity, pity. Occasionally she pounces—she'll find Nora alone in the kitchen and hop onto the counter, or she'll wander into Nora's bedroom and sit on the edge of her bed, subjecting her to increasingly weird lectures and conjectures about space and time and the end of civilization. One morning she says life is like a record that you listen to over and over, unable to remember each time that you've heard this before. Two hours pass and she has changed her mind: no, time is moving backward. They have already eaten lunch, already gone to bed, already gone for this walk, which is why they experience déjà vu when they pass a busker playing Glen Hansard songs in front of Taleh Thai. Only half a day later she has decided that all of reality and eternity and existence is the moment they're in, and she seems to really believe this, really thinks that the two of them sitting in their apartment right now is all there is, that any memory of doing anything other than this is simply made up.

And when it's not a fancy speech, it's a field trip. She's like a demented kindergarten teacher. Today's agenda: Berghain. A place Nora has never heard of, but which, she suspects, is not a shopping mall or anything remotely equivalent.

"I don't know what that is."

Nora is half passed out on the couch. She has finally given up on the credit card company, at least for the moment (hope comes and goes, like Petra, sometimes interested in her but only in a self-serving way). Begonia is still closed, and she still hasn't called her parents; it still feels like she can't until she has sorted it all out on her own—which might mean she'll never speak to them again. Jacob hasn't called. Derek hasn't even texted her back. In light of all of this, she wants Petra to go away.

But Petra isn't good at reading social cues, and she seems to be getting worse at it with every passing day, as though she doesn't see the point in trying anymore.

"I am sure you have heard of it. *Berghain.*"

"Never," Nora mumbles, but Petra doesn't hear her. Nora misses Sonja. Infinite, unintentionally ironic, nauseous Sonja, with her obliviousness, her ability to temper Petra's obnoxiousness.

Nora rakes her fingers through her hair. She is 92 percent sure she has never heard of Berghain, but somehow she knows how much she would hate being there. She can tell by the way Petra's dressed—satin shirt, fishnets, running shoes, black lipstick. She looks like she's going to run a marathon at a black-tie goth gym. If such a thing exists. Maybe it does. Maybe its name is Berghain.

"It is Berlin's most exclusive night *club.*" She breaks the word *nightclub* in half, landing heavily on the second syllable. "Very difficult to get in . . . but I can get us in."

"I'm not really a nightclub person," says Nora. She has no idea if this is true. They don't have nightclubs in rural Saskatchewan, and if they did, they couldn't make them exclusive, or there wouldn't be enough people to make the endeavor worthwhile.

Petra looks her up and down, eyes lingering on Nora's three-year-old leggings, bagging at the knees. "No." That smirk. "You are not a night *club* person, are you?"

Before Nora can answer, Petra gathers her bags and purses her lips; she looks like she has had a pen explode in her mouth. "Well, if we are not going night *club*bing, I am just going to go home. It was nice knowing you, Nora."

"Oh . . ." Nora feels somewhat scrambled now. She wants Petra to leave, of course, but it's just now dawning on her how lonely she's going to be—she could conceivably be alone in this apartment for the rest of her life. She wants simultaneously to shove Petra out the door and cling to her, begging her not to go just yet. "You too. Have a safe trip."

She stands, uncertain. Will Petra want to hug her?

No. The door's already shut. Petra is gone forever.

Nora frowns, trying to drum up enthusiasm. This is fine. It's *good*. It's good that Petra's gone. She's mean. She's scary. And her weird theories had been exhausting—that one where time is fixed and movement is an illusion—what is that? Time has to move! It's impossible that nothing moves, that everything is nothing more than a moment, a droplet suspended in space and time, full of impotent hope and false history. You couldn't feel so strongly about things that hadn't actually *happened*.

Nora's cat jumps onto her lap, sinking its nails into her thighs. She frowns and pushes it off, and it drags its nails across her inner arm, right through the tattoo, as though it disapproves of the unauthorized use of its likeness. "*Thanks,*" says Nora. "That felt great."

From the floor, the cat peers at her with an air of superiority, curiosity, pity. As though it's thinking, *Poor girl. All alone at the end of the world, talking to her cat.*

20

Hilda can't find her necklace.

It was a present from Nora last Christmas (or maybe Mother's Day? She can't remember), a cheap silver locket, the kind you'd get at a drugstore on a jewelry tree by the cash register, but precious in the way presents from your children always are.

She has checked everywhere. The floor of the car, behind the dresser, under the night table, all the places tiny lost items have been found before. One might think that in the face of your own demise and that of everyone you know and love, your priorities would shift, and something as idiotically vain as a necklace would cease to matter, but for some reason it's the opposite. The necklace feels symbolic, like a placeholder for her daughter, whom she might never see again, might never even talk to again. She has cried over it twice today. She feels desperate to find it. She goes outside looking for Marlen.

"Marlen, are you sure you haven't seen my necklace?"

He looks up at her, startled. He's chopping wood for a fire tonight, inspired by the fire starter on the shelf at the Pot Hole and by Alfie's comments about what everyone should be doing right now. Chopping wood is harder than it used to be, and he's winded, but it feels great to be winded with good reason, not because he walked up the front steps or stood up from the supper table. It's exhilarating for Marlen, to have added a new thing to his schedule. He'd been starting to look at his life as a series of dropping offs.

"What necklace?" He leans on the axe, attempting to catch his breath. He's not sure he can. He might actually be winded for the rest of his life.

"The one Nora gave me. Silver. A heart. I asked you before, at supper." She's got that phone in her hand still, redialing, redialing . . .

He shakes his head, not sure which necklace she's talking about. She has a lot of jewelry.

She sighs, exasperated.

He wants to be helpful. It's why he's chopping wood even though it feels like it might actually kill him here and now. "Did you check under the night table?"

"Yes, and behind the dresser."

"And on the floor of the car?"

"*Yes*, Marlen. Everywhere."

"You could wear the . . . your other one? The, uh . . ." He racks his brain for a mental image, just one necklace he's seen her wear before. "The . . . gold . . . chain . . . ?"

He doesn't know if she owns one like that, but when he thinks *necklace*, this is the stock image his brain pulls up.

She takes a breath and touches her temples. "Never mind. It's fine. I'm sure it'll turn up."

"For sure it will. You just set it down somewhere and forgot. It'll come to you." He looks at the pile of wood next to the firepit. "I think I've got enough here. Come sit with me?"

She hesitates. "Okay. Yeah. I'll look for it tomorrow."

They settle in and Marlen smiles contentedly. Conversation comes easily tonight; he had forgotten how clarifying it is to sit outside when it's getting colder, how it wakes you up and makes your mind feel bright.

He watches Hilda while she talks, her face lit first by the sunset, then by the fire, noticing the mannerisms that have become so familiar they've almost disappeared over the years. The way she brushes the corner of her mouth every so often, like she's been eating chips and there might be crumbs there, or the way she peeks at him out of the corner of her eye when she makes a joke, like she wants to see if he thinks she's funny even though he feels like he has made it clear that he does.

He wishes he could edit his book and add these details in. This is the problem with trying to capture a real person inside a book—no one fits. It's something that should be immediately obvious: people are quite a lot bigger than books.

What he'd wanted was for her to read the book and see herself in it—and not just in the character that was obviously her, but in every character and place and scene and part of the book that was good, or cheerful, or thoughtful, or smart. He wanted her to see how much he'd noticed about her, because he knew that being noticed made a person feel cherished. He wanted her to know how much he'd cherished her.

Tonight the air is chilly. Hilda goes back in and brings out two large comforters, one from the spare bedroom, and one from Nora's old bed. Marlen wraps himself in that one. It's neon pink and covered in tie-dye peace signs and makes him ache to hold his daughter. He feels the ache in the back of his jaw, radiating down into his stomach.

"You okay, Dad?" Nora squints at him, then back at the marshmallow turning brown on the end of her stick. The crickets are suddenly so loud, like a parking lot full of cars with their alarms going off, like a choir of sopranos relentlessly hitting one note. It makes him feel unreasonably anxious.

Marlen nods and pedals his heels into the soft dirt, trying to bring himself firmly into the present. He's been having so many moments like this lately, strange visions—of the future? He hopes not. It would make him laugh if it weren't so frightening—a future where his little girl is abroad without him while he's dying and the world is ending? It's not the actual future. It can't be; it's too absurd. It's just fear, vividly picturing the worst that could happen. He's always been prone to this, for as long as he can remember. He's an English major, an aspiring writer, a daydreamer. Of course his worst-case scenarios are going to be overblown. Nora smiles at him, then over at her boyfriend sitting on a tree stump across the fire, this scrawny kid she brought home with her at the beginning of her grade eleven year, who has not left her side. Marlen tried to hate him for a while, but the kid's nice, respectful, very funny. He listens with rapt attention to Marlen's trivia and can hold a competent, interesting conversation about music. No one could ever hate this kid.

This kid. Marlen's brain is malfunctioning; it's the crickets or the late hour. He can't think of Nora's boyfriend's name. It's not concerning, just funny. Your brain starts to do this when you get to a certain age. One time he forgot the word *pickle*. One time he put his car keys in the fridge. It doesn't mean anything.

The kid is openly staring at Nora with unabashed admiration written all over his face. They've been dating, what, a year and a half now? And the kid still looks at her like that, like she is the first human female he has ever seen. It's very cute. Marlen doesn't believe in high school relationships—he's been a high school teacher for too long—but if his daughter has to have some kid over here all the time, it's good that it's this kid. What *is* his name? Jacob?

He's sure that's it, but it feels wrong.

Hilda pats his arm and he blinks heavily. Had he been falling asleep? Possibly. The steady background trill of crickets is hypnotic.

He leans toward the fire and watches the cracks in the wood turn orange, stray pieces of ash flying into the air like wish paper. He misses Nora. She's impossibly far away. He feels the ache in his jaw. The present situation is a nightmare, the likes of which not even he could have dreamed up.

"I should go to bed," he says. He feels Hilda stiffen beside him. She has gotten greedy for his time. He wants to be able to give it to her, but he's just so tired.

"Okay," she says. It's her pretending-to-be-okay okay.

"No, actually, I'll stay up a few more minutes," he says. "It's not the end of the world if I'm tired tomorrow. I can sleep when I'm dead." He laughs; she doesn't. He throws a couple more logs on the fire, sending up a burst of sparks, a message to his wife that he isn't going anywhere just yet. He changes the subject. "Talked to Jerry today. Told me he saw a cougar out there this summer, by his bins."

"Weird to think they come out here sometimes. I haven't seen one since that time when I was a kid, with Irene," says Hilda.

Marlen's just a shadow, but she can see his head tilted back, taking in the stars. Looking for the dangerous one. Strange to think it's out there, that it's harmless and will be harmless right up until it kills them all. A cougar feels more dangerous at this point. It feels more plausible. Hilda's mother had always been so afraid of cougars.

21

Iver has fallen neatly through a crack in time; it must have opened up as he walked over it on the way to see who rang the doorbell, and he didn't notice he was falling until he'd opened the door and realized he'd gone back thirty or forty years.

His son is standing there in front of him, the tips of his scraggly blond hair poking out from under his toque, his cheeks red, the rest of him hidden beneath a bulky winter coat.

Iver is not sure what to do. He straightens up, like someone has told him to. He clears his throat and says the only thing that makes sense. "Come in."

He realizes he's frowning. He tries to look how he feels, but he can't do it because he doesn't know how to translate this feeling from the inside to the outside. He has dreamed about this moment for years and years, but now that it's here it's very complicated—because it can't possibly be real. It's either a dream or the end of the world has come early and this is heaven.

He checks in with himself: Is the usual pain still there? The foggy vision and hearing, the knee that feels like it's going to snap in half at any moment?

It's all still there. He's very much alive.

Then it's either a dream, or someone's playing a joke on him, or he's living in the past in his mind only, like his father had before he died with Alzheimer's.

Iver doesn't like the thought of that. People watching him step out of reality, not having control of their perception of him. But if this is the lived experience of it . . . it's not terrible. Worse for the onlooker.

He becomes aware that he's walking back into his house. His son has shrugged off his jacket, hung it up, and is now following him into the living room. They're not huggers, either of them, so they just sit stiffly across from each other, Iver in his plaid armchair and his son on the sagging blue couch. Iver feels as though he's been plunged into an ice-cold bath—the first few minutes were pure shock, but now that's wearing off, and he's feeling pain and euphoria and a million other things. Frozen solid on the outside.

Here's another thing that's wrong—if this is the past, where is Iver's wife? Why is the house still all musty, the TV tray in the middle of the room with last night's supper on it?

Iver has not done the traveling, it would seem. His son has come to him, back from the dead and through the years and into the living room, where he sits with his legs crossed under him, chewing on his fingernails, unaged. He has strong fingernails; they make loud cracking noises when he bites down on them, as though he's biting right into his finger bones. Iver had forgotten that his son did this and that he hated it so much, but now he feels conflicted. He still hates it, but now it's also the best sound in the world, one he would miss if it went away again.

"So? How are you?" A stupid question to ask someone who has been dead for such a long time.

His son shrugs.

Fair.

"You want something to eat?" This feels like a more appropriate question. Iver thinks that if he were to die and then come back to life, the first thing he'd want is a meal. Get everything moving again.

His son nods. "Sure."

Iver doesn't have a lot to offer. He makes a sandwich with just a few things on it, pickles and cheese and ketchup. Almost a hamburger, minus the most important ingredient. His son scarfs it down and accepts a second sandwich without hesitation, and then a third.

"You haven't changed at all," says Iver. Saying this out loud makes him choke, and he pretends to cough to cover it up. Good grief. Is he not allowed to get a little emotional? His son has come back to life! But his son is not emotional—maybe he doesn't even know he was dead in the first place. A big dramatic display would be awkward and one-sided.

His son has finished eating his last sandwich and is leaning back in his chair, eating his finger bones again. "Can I, like, stay with you for a few days?"

"Of course," says Iver, as baffled by the request as by the rest of it. He has to fake another cough. "You can stay as long as you'd like."

"Cool. Thanks."

It makes so little sense it *has* to be a dream. Iver decides to let it unfold and enjoy it. What else is there to do?

Ole feels his body relax. He'll call his parents soon enough and let them know where he is; maybe they'll make him come back, or maybe they'll be glad to have him out of the house so they can yell even louder, say all the things they don't want him to hear. He's okay to just be here for a bit. This house is comforting. His grandfather has lived here since long before Ole was born, and it's one of those places that never changes. The itchy couch fabric, the disconcerting red shag carpet, the large wooden clock in the corner that plays a fragment of a tune every hour on the hour.

But, most importantly: his grandfather, who is neither panicking about the end of the world nor pretending it's not happening. He's somewhere in the middle, and that's where Ole wants to be too. Here in the middle with his grandpa.

22

Petra peers at Nora over her glasses, her eyes narrow and dark, her pupils too large. "Is it possible," she's saying, "that memory is a construct relating to gravity and entropy and complexity, and there could be moments of misplaced complexity that make memory happen in the opposite direction?" What is she? Not a hallucination, because Nora is fully aware that she's not real. She's here because Nora needs *someone* to be here. She has summoned her, like a ghost, to fill a very specific role.

Pretend Petra moves around the apartment exactly the same way Real Petra had, theorizing and issuing bizarre challenges. Pretend Petra thinks the end of the world is *gorgeous* and *intriguing*, and she thinks Nora is an absolute child. And when Nora can't stand her anymore, she summons Pretend Sonja instead, a space-cadetty mother hen, saying, *Heyyyyy hey hey hey you're going to be okay, everything's going to be okay* and reminding Nora to eat and sleep. An antagonist to keep her sharp, a comforter to keep her sane. The human brain tries so hard to take care of itself.

Then, sometimes mid somebody's sentence, the house is silent. Nora is alone, save for her cat, and she can't summon anyone. Not the credit card company, not the courage to call her mother after leaving it this long. Not even Jacob.

But now, it would seem, she has been able to summon one other person. Her phone lights up, a message from Derek.

nice pic

She rolls her eyes. She sent that picture days ago, in a moment of weakness. The moment has very much passed.

saw ur parents at ph. ur dad hates me

Pretend Petra is still going. "Perhaps there could be a glitch in the way time goes, and you could remember something that has not happened yet, people you have not met. Like you and that guy . . ."

my dad doesn't hate anyone

he hates me

What is she supposed to say to this? *I don't blame him? I hate you too?* This is why you don't text your exes, not even in end times.

what did he do

nthng. just acted mad

She stares at the phone. Types,

sry

Is that what he wants? An apology from her on behalf of her father? He doesn't reply.

She searches him on social media, something she has managed to avoid doing for most of the time she's been abroad. He has TikTok now, a platform he'd mocked ruthlessly the entire time she'd dated him, and Sophia, the girl he'd dumped her for, is in almost every one of his videos. They do a lot of road trips, a lot of annoying pranks, always showing their best angles, watching the camera out of the corner of their eye as though it's the third member of their relationship—it has the effect of making the viewer, in this case Nora, feel like *they* are the third member. Nora watches his face on the screen, wondering if she misses him or if she just misses . . . everything. The way she misses home, her parents in the kitchen and her familiar bed and the drafty windows in her bedroom and the mice that live in the walls, where she wouldn't necessarily want the mice, and the windows, but if it meant having the house and the parents and the bed, she'd take those things too. Is Derek more like the familiar bed or the mice in the walls? She's not sure.

Her social media stalking is interrupted by a knock at the door, such an improbable sound that it is either also imagined or a mistake, someone thinking they're on the fourth floor visiting their grandmother, about to get a little jolt when Nora opens the door instead. It's the most depressing thought she has had in a long time—and that's saying something—that she is so far from home that the odds of someone dropping in just to say hello are less than that of winning the lottery.

Almost.

She opens the door and wins the lottery: it's the only person it possibly could be.

He's smiling, but the smile is anxious or, she hopes, sheepish, like he's aware of how long it's been since he said he might call her. He crosses his arms, uncrosses them. He looks wrong here, like a character from one sitcom showing up in another one. "Hey, Nora." He leans against the doorframe, then quickly corrects this too. His body wants to relax, but his brain knows relaxation is inappropriate. "May I come in?"

"Of course." She sounds very calm, very sane, as though she has not been texting and stalking her ex-boyfriend and carrying on actual out-loud conversations with imaginary ex-roommates.

Pretend Petra still sits at the table, waiting expectantly. Jacob walks over and sits beside her. She wiggles her eyebrows at Nora suggestively.

Nora tries to ignore her, but seeing as she is also the one conjuring her, this is difficult.

"Oh, hello," he says.

For a second Nora stupidly thinks he's addressing Petra, but then she realizes he's talking to her cat, who has appeared at his feet, rubbing against his legs, purring softly. She reaches out her hand, but the cat ignores her. On brand.

Jacob rubs his forehead with both hands. "So? How've you been?"

"Oh, you know . . ." She tries to remember what has happened in the days since she last saw him. She has gotten an obnoxious cat tattoo. She has gone skydiving. She has called her credit card company hundreds of times and her mother zero times.

She has given up on ever getting home. That's a big one.

"I'm okay," she says. "You?"

"Well." He looks out the window, at the invisible panic. "I'm doing okay too."

There is a silent sense of knowing that no one is, in fact, doing okay, but no one knows how to say this without sounding pitiful.

"I'm sorry I haven't called," he says. "It's kind of a weird time."

What a strange way to put it, she thinks.

"Real weird," she says. "It's okay. I didn't call either."

"So I have a favor to ask," he says.

She feels disappointed. He's not here to see her for the sake of seeing her. He's here to ask her for something, though she can't imagine what she could have to offer. "Okay?"

"It's a weird one."

"Okay."

"Okay, so brace yourself for a really weird favor."

"I'm braced."

He shakes his head and mumbles something under his breath. "Sorry?"

"I said, 'You can't possibly brace yourself hard enough for this.'"

"Well, now I'm starting to feel a little bit curious." She tries to sound jokey, unbothered, but she's becoming more bothered by the second. He shows up, after all of that annoying not showing up, with this apparently preposterous favor he can't even say—

"I'm here to ask you to marry me."

Her ears are ringing, as though he'd screamed the words into the quiet apartment. Instantaneously he has turned red, and she has gone white, as though all the blood has rushed out of her and into him.

"Is that, like, the joke favor, meant to prepare me for the real one?"

He can't meet her eyes now; he's staring at a poster on the wall, one of Petra's, a glam rock band sporting lots of thick black eyeliner and metal hair. "Nope. That's it. That's the favor."

Nora is experiencing a welcome rush of emotions that are not related in any way to the end of the world. Confusion and flattery and curiosity. Feelings from Before Times.

But Jacob looks like he wants to jump out the window. "Believe it or not, there's actually a fairly decent explanation."

She almost doesn't want a fairly decent explanation. Why not something outlandish? Something like, "I've fallen madly in love with you!" *Is* there any other explanation for wanting to marry someone?

"You're from Canada."

This information seems as though it were meant to be helpful, explanatory. All on its own.

"And it's on your bucket list to marry a Canadian . . . ?"

He shakes his head, looking impatient, but his impatience is not directed at her. "Okay, so here's the thing: they—your government, the Canadian government—aren't allowing almost anyone to enter Canada right now except Canadians. Did you know that? They've put an emergency travel ban in place."

She nods. "It's on all the airline websites." A small yellow box at the bottom of every page, explaining how the policy has to do with prioritizing the homecoming of Canadian citizens, keeping what few flights are left for those people as pilots quit and airlines shutter.

She doesn't know where the blood has gone now; he's as white as a sheet, and she's worried he's going to pass out. "So if you want to go to Canada right now, you either need to be a Canadian citizen, or—"

"Okay." Has he come here because he thinks she doesn't know this? "Well, I *am* a Canadian citizen, so it should be okay, as long as I can get my credit card sorted out. That's actually my problem at the moment—"

"No, that's not what I'm—" He regroups. "I know *you're* Canadian. *I'm* not."

It takes her a minute. "You want to go to Canada, Jacob? But why?"

"My sister, Anna—I think I mentioned her?"

Nora nods. Right. He had mentioned her that first day in the café. Roughly a week ago—or two?—though it feels now like a different lifetime.

"She's in Montreal. For school. And if you think it's hard to get from here to there—it's impossible, *impossible* to get from there to here. At the beginning of all of this, someone on some blog or on the news or something made it seem like North America was going to be most directly hit, and lots of people still seem to think this part of the world is safer. So while people like you are trying to get to their loved ones, a huge portion of the population is fleeing here. And there are so few flights, with pilots and airport staff quitting . . . Anna's been trying desperately to get home, and my family's talked it over, and we've decided I've got to go be with her so at least she's not alone. You know, if . . . or when . . . or . . . and then we'll try to come back together. And if we don't make it . . . we're together. She has someone with her."

What a bizarre trajectory their lives have taken, where the priority is not survival but emotional comfort.

"So anyway," says Jacob, suddenly talking very quickly, "that's why my mom wants us—you and I—to get married."

Her mind clatters along a track, and suddenly she knows where the track will end. Somehow she already knew it when she met this man at Begonia. She thinks of Petra and her beloved physicists and the idea that they have been here before. It really does feel that way.

Still. It's weird.

"And it shouldn't actually be that complicated," Jacob continues. "In—normal times—there'd be a lot of red tape. You'd need all the usual documents as well as something called a *Ehefähigkeitszeugnis*, a certificate showing that you're legally free to marry. But my mother knows someone at the civil registrar's office, and they're going to shortcut us. I mean"—he flushes deep red—"they will—they *would*, if we decide to do it. We'd just have to go in and sign some things."

"That's something."

"Isn't it?"

"Like, really, *really* something."

"My mother is really something. She's very . . . creative . . ."

"She wants us to get *married*."

"Well, not really married so much as—legally *wed*."

"*Wed* is different than *married*?"

"*Legally* wed."

"Again, *legally wed* is different than *married*?"

"Well, yes, because the emphasis is on the *legally* part. The *wed* part is just . . . there for decoration." Jacob's voice has become deeply sad, as though he's recognized the stupidity of this plan and is prepared to go back home and tell his mother it failed. "I know it's weird. It wasn't my idea. It was my mom's."

She looks back at his hands, shaking on the table in front of her. Poor guy. He's taking this too seriously. They'll all be dead in two months. What does marriage even mean now? How hard would it be to commit yourself to another person for the rest of your life, at this point? And if not being married is the only thing stopping you from being with your family, why *wouldn't* you get married? She's the only person in Jacob's world who can make this happen. It's really more of a good deed than anything else. But in a shallow way, she can't help but bemoan the fact that she is only ever going to be proposed to one time in her short life, and that proposal contains the phrases *I know it's weird. It wasn't my idea. It was my mom's.*

She wonders what Derek would say if she texted him and told him the news. *I'm getting married! To a man I met a week ago! Love at first sight, unlike anything I've ever felt before!*

And, of course, she thinks of Petra, who is, in spirit, sitting at the table with them, watching this play out. What's more adult than getting married?

"Okay," she says. She wants to ask him to do it again, more romantically, but that would be weirder than anything to this point.

"What? You'll *marry* me?" Now he looks incredulous, as though she were the one who showed up at his apartment and proposed after less than a month of knowing each other.

"I mean. *Yes.* I get the desperation thing. I'm desperate too. I've been trying to book tickets home for ages, but my credit card has been offline—"

He lets out a giant sigh of relief and holds up a hand. "Wow. Okay. Nora, thank you. Thank you. And don't worry about the tickets; my father's taking care of that."

He has very casually granted her a wish, and he doesn't seem to understand the magnitude of it. She must have misunderstood him.

"What do you mean?"

"My father is on it. Plane tickets."

"For me?"

"Yes."

"Wait—but what if I had said no? To you?"

"I was prepared to beg." His face is red again, remembering his embarrassing desperation. "And in the event that you hadn't already found a ticket, I was prepared to bribe."

"Wow."

"Again, I'm very aware of how weird this all is."

"No, I mean, 'Wow, I don't know how to thank you.' Or your father."

He sits back in his chair, at last allowing himself to relax, and as he does he catches her coffee mug with the back of his hand, sending it flying off the table. It shatters, and he jumps out of his seat, apologizing and picking at the pieces of broken pottery.

"Don't worry about it," she says, stooping to help him. "It's just a mug. It's not the end of the world."

He laughs heartily at her weak attempt at humor, and the sound of it is thrilling, like the actual beginning of something. Or the middle. Not the end, not yet.

23

Marlen has never been this nervous.

Well, that might not be entirely true. Surely he was this nervous when he'd asked Hilda out on their first date in grade eleven. The Pot Hole hadn't existed then; they'd driven forty-five minutes to the nearest movie theater in a neighboring town. Surely he was this nervous when he'd asked her to marry him. And again when she'd given birth to Nora. (He wouldn't have been so nervous then if it hadn't been for the videos they'd watched in the birth classes Hilda insisted they take beforehand. Graphic horror movies about episiotomies and emergency C-sections. Hilda just wanted to be informed, she said. He had not wished to be informed. He had hoped the doctors would be informed enough for all three of them. But when it comes to childbirth, you let the person who's doing the birthing make the decisions, and now he has an encyclopedic knowledge of all the things that could go wrong during childbirth, the one topic he'd never felt compelled to study independently.)

Anyway, Nora was born twenty years ago, so it's been a long time since he was this nervous.

"Are you okay?" Hilda looks equally nervous, like she thinks he's called her down here to confess something, to get something huge off his chest before they go. She'd been getting ready for bed; her hair is slicked back into a tiny nub of a ponytail, and her face is freshly scrubbed, slightly red. Phone in hand, as always. Redialing, still, the stubborn persistence only a mother could possess.

"Oh, you know—" He stops himself. Maybe now is not the time to make jokes about dying. "Yes, I'm great." But he says this so woodenly it just makes her more nervous.

She sits beside him on the couch. "What's up?"

With shaking hands, he hands her a package, wrapped in newspaper. "What's this?"

"Open it and see." His voice cracks, like he's twelve.

She pulls back the paper, revealing the glossy cover of his book, the exploding stars, his name in huge block letters. "Oh," she says, her expression completely neutral, "thank you."

Hilda's confused now. Why does he look like he's about to admit to murder? And why has he given her a book about—she glances down at it—space?

He clears his throat. He looks immensely disappointed in her reaction. "You're welcome," he says hoarsely.

Clearly she's missing something. She looks back down at the book. *It's Not the End of the World* by—she gasps.

"Oh! Marlen—*oh*, I didn't notice that!"

He breaks into a relieved grin . . .

"Where did you find this?"

. . . and freezes in confusion.

"Huh?"

"Where did you find a book written by someone with the same name as you? That's hilarious."

"I wrote it." His voice is quiet; he has not yet admitted this out loud to anyone.

She flips the book over and gasps again. "OH! MARLEN!"

Because a book written by someone with the same name as your husband is a funny coincidence. A book written by someone with the same name *and face* as your husband is . . . most likely a book written by your husband.

"This is *your* book," she says reverently, holding it as though it's an ancient artifact. It feels like it is, for how long it has existed in his head, and she knows this, that there has always been a book in him. Since their first date she's known about his desire to write it, though he has been too bashful to discuss the details. She knows what a big deal this is—which is probably why she's coming all unglued.

"When did you *do* this?" She flips open the front cover to check the copyright date.

He feels like he's going to burst. Here it is—*this* is the feeling he'd wanted when he'd first opened the box.

"Can I read it?" She has to set the book down on the couch and reach for a Kleenex. She's much more emotional than he'd anticipated.

"About that . . ." He takes a deep breath. The nerves are back. "It might be a strange one to read right now."

She laughs through her tears. Looks out the window. "I don't know that there's going to be a better time, Marlen."

"Right. Well . . ."

So he has to explain to her why, exactly, the book is "a strange one to read right now." He leads with the story about the kid with the Pentecostal aunt, which seems to be more confusing than helpful, and ends with a sort of toned-down version of the morning he woke up and knew he had to write this book *now*, glossing over the bit about knowing he was going to die. He watches her eyes widen when he tells her that the book deals with a gamma ray burst and the end of civilization. When he's finished, she shakes her head, almost speechless.

"I don't know what to say about any of that," she says at last. "But I really am so proud of you, Marlen." She's starting to cry a little, and Marlen has to focus on the cover of his book so he won't start up too.

Mindlessly, reflexively, she picks up the phone to press the redial button, but it rings in her hand before she can, confusing her. The number on the screen: Nora's. She shrieks at it, forgets how to answer it. She fumbles it and drops it on the floor.

But at last she has it in her hands, and she has managed to push the right button and put it on speaker so Marlen can hear his daughter's voice.

Nora's voice, blown out and distorted because she seems to be yelling directly into the receiver: "I'm coming home!"

And though Marlen is deliriously happy, out of his mind with joy, a feeling that might physically lift him up into the air, he doesn't feel at all surprised.

24

It's a small town. No one has ever gone *missing*, not in the face-on-a-milk-carton *60 Minutes* way kids go missing in cities. Here kids go funny-story-for-later missing—both parents thought the other would pick the kid up from hockey practice; there was a miscommunication between the parents and the kid about where exactly they were supposed to meet; the kid fell asleep on the school bus and woke up confused and disoriented at the bus driver's farm, parked behind the barn.

But this time Hank's worried there won't be a funny story for later—whether or not there's a later to be had. When Ole doesn't come home on the bus, Hank calls the school, and that's how he finds out Ole didn't go to school today. He calls around to some of Ole's friends' parents, but no one can help; no one has seen him. Hank doesn't know what to do next. Irene suggests they call the police, but Hank is disturbed at the idea. People don't call the police here; it feels like the kind of thing that would be an overreaction in any event. The nearest station is over an hour away; sometimes they send an officer down to check for seat belts and hand out speeding tickets, but for all intents and purposes it's not a place where you call the police when you need help. You call your neighbor.

So that's what Hank and Irene do first.

They call the neighbors three miles to their left and the neighbors four miles to their right and the ones five miles up the road. They call the grocery store and the bank (now, ominously, closed) and the Pot Hole (no one answers).

Hank and Irene begin moving around the kitchen, cleaning it as they go—an excuse to slam cupboards and set things down a little harder than usual. Irene wants to call the police, but Hank is still holding out—*What if he's with a friend? Wouldn't that be embarrassing, to get those guys all the way down here for no reason?* Irene walks over to a wall, firmly plants her palm against it, and begins emphasizing every syllable with a gentle thud, a controlled but assertive move, like a judge with a gavel.

"We"—*thud*—"need"—*thud*—"to call"—*thud thud*—"the police"—*thud thud thud*.

So Hank calls the police, but the police don't come. They take a statement over the phone, say he should call again tomorrow if the kid hasn't returned. *Twenty-four hours,* they say. *Give it twenty-four hours.* Irene, who can hear the officer's voice loud and clear from across the kitchen, raises her palm to the wall, as though she is going to start *thud thud thud*ding again, this time at the police, but it's too late; they've hung up. Hank looks helplessly at her. "I'm sorry, Irene," he says. "That's about all they can do."

"Not *can. Want to,*" says Irene. (*Thud thud. Thud thud.*)

She sits at the table, defeated. What do you do with those awful in-between hours where your child is missing but not missing enough for the police to care? Take flashlights and walk around fields? Drive up and down dirt roads, yelling Ole's name out the windows? Call one of the church ladies and start a prayer chain? (If there is one single thing you can count on to spread some news in a small Saskatchewan town, it's a prayer chain.) Hank calls Marlen and Hilda to let them know, and they say the obligatory thing about telling them if there is anything they can do to help (of course, there is nothing and they know that). Irene is about to call Iver, but she changes her mind at the last minute, right as she's about to dial the final digit in his phone number—best not to worry him.

That's everything. There's nothing more to do today. Hank pulls Irene into a hug, the first they've shared in days. The letter does not matter right now; the end of the world does not matter. This is the actual end of the world, and neither of them can bear to be alone in it.

The next morning Hank calls the police again, and an officer finally comes. He arrives in plain clothes, driving his truck, which for some reason shatters any illusions Irene had about the police being able to fix anything.

"Sorry, Irene," says the officer, someone she has met a handful of times before now but never seen in jeans and a T-shirt. "I came down here because I couldn't stand saying it to you over the phone, but . . . we don't have the resources for this right now. It's—well, I'm sure you can imagine. I'll do what I can, personally, of course, but . . ."

She wishes he had said all of this to her over the phone. Then she wouldn't have to see the look of absolute hopelessness on his face.

25

Nora drinks so many cups of coffee she starts to have heart palpitations. She rests her head on the seat of the couch and lets her arms hang limply to the floor, trying to breathe deeply, trying to signal to her body that there is no immediate emergency, just a lot of caffeine. Her tattoo is starting to scab under the Saniderm wrap. She's not sure when she's meant to take it off, expose Yannick's artwork to the elements. He had explained it all to her, how to care for the cat, but as the words came out of his mouth, she forgot them, like he was handing important things to her and she was immediately throwing them into the garbage. Her real cat still doesn't like it. It climbs over Nora's body, taking great pains to step on the ink likeness of itself.

"I'm getting married tomorrow," Nora says to the empty room. "To Jacob."

"Congratulations," says Pretend Petra, even more sarcastically than she says everything else. Nora hadn't thought this possible.

Pretend Sonja is trying to be chipper, as usual. "It's exciting," she says. "Even if it's fake."

"It's not fake," says Nora defensively. "There will be paperwork."

"Okay." Petra hums, a sound that vibrates in Nora's head like Yannick's tattoo gun.

They sit in awkward silence for a while. Nora had not known it was possible to feel awkward with just yourself. She wanders over to the window. She hadn't noticed this before now, but she can see the bird mural from here, the same one visible from the front window of Begonia. Not the whole thing, and not very well, just a sliver of it through the buildings, part of a blue jay, part of a parrot, part of a robin. It's a bit disorienting; she hasn't gained a sense of the city yet and would not have thought it possible to see that street from this vantage point. But it's comforting. Grounding. Something about that mural feels nostalgic, like when you come across a children's book in a used bookstore that you vaguely remember your mother reading to you when you were small.

"I am bored," announces Pretend Petra. "You should text Derek."

"Why would I do that?"

"To ask him if he cheated on you."

"I don't care if he cheated on me. Why would I care about that now? It's not like we're getting back together. Doesn't matter anymore."

Pretend Petra snorts. "But you are curious."

"Obviously."

"So? It is the end of the world! Indulge your curiosity!"

Petra has a point. Nora types it before she can second-guess herself anymore.

When did u start dating Sophia?

26

Irene snags the good table at the Pot Hole—less of a feat than it used to be with all the families leaving, and the fact that no one really feels like going out on the town right now. Hilda is meeting her in ten minutes, but Irene has come early to take some deep breaths.

She has the letter in her purse.

Hilda is a reasonable woman and a good sister. She knows Irene better than anyone and always believes the best of her. Still, Irene is anxious. She doesn't understand why her position would be inflammatory or controversial—it makes sense to her; other reputable people hold the same opinion; it's not going to hurt anyone if she's wrong—but just look what it's done to her and Hank.

Hilda shows up exactly two minutes early. When she sees Irene, she rushes forward to pull her into a hug.

"How are you holding up?" Hilda's hugs have become very clutchy and examining. She's been turning into their mother ever since the position became available, but recent events seem to be fast-tracking the process. "How's Hank?"

"Oh, we're . . ." Irene pulls away from her sister. She pours two cups of coffee, adds cream to one, passes it to Hilda. "Miserable. It's awful, not knowing where he is or if he's okay. I can't explain how awful it is." Technically this is a lie: she lets her sister think they're miserable only because their son is missing. She doesn't mention the fact that they were miserable before that too. That she worries his absence might be in some way related to that miserableness and that this is the worst part of any of it, the thought that her son's disappearance might be her fault.

Hilda almost says she understands—after all, for almost two weeks she didn't know where Nora was or whether she was okay or whether she'd ever see her again—but she stops herself. It's not the same, especially now that her story has a happy ending.

(She almost laughs out loud at this thought but stops herself. *Happy ending. Ha ha. Nobody's getting one of those.*)

Funny how, even though everyone is living through the same tragedy, there are still hierarchies of pain and trauma, and people still try to respect them, and a missing child is uncontestably higher on the ladder than the end of humanity.

"I'm so sorry," says Hilda after a moment of tentative coffee sipping. "I can't even begin to imagine."

"My brain keeps doing the strangest things," Irene says quietly, tracing the lid of the paper cup with her finger. "I picture him as a baby, even though I know he's not a baby. I know he's old enough to take care of himself, and I know he's smart enough not to do anything too dumb. But every time I shut my eyes I picture him, tiny and naked, lying on my chest for the first time, completely helpless . . . and I get that feeling I had when he was first born, that terror when you realize you have to go to sleep and leave them . . . alone, sort of—you know what I mean? And closing your eyes feels like you're neglecting them, like something bad's going to happen if you're not staring at them . . . ?"

Hilda nods, even though she knows Irene had a much harder time with that stage of motherhood. Terror wasn't a dominant emotion in her first few days with Nora. It had been mostly joyful for her, unfathomable physical pain aside. But it seemed as though everything about that time evoked fear for Irene—the depth and intensity of which Hilda generally associates with nightmares, not babies.

"I get that same feeling now," Irene continues. "That fear. It's awful. And I can't sleep because he's on the backs of my eyelids when I close my eyes, tiny and naked, lying in a field, crying so hard his face is red and wrinkled, and his little fists are shaking, and I just want to hold—and I *can't*—"

She breaks off.

This is not why she came here.

"Actually, Hilda," she says, sniffling, trying to regain her composure. It takes a few minutes, during which Hilda won't stop reaching across the table, touching her shoulders, like she's trying to find an off switch for the tears. "There's something else I want to talk to you about today. And I don't have a lot of time—I want to be home in case—when—Ole comes back. I just came in to ask around town some more, drop by a few of his friends' houses, and talk to Dad."

"You've decided to tell Dad?"

Irene nods. "I know we said we didn't want to worry him, but it's not fair to keep him in the dark. He's not a child."

"Mm-hmm."

Hilda waits expectantly. Irene seems to be psyching herself up for something, like she's about to ask for money or say something confrontational. Like Marlen the other day with the book. Maybe Irene wrote a book too? Hilda hopes not. She doesn't particularly want to spend the rest of her life reading.

But it's not a book—or if it is, it's a very short one, a single page long. Irene produces a paper from her purse and slides it across the table with a sheepish smile.

"What's this?"

"A letter. It was in my mailbox."

Hilda picks it up and reads it, her expression indecipherable. Irene tries not to read into the quick twitch of her eyebrow, a momentary wrinkle of her nose.

"Wow," Hilda says at last, setting the letter down and picking up her coffee again. "That's quite something, isn't it?" But she knows her sister well enough to know that she didn't ask her here just to share something she thought of as a joke. Something about this letter is important to her, meaningful in some way. Maybe a friend of hers wrote it, and Irene is looking for advice on how to address this silliness in a loving way.

"Quite something in, in what way, do you mean?" Irene stammers, looking at the letter instead of Hilda.

Oh no.

Hilda, it would seem, is the one who needs advice on how to address this silliness in a loving way. Probably she needs to start by reframing it, even in the quiet of her brain, as something other than silliness.

"I mean . . ." Hilda drinks the rest of her coffee in three gulps and has to go back for another cup. She has to hunt in her bag for another loonie. She has to pour the cream. She has to blow her nose. How many more tasks can she come up with before she has to answer this question?

Quite something in what way?

Quite something in *every* way!

It feels as absurd as if Irene had invited her here and passed her a letter from a random internet person claiming that grass and trees are artificial and real nature involves skyscrapers and parking lots and streetlights. But maybe there are people out there who believe that too. Maybe it's unfair to judge anyone for what they believe, if they have come to that belief honestly—and is it even possible to come to a belief *dis*honestly? People aren't out there *trying* to believe ridiculous things, are they?

She can't put it off any longer. She sits and faces her sister, softens her voice. "I mean, I just feel like this is wishful thinking. I want to believe it, because it sounds so lovely, but I don't."

Irene's face falls. She stuffs the paper back into her purse and stands. "I don't understand how you can be so sure, so quickly," she says, her voice hoarse. "You haven't even read the articles on the website."

"Irene—"

"Never mind. I should go. I need to stop by Dad's place still."

Hilda doesn't know what to do. Should she offer to read the articles? Not that they'd change her mind—then again, maybe she should be open to having her mind changed. The letter reminds her of ones she's received from Jehovah's Witnesses over the years, only instead of trying to convince her the end is near, this one preaches the opposite. She pictures a grizzled old man with unwashed hair, standing on a street corner, calling to passersby, wearing a sandwich board that reads THE END IS FAR AWAY. Perhaps it's simply this association for her, something she's already shut the door on that makes it hard to open her mind to a different view.

Irene's trying not to cry now; she's always been bad at this. Is she embarrassed? Angry? Hurt? This letter convinced her. Clearly she'd thought it would have the same effect on Hilda, and Hilda almost wishes it had. It would be nice, actually, to believe the world wasn't ending. To carry on as though everything is normal until, well, it's not. She thinks of Marlen's book, which she has to read in very short spurts because it's too real. It seems to be the best evidence she has for the fact that the world is ending. But if she were to offer it up as evidence, she knows she'd be met with the same skepticism she's showing her sister right now. *Your husband wrote a book and you're taking that over my scientists?*

"I'll read the articles," Hilda says. She wants to be open-minded. Or, at least, she wants Irene to feel that she is, and she wants to believe this about herself even if it's not true.

Irene can't meet her eyes. She thrusts the letter at her sister and hurries out of the shop, nearly colliding with Alfie on the sidewalk.

Alfie is carrying a box. Alfie is always carrying a box. A box of carafes, a box of library books, a box of groceries, of hymnals, of flowers, of coffee cups. If there is a small collection of anything that needs to travel from one end of town to the other, chances are it's in a box in Alfie's arms.

Irene tries to brighten and smile at her, but Alfie is much too perceptive for fake smiles. She's like a shark, and sadness is blood in the water. She gets right in Irene's way.

"What's wrong, Irene?" She doesn't even say hello first. Just *What's wrong?* This is Alfie's way. She runs this town; she's too busy not to go straight to the important part of the conversation (but never too busy to go there).

Irene shakes her head and Alfie lets it go. She is nosy, but, to her credit, she is also respectful.

"How's Ole?" Alfie knows he was not at home at one point, because it is her business to know everything, but the village's communication chain has suffered this week in light of the upcoming apocalypse (for which Alfie is completely unprepared; she has three baby showers on her plate this month alone, plus Christmas is coming *and* she's running the gas station now that Craig has left town to be with his parents in Moose Jaw); so she has not received an update on Hank and Irene's boy. She assumes he's back home, because this is a tiny town in the middle of nowhere where nothing bad ever happens. Why should it start now?

"He's . . . we don't know where he is, actually," says Irene, and Alfie bites her lip. She considers herself assertive, efficient, never insensitive. Usually. She works as hard to keep her feet out of her mouth as she does at everything else.

"Oh, Irene . . . I'm . . . I'm so sorry. I honestly didn't know—"

"No"—Irene can't stand the thought of making Alfie feel bad—"I'm sure he's fine. We're not worried; he's probably just with a friend . . ."

Alfie nods vigorously. "Of course he is. Of *course* he is. Absolutely."

"Okay—well, I'm on my way to see my dad, so I should—" She motions in the general direction of her father's house.

"Right, of course—have a nice time with him."

"Thank you. I will. Have a nice day, Alfie." They turn to go their separate ways, but suddenly Irene needs to know what Alfie thinks of the letter. Of all the people in this town, Alfie, with her altruism and her generosity, would at least give it serious consideration.

"Alfie," she says, turning around again, "one question, actually?"

"Yes?"

The box looks heavy, but it seems like Alfie could stand there holding it all day, if that would be helpful to someone in some way.

Irene can't go through with it. She can't stand one more person—and especially not Alfie—looking at her with that weird mix of pity and bewilderment, like, *You, Irene, are a conspiracy theorist now?* As though Irene were not an intelligent woman who has always thought things through with great care. People have always respected her—why should that change just because she's adopted one single unpopular opinion?

"I was just wondering . . . if you didn't believe all of this stuff, about how the world's ending, what would you do differently?"

Alfie shifts the box onto her hip. "Hmm. I'm not sure. I don't feel as though my life changed very much when I found out it was ending, so I guess it also wouldn't change if it wasn't. I'd just keep on doing what I feel is needed."

Irene stops at her father's house on the way out of town. She tries to think of a way to tell him about Ole that doesn't sound hysterical. She doesn't want to worry him, but she doesn't want to treat him like a kid who isn't allowed in on the grown-up conversations.

She knocks on the door, and it creaks open almost instantly, but not all the way. Iver peers at her, almost suspiciously, as if she's a door-to-door salesperson. Irene has a moment of terror—had Hilda called ahead and warned him that Irene had, what, joined a death cult? The opposite of a death cult? A "the world's not going to end" cult? Would that really be the worst cult to be a part of?

Usually when Irene visits her father, she is sucked into the house, as into a black hole. He opens the door wide and all but drags her in, offering food and store-bought cookies and awful coffee, and she always leaves feeling acutely aware that she does not visit enough, and that she doesn't stay long enough when she does, and that one of these times she needs to clean his coffee maker for him.

Today he offers a quick smile but keeps his body wedged in the door.

"Hi," he says, the way you'd say hi to the grim reaper. Like, *Please don't think I'm being disrespectful, but please go away.*

"Hi, Dad," she says. "Are you okay?"

"I'm great!" He kind of shouts this at her.

"Can I come in?"

He looks panicked. "Actually . . . I was just . . . heading out." He slides out through the small opening and shuts the door behind him.

It's not proper for a daughter to question her parent, so Irene accepts this with a shrug.

He's standing on the porch in his socks. She looks down at them, and he follows her gaze. He gulps.

"What are you up to today?" He offers a shaky smile. He looks . . . guilty?

"Actually, Dad, I just wanted to let you know that . . ." Now it's her turn to be flustered. No, she realizes, it wouldn't be kind to worry this man. He looks so fragile right now. He has lost so much in his lifetime. He doesn't need to worry about anyone but himself. "I wanted to check on you and make sure you're doing okay."

"Thank you," he says brightly.

They stand there and contemplate each other. Sometimes it really strikes her how strange it is to be an adult daughter, to stand in front of the person who has known you your whole life and finally understand what it's like to see things from the perspective they had when you were a kid, but to also understand that they have lived another whole lifetime since then. And *she's* trying to protect *him*?

For reasons she can't articulate, yes. Nothing makes much sense if you think too hard about it.

"Anyway, I should go. And you—" She looks down again at his socks.

"I should go too," he says, moving toward the steps, guiding her away from the house.

"Are you going to put some shoes on first, Dad?" She tries not to be too motherly about it.

Another glance behind him. "You know what, Irene, my shoes are pinching me in a strange place, and the leather . . ." He makes a face and gestures at his feet. "This is fine."

She hesitates but doesn't want to push, so she follows him reluctantly down the porch steps. He walks her to her car and won't even accept a ride to wherever he's going. She sits behind the steering wheel and watches him painfully pick his way across the gravel.

She follows him at a distance to make sure he's okay. Much to her surprise, he just circles his block—it takes him a long time in his socks—and returns home again, as though he has forgotten where he was going and given up altogether. She smiles sadly. It's hard to see your parents start to slip. She thinks of a friend who had to put her aging parents into a home this past summer, how awful that whole process had been for everyone. This is where it could be nice to believe the same thing as everyone else; she could see the end of the world as a comfort in this one small way. In that reality, there are no retirement homes, no dementia, no end-of-life care. She thinks of Marlen and his cancer, and it clicks. Hilda *wants* to believe the world is ending because, for her, it is.

27

Hilda is halfway through Marlen's book. She picks it up a lot, but she sets it down within minutes every time. It's a hard book to read.

Not that Marlen's not a wonderful writer—he's weird and funny and insightful—it's the subject matter.

Or that's what she tells him when he asks if she's finished it yet.

"It's weird and funny and insightful," she keeps saying. "It's just that it's so hard to read about the end of the world when you're at the end of the world. It's like how it would be hard to read a book about sharks if I were on a cruise ship."

But that's not it, not completely.

If she were honest with him, and with herself, she would admit that there's something else that forces her to put the book down, to physically remove herself from its presence moments after she's entered into it.

When he'd given her the book, when she realized what it was, she couldn't stop crying—and in large part it was joy, admiration, excitement for him—pride. He'd accomplished the one dream he'd had the whole time she'd known him. He done it *in time*. It occurred to her: maybe that was why he was so okay with dying, so "used to the idea of it," as he put it.

So part of the reason she couldn't stop crying then, and part of the reason it's so hard to read his book now, is because she can't get there herself.

She and Marlen have always gone everywhere together, ever since they started dating in high school. But now Marlen has gone off somewhere Hilda can't get to. He didn't wait for her; he didn't pull her along with him.

That's not fair.

✳

Ole has been gone now for almost four whole days. Hilda has just gotten off the phone with Irene—a short, terse exchange, just an update: no Ole; Hank's still looking. Neither of them mentioned the letter, though it shouted at them both throughout the phone call, probably why they'd needed to keep it brief, too hard to hear over the silent racket.

In light of this, Hilda feels guilty about her excitement at collecting Nora from the airport. But she *is* excited; she can't help it. She sets the phone down on the kitchen counter and surveys the room. Marlen's book on the table, the walls desperately in need of a coat of paint.

Maybe she *should* paint the kitchen, if only as an excuse not to read the book. Sure, it won't last very long, but it'll look nice for Nora's homecoming.

She makes the trip into town, to the hardware store. She hopes it'll be open, that someone will have bothered to come into work today. This is becoming a more normal mindset, hoping things will be as they've always been but not expecting too much. For the more pessimistic people it's probably not all that unfamiliar. For Hilda it's like suddenly going blind in one eye. Her depth perception is off; she goes to take a step, and it doesn't get her as far as she feels it should. Her peripheral vision is narrowed considerably. Everything's just a little darker, and there's nothing she can do about it.

But today she's in luck: there's a teenager behind the counter, a girl with long brown hair and dried paint all over her jeans, the daughter of the lady who works at the post office.

"I'm surprised you're open," says Hilda.

"Oh yeah," says the girl with a grin. "And I've been busy. The grade twelve class is painting a mural on the side of the rec center."

"A mural?" Hilda perks up. When she was in high school, she and her best friend had been commissioned by the art teacher to paint murals all along the senior high hallway. It was one of her fondest memories of that time, staying late after school, planning the pictures out on paper, and then trying to bring them to life in a much larger format, from the smooth page to dimpled concrete.

"Yeah. They're doing it to cheer everyone up, you know? The adults were like, 'Well, it's going to disintegrate in two months anyway, so go for it.'" The girl laughs, like she doesn't really grasp the gravity of *it's going to disintegrate in two months.*

"That's such a nice idea," says Hilda, trying not to look dismayed.

"It's fun. And like . . ." The girl pauses, moving gum around in her mouth. "Our art teacher was saying, the game has really changed, you know? It's like suddenly nothing matters more than anything else. Because longevity isn't a thing anymore; it doesn't matter how old anything is or how long it's going to stay relevant. Money isn't a thing anymore. Demand. Reputation. So it's like, everything matters the same amount. So this mural they're doing matters as much as, like . . . an Andy Warhol painting. Or the *Mona Lisa*. Right?"

Hilda thinks this over. She's been much more inclined to think that, in light of the end of all things, nothing matters, period. But maybe it's nicer to think that everything matters the same amount. Maybe optimism is still a possibility in certain small pockets of reality. "Actually, yes. That's beautiful."

The girl looks pleased. "Right?"

At some point in this conversation, Hilda had absentmindedly plucked a paint swatch from the small selection by the counter. She chose a soft eggshell cream. She'd come looking for paint that would brighten up her kitchen, and as a force of habit she'd gone for something affordable and durable, something that wouldn't need repainting for a long time, something timeless so that it wouldn't go out of date before it started peeling.

But now her eye is being drawn elsewhere.

That shade of green there is so fun, so effervescent, like clover or fresh-cut grass, the color of life. The blue is so deep and beautiful, like Marlen's eyes, the ones he'd given to their daughter. The purple is outrageous, not a kitchen color at all—and this makes Hilda want it.

The girl behind the counter sees the swatch in Hilda's hand. "Looking for white paint?"

"Actually, no . . ." Hilda folds it in half, creasing it with her thumbnail, folding it again. "I'm going to need a few more minutes, I think."

Affordable. Durable. Timeless.

She laughs to herself as concepts that once felt very important lose their meaning altogether, instantly, like they've been incinerated by exploding stars.

28

Derek's response to Nora's question takes a little over twenty-four hours, and when it comes it's terse, even by teenage-boy text-message standards:

not rly ur busness

She frowns at the screen. *Bus-ness.*

Idiot.

She has more important things to worry about right now: it's her wedding day. Their future as a couple is crystal clear: they'll get married at the civil registry center; then they'll spend almost three weeks apart, and then they'll meet at the airport, taking off to start their new life as husband and wife for all of fourteen hours and fifteen minutes. In Toronto, they will, for all intents and purposes, divorce.

Classic love story!

She thinks she might wear a dress. Is that weird? She goes back and forth. Will he think she's making too much of something that's really just a formality? Then again, maybe it doesn't matter what he thinks. The world is ending!

Anyway, if you're going to propose to someone, it's solidly your fault when they show up to your wedding wearing a wedding dress.

The dress is white.

That's weird, though, right?

But when Jacob arrives, he's wearing a suit. She feels worse and better.

"Hi!" He's three rapid breaths from hyperventilating. "Is it weird that I wore a suit? Tell me honestly." His face is frozen in a petrified grin. Does he think she's going to back out? She smiles reassuringly, even though her stomach is doing flips. A fake wedding day feels strangely similar to how she's always imagined a real wedding day would feel.

✳

They decide to walk to the civil registry center.

"It's about a half hour on foot," he tells her. "And it's beautiful outside for this time of year—we don't have many of these beautiful days left." There's an elongated pause, and then he stammers, "Before winter gets here, I mean." He's trying to be optimistic.

The air is cool, but the sun finds its way to them through all the buildings, diffused and yellowy orange. She's still not used to this, the way the city refracts light, blocks wind. Back home, there are few trees, planted in strategic rows here and there. The wind and the sun have free rein.

Jacob suggests a stop at Begonia for a coffee—he still has the keys—on the way to the registrar's office, and Nora nods, feeling herself relax. They're running an errand, that's all. Getting coffee, then signing some papers. He's gotten a haircut, and it crosses her mind that she has always liked his hair like this, even though she knows she's never seen it like this before. She wonders if these flashes of false familiarity will decrease as she gets to know him, replaced by actual memories and knowledge.

He lets them into the abandoned coffee shop. She hasn't been here since News Day, and now it's one of those places that feels haunted, like everyone there that day had left an emotional imprint.

She leans on the counter while he makes their drinks, trying to think of something to say. He must be doing the same thing, and they're both coming up empty. Instead, they listen to the hiss of the espresso machine, and she watches him measure out the grounds and steam the milk. It's mesmerizing; he doesn't hurry through the process like the rainbow-haired teenagers. He seems to enjoy every part of it. He can't do a Freddie Mercury, but he does a heart, and she tries not to read too much into it.

When he locks the door behind them, he smiles sadly. "Might be the last time I do that," he says.

Soon, half-empty coffee cups in hand, they stand in front of the civil registry center. The doors are recessed, set behind large arches and at the top of a short set of stairs, as though to make you think twice about entering.

"I've seen huge lines of people waiting here on Saturdays," says Jacob. "To elope."

"Looks like we have it to ourselves today," says Nora. Neither of them states the obvious, that romantic things like elopements are nobody's priorities right now.

There's a woman sitting on a chair just inside who stands when she sees them. She's kind looking and has hair so dazzlingly silver it might be tinsel. It's pulled back into a low bun, and though her face seems to sag with grief and apprehension, her eyes are happy. "Jacob?" She reaches forward to shake his hand. "I have not seen you in twelve years. Your mother said you were all grown up, but I still cannot believe my eyes. And Nora? Good."

She doesn't shake Nora's hand; she's all pleasantried out.

But she's efficient; she moves quickly, almost frantically, like she is possibly the only person left working here, running the whole place, and has a lot to do today. She reminds them that they can't tell anyone what she's doing, but the warning isn't overly urgent. They all know consequences are a thing of the past. She leads them over to a reception desk and begins to leaf through a pile of papers, mumbling to herself. "Normally I would need your birth certificates . . . we will just skip this part . . . and this part . . . maybe sign these . . . oh, who will even care?" She gives them a quick, good-natured eye roll and licks her fingers, extracting a couple of pages and setting them in front of Nora, jabbing a long, crooked finger at the lines that need signing. The finger comes to rest on her top lip. She furrows her brow. "I think that is it. That should be enough. I printed this"—she taps another paper on the desk—"off for you in case you have any trouble boarding the plane. It is to show that you are legally married. Actual marriage certificates are slow; they know that. They will not care at all."

Finally she shoves the remaining papers in a folder and pushes them at Jacob. "Those are the copies I would usually send away or file for our records; you just get rid of them however you want." She straightens. "Okay! That is that. Tell your mother 'you are welcome.' Tell her hello, and goodbye." The woman says this matter-of-factly, like it's neither tragic nor meant to be funny. "I now pronounce you husband and wife. You may kiss the bride and everything." She pats them both on the shoulders and shuffles off down the quiet hallway, off to marry someone else, perhaps, or to file her useless paperwork.

A very efficient wedding. Maybe too efficient. They don't kiss, obviously; they can't even make eye contact.

Once again, Nora has the vague feeling that she has been cheated out of something. A wedding with a calm, present officiant, someone who cares about the correct paperwork. A wedding with a kiss at the end. But when Jacob turns to her, she senses his relief. "Thank you," he says. "Again, I really appreciate this—my whole family does." Such a charming line to deliver to your new bride.

"No problem. Seriously." She raises her half-finished latte. "Cheers, Mr. Schmidt." She raises her latte again and he taps it with his.

"And to you, Mrs. . . . ." He shrugs. "I don't even know your last name."

"I'll take yours," she says. "My parents are old school; they'd like that."

He nods, and they tap their paper cups together again.

They drink to their strange union, and then they walk back out the doors of the civil registry center, down the stairs, through the arches.

The sun is bending through the streets in a different way now, more pink than orange.

"Now what?" Nora feels unmoored. This strange little civil ceremony had been, at least, something to look forward to. Now she's staring ahead at twenty empty, lonely days. What's she supposed to do with that much time? It feels important that she use it well, but she doesn't know what it means to use time well. Would it be a good use of time to figure that out? Or has she already wasted her only two decades *not* figuring that out, and now it's too late and she's doomed to spend the last two months with the knowledge of what she should've done but without enough time to do it?

"Now . . ." Jacob looks lost for only a moment. "Now I guess we plan the honeymoon?"

"The honeymoon?" Nora stares at him.

"Mrs. Schmidt! We're going to need to book hotels, look online for good restaurants, things to do." He starts walking back toward her apartment. "Then it's Christmas right as soon as we get back. Busy season to get married. What were we thinking, right?"

For a split second Nora thinks she's lost her mind, that all her imaginary conversing with her absent roommates has finally pushed her off the edge of a mental cliff. Or maybe, she thinks, he's lost *his* mind?

He starts laughing at the look on her face. "Hey, I'm just trying to be optimistic here. Your idea."

And she understands: the only way to keep themselves sane is not to picture frying or sit around worrying about the best way to use their last days—it's to throw themselves into those days with purpose, to construct a narrative that doesn't include dying. To play house, to act like they have a happily ever after ahead of them, full of real-life responsibilities, stressful, busy weeks, and blissful, relaxing stretches of reprieve. A honeymoon. Christmas. Library books to return, a kitchen to clean, a bed to make. A marriage.

As it turns out, the way to keep sane when the world is ending is the exact same as when it's not.

29

Iver has never bought something online before, wild as that sounds. He's never had to! He has everything he needs here in town—there's a hardware store, a grocery store, and a gas station. His late wife bought him all the clothes he needed (she'd liked shopping online *and* going into the city), and sometimes his daughters bring him even more clothes. He has enough clothes for ten men, but only one shirt he actually likes to wear.

He's never bought plane tickets or . . . he can't think of anything else you'd need to buy online that you couldn't either find in town or get someone in town to find for you and bring into their store for you to pick up and pay for in person.

His friend Arnold *loves* buying things online. He buys gum(!) online, even though he could get gum, in person, at the grocery store *or* the gas station *or* the hardware store. He buys clothes online even though he already has clothes. He buys toilet paper online.

Toilet paper!

But today Iver is following suit and making his first online purchase—and what a purchase it is: arcade machines.

Yes, plural. A verifiable *fleet* of arcade machines.

It started with the Arcade1UP Atari Legacy Edition: $599.96 from Walmart.ca. Free shipping, expected to arrive by the end of November! He'd thought it would cost a lot more than that, to have it come all the way out here, but no. Six hundred dollars (plus tax). He had intended to buy only the one, but he also thought he'd be able to afford only the one. But now—$600?!—the world has opened up to him. After all, he had a life savings to spend and years—years!—of missed birthdays to make up for. He added *Ms. Pac-Man* to the cart, and a Simpsons one, and a Ninja Turtles one, and a couple of pinball machines for good measure. And then he looked around his living room, wondering where to put it all, and thought, *I'll just throw all of this furniture on the lawn.* The end of days is kind of a fun time in some respects! It's not all dragons and brimstone.

He's entered all the numbers on his credit card, including the security code, which took him a few minutes to find, as well as his address and postal code, but right as he's about to click the purchase button he thinks, *Why not buy a few more things while I'm here and putting in all this effort? Socks,* he types in, and behold, there are socks of all colors and styles and thicknesses and lengths. *Cheerios,* he types, and discovers with pleasure that Walmart.ca stocks more varieties of Cheerios than he knew existed. Strawberry Cheerios? Why?

Why not?!

Toothpaste, he types, and he buys one of every flavor, just for fun, Winterfresh and Aquagreen and Sour Apple and Bubblemint 4 Kids and so on. He's going to brush his teeth with a different kind of toothpaste every day for the rest of his life. What an absolute luxury. Millionaires probably do this kind of thing!

It's the end of the world, he thinks, *and my inheritance isn't going to be useful to anyone anymore, so why not keep going?* He thinks of Alfie first; what do you get for the woman who takes care of everyone and everything? How about this mug that says VVVVVVIP (VERY VERY VERY VERY VERY VERY IMPORTANT PERSON) on the side? For the grandkids—Monopoly and candy and some books to balance it out. For his daughters—watches and earrings and a dress in every size so they can try them all on and throw out the ones that don't fit. His sons-in-law get new wallets and ties and noise-canceling headphones. For the neighbor who has never liked him and who ardently refuses to say hello if they are ever outside at the same time—a bird feeder.

Because the neighbor does like birds; Iver knows that. He sees him out there smiling at birds all the time; birds are the only living thing he ever smiles at. For Arnold . . . well, what do you get for the guy who has internet access and can buy anything he wants already? A Walmart gift card? Sure!

Iver is sad that it has taken him until the end of his life and the end of the world to experience the joys of online shopping. And when he finally pushes the purchase button, he has spent more than he thought possible, but he feels a rush of adrenaline; he hasn't felt like this since the last time he went car shopping.

This is the most fun he's had in a long time. He feels like he's smiling even though he knows he probably looks neutral, or even cranky. Hilda has told him this is a thing his face is often guilty of. He wonders if this is his neighbor's problem too—maybe the neighbor has always really liked him; he just has a cranky face too! What a pleasant little thought.

The door to his house creaks open, and he hears his son—his son! Not a dream, not a hallucination, not a postlife reality; he knows this because food is rapidly disappearing from his fridge, and he doesn't feel more full than usual—removing his boots and jacket in the hallway. He hurriedly closes the Walmart window and shuts the laptop gingerly, feeling another jolt of excitement at the thought of what he'll do when all this stuff gets here. He makes his way to the kitchen to boil a pot for elbow macaroni. For two.

"Hi, son," says Iver.

"Hey," says his son.

What a week it's been.

Ole sits at the table. They eat macaroni for almost every meal—and Ole isn't sure if this is an end-of-the-world thing or if this has been on the menu for his grandfather every day since his grandma died—but that's okay. The predictability is nice. The meals are almost silent, a comfortable quiet that sits with them like a third party, like space being purposely held for his grandma, who would fill it easily if she were still here. Ole keeps thinking every day that he'll call his parents; he wonders if they're worried about him. But his father's face looms in his head, angry—his mother's, worried.

These faces are supposed to be kind, comforting; they are supposed to help him contain *his* anger, calm *his* worries. He has a fuzzy recollection of being very young and visiting the city with them; his mother holding his hand as they used a crosswalk, pointing at the traffic lights and explaining how to safely navigate the city. That's what he wants now—help navigating. Something is broken there, and he doesn't know how to fix it, so he just waits, one more day, and then one more day, and then one more day. For now he crawls inside the memory of the city trip and holds his mother's hand.

His grandfather is standing at the stove, stirring the macaroni. His face is set in something that is not exactly a smile, might even be misconstrued as a frown, but which is still, somehow, full of joy. It has the comfort of Ole's mother and the calm of Ole's father. This is the one face doing exactly what it's supposed to do.

30

Hank hasn't been sleeping very much since Ole went missing. He stays up late and wakes up early, driving down back roads, shining flashlights into old buildings, calling hospitals, listening to podcasts about parenting and marriage and conflict resolution—because he knows he's going to find Ole, and when he does, he is going to parent the crap out of that kid and fix this family. He's going to be the best dad Ole could ever imagine, the best husband Irene could imagine; he's going to do everything right, and it's probably going to be a little annoying for everyone, but he doesn't care, and his family won't either. The last two months they have together are going to be perfect. And when the asteroid or the heat rays or the . . . whatever the thing is, when it comes, right before it hits them, there's going to be a moment of beautiful, blinding clarity, where they all look at each other, and they're proud of themselves and each other, and they have no regrets. Hank will think of the day Ole was born, when he fit on Hank's forearms, when he was perfect in every way and Hank could not imagine so much as frowning in his direction. He'll think of Irene, his beautiful wife, her hair all squashed flat on her head, her happy, tired, sweaty face beaming up at him from the hospital bed. He'll think of Ole's first laughs and steps and sentences and the way Irene held his tiny hands and walked him across the living room, and he'll think of the way Ole watched him back then, the way his little eyes studied him as he tried to emulate him, something that was both amazing and terrifying. Maybe Ole will think of games of catch in the backyard and building stuff together and that chunk of time when he was five or so, when he used to get up every morning at about 4:00 a.m., crawl into bed with his parents, and talk their ears off until the alarm rang.

Hank will think of that too. When had that stopped, exactly? He had wished it away at the time. He'd been so tired. He'd just wanted to sleep. Now it sounds like the best thing in the world: a dark room, a heavy comforter, reaching over to scratch Irene's back as they lie there, and that tiny body snuggled into his side, that precious little voice floating through the haze of sleep, on and on, never ending. It had actually felt like that at the time, never ending. And now Hank knows better, only *better* is not the word he'd use.

Today Hank is almost fifteen miles from home—he's sweeping fields and abandoned yards in concentric circles, certain his son is hiding in somebody's deserted house. The police may not have the resources to look for him, but the fields and farms are what Hank knows, what Ole knows too. If Ole is out here, and Hank is sure he is, Hank will find him.

Hank knows the people who own this land. They were friends with his dad; he used to come here as a kid for harvest suppers. There's an old farmhouse on the edge of it, where *their* parents lived a long time ago, which has long since fallen into disrepair, downright unsafe for anyone to wander around in. The front porch has fallen in on itself, so the front door is inaccessible, but the back door makes up for it by being gone altogether. Hank walks right in, careful to watch for rusty nails and rotted wood—if he falls into the basement, he'll be the second missing member of the family. Irene doesn't need that right now.

The house smells musty; wallpaper hangs from the walls like vines. Things are growing in here; animals have been living in it. He creeps forward, testing each step, and calls for his son as he moves. "Ole! Are you in here, son? Please answer me if you're here!" There's a creak upstairs, directly above Hank's head, and he realizes this is a sound that, to him, has come to represent Ole. Creaks and steps and shuffles. Slight movement, vague signs of life. Forgetting to be cautious, Hank bursts ahead, lunging for the staircase.

His foot bursts through the bottom step, rotted wood disintegrating beneath his boot. He calls out again, "Ole! Is that you?"

Silence.

More carefully, he makes his way up the staircase, stepping as close to the baseboards as he can, heart pounding at the thought of arriving at the top, turning a corner, finding his son tucked into a sleeping bag. They could start fixing things right now; they could talk on the way home—on the way to the truck even. Ole might not want to at first, but that's okay—Hank's the parent, the adult. The podcasts he's been listening to remind him of that often. It's not the kid's responsibility to initiate or nurture or maintain the relationship. He's the dad. He can steer the ship, no matter how big the ship is or how stubborn the ship is or how much the ship seems to not like him.

"Ole? You up here?"

He reaches the top. There's a hole in the roof, and birds have been flying in and out; the floor is many layers of white and black. Another creak, coming from the end of the hall. He moves toward it, swallowing hard, trying to step where the beams are. Ole hasn't replied, which means he doesn't want to be found yet. That's okay. It's not Ole's job to want to be found; it's Hank's job to find him. It's Hank's job to reach out in love and respect. So sayeth the parenting podcasts. There are two rooms at the end of the hall. The right one has soft pink wallpaper, pink wood trim, a matching pink radiator; there's still an old iron bed frame in the corner, yellowing lace curtains over the window, sunlight flowers shimmering on the floor. No Ole. Movement catches his eye as he turns into the other bedroom, and for a moment his sleep-deprived brain sees Ole sitting in the corner, waiting for him. Smiling.

But it's not Ole. It's a dog. A huge brown dog.

The dog and Hank look at each other. The dog whimpers.

"Shouldn't be in here," says Hank, disappointment battering him like hail. He feels angry at the dog, like it played a trick on him. "You could fall through the floor." When he heads back down the stairs, the dog follows him. It follows him right out the door and back to his pickup truck. When they get to the truck, Hank looks around. "Nearest farm is the Jensens'," he says. "And you're not their dog. Their dog's half the size of you. Who do you belong to?"

The dog cocks his head to the side, so slowly, like he's saying, *I'm too tired to have this conversation.* He's an old, old dog.

"Hop in," says Hank, opening the truck door, patting the seat. "Let's find your family. At least someone's going home today."

31

Mr. and Mrs. Schmidt sit across from each other at the kitchen table, so still they could be a painting. Now that they're here, in the quiet of this apartment, it's occurring to each of them how intimate a thing it is to be married, even if the marriage is not completely real (though Mr. Schmidt is doing everything he can to nurture the illusion). How do you pretend to be married without the physical stuff? Or, worse, the emotional stuff? It's like going door to door on Halloween, wearing your regular clothes, your regular makeup, telling people you're a peacock. Your earnestness would make you look silly if you were not also wearing feathers.

It doesn't help that Mrs. Schmidt is attracted to her husband. She has been trying to deny this, but there it is anyway. The truth is the truth whether she admits it or not. It doesn't help that he's so beautiful, so sweet and unassuming. It doesn't help that sometimes she remembers him putting his arms around her, even though she knows—she knows!—it has never happened. The truth, it turns out, is sometimes the truth whether it is even *true* or not.

Mrs. Schmidt makes a french press just so she has something to do, a quick reversal of roles. Now he watches her measure and grind the beans, boil the water, let it bloom. Mr. Schmidt smiles appreciatively when the cup is set down in front of him even though it's been less than an hour since he finished the coffee from Begonia.

"So," he says, staring intently into his coffee, as though she's swimming around in there.

"So?"

"Now that we're married," he says slowly, "I don't want to become one of those couples that stops getting to know each other. I don't want to assume I know all there is to know about you and stop asking questions."

Mrs. Schmidt doesn't know very many married couples. Not her age, anyway. But she can see how that might be a problem. She nods and says, "Agree."

"So," he says again. "Let's go around the table and say one thing about ourselves the other person might not already know."

"Go around the table?" she says. "There are only two of us."

"Clockwise," he says.

"Okay . . ."

"Or counterclockwise, if you want. Not trying to be bossy."

"Clockwise is fine."

"Okay."

"You first," she says.

"Right. Okay." He thinks for a moment. "I'm twenty."

"Same."

"Cool."

"Yep."

"Funny that hasn't come up before now," he says.

She shrugs. "Lots of people don't know how old their spouses are."

"True."

"What else?"

"Hmm. Okay. My first car was a fifth-hand 1986 VW Golf."

"Where's that car now?"

"It turned into a brand-new BMW."

She frowns at him. "In real life or is this part of the pretend-marriage thing?"

"Both," he says. "Though I'm not sure what you mean by 'pretend.' We have a very legal, real marriage. But, yeah, I literally turned my VW into a BMW. Totaled it. Totaled the BMW too."

"Oh." His jokes are hard to recognize because his face is so straight. She feels awkward laughing at them because he doesn't seem to notice he's telling them.

"Your turn."

She leans back in her chair, studying her new husband. If their relationship was strange at first sight, getting married has definitely complicated things. She can't shake the feeling that anything she has to throw at him will be something he already knows, yet she feels nervous to wade into deeper conversational waters. He is too familiar; he is not familiar enough.

"Well . . . I'm allergic to dogs."

"I do know that already," says Mr. Schmidt.

This catches her off guard even though she'd been expecting it. *See? It's not just my imagination!*

"You mentioned it the other day at work."

"Right." *Never mind!*

Her phone lights up, and she tilts the screen to see who it is. Derek. It has taken him another few hours to think of a follow-up to his earlier text. This one says,

we didn't start dating til after i broke up with u

She turns the phone face down, too quickly, as though her pretend husband might care that she's texting with her ex behind his back. Is it possible to cheat on a pretend husband? The legal aspect of it makes things feel morally murky.

"You okay?"

"Well . . . yes, but . . ." She doesn't want Derek interrupting this conversation, even by text message. "I can't think of anything else about myself. I'm allergic to dogs. That's it."

"That's not true."

She gives him a look. "How would you know?"

"I don't know," he admits. "But I *sense* there's more to you than 'allergic to dogs.' I've thought that since I first met you." Is it just her imagination? He seems like he wants to say something else. "You seem like a very interesting person."

She tries to stay calm and keep her smile a normal size. "Thanks," she squeaks, trying to breathe in and out at the same time.

As the conversation progresses, they venture into deeper waters, which is where they remember, once again, exactly how old their relationship is—which is not old at all, and certainly not old enough to swim in the deep end. She asks him a vague question about past relationships, and he dodges it. He asks her how she's doing living so far away from her parents, and she dodges that. They swim to shore and rest for a minute.

"Sorry," he says.

"For what?"

"I don't know, honestly. I think—mentioning your parents?"

"Oh. No. It's just . . ." She doesn't know what it is. "It's a sore spot. People keep asking me if I'm okay being so far from them and . . . I'm not, honestly? And I feel like a child. I feel like I should be more independent by now."

"You're talking to a guy who has never lived more than ten kilometers from his parents' house," says Mr. Schmidt, "if that makes you feel any better."

She smiles gratefully.

"We're twenty," says Mr. Schmidt. "By the time we're thirty we'll have it figured out."

"You're right," says Mrs. Schmidt. She can see that, if they keep this up, they are both going to become very good at lying. To each other, to themselves.

32

Marlen bought a radio the other day.

He came into the kitchen with bags of stuff, more than a dozen trips from the truck with his arms full, quite the task for someone who's been feeling so rotten. He set the stuff on the floor and on the counters and on the kitchen table next to Hilda's painting supplies, then caught his breath and began to unpack, lining it up in neat rows. A radio, large jugs of water, canned goods, candles. A bigger flashlight than the one they already owned. Extra toilet paper. Batteries. Etcetera. Things kept appearing until Hilda started to feel ill.

"What's all this? Are you becoming one of those people who—what are they called? Preppers?"

He shrugged. "Preppers? If you mean, am I *preparing* for the end of the world? I guess so. It's kind of lost its negative connotation now, hasn't it?"

"You think we're going to need all this? You think this is going to help?"

"Well . . . yeah? Haven't you been paying attention?"

"Here and there. Yes?" She thought she'd been paying attention. What more was there to know than what she knew? "Maybe not like you—"

Marlen continued to stack cans. Tomato soup, chicken soup, peas, corn. "They say it's going to happen in two phases. Two quick, subsequent blasts; *how* subsequent, they don't know yet. We'll survive the first, but we'll be stuck inside until the second. And I don't know about you but"—he shook a bag of chips at her—"I'll probably want snacks for that part." He pulled out a few bottles of sunblock, and she stared at him incredulously.

"What?" She'd thought it would be quick. She'd been banking on that. She'd even come to like the idea—after all, a slow, painful death of natural causes was the most likely alternative. "I didn't hear any of that."

He unloaded Alphagetties and Beefaronis. Nora's cat jumped on the counter and began poking at the cans with her nose. "I heard it on the radio this morning on my way into town."

"I don't listen to the radio." Why was everyone suddenly so obsessed with the radio? She wrapped her arms around the cat and gently lowered it to the floor. It didn't mind or resist, but it looked her straight in the eye and jumped back up onto the table.

"Now might be a good time to start, honey." That was when he pulled out the new radio. "It's nice to have a sense of what's going on—and I think we've all forgotten the joy of not knowing what song is next, you know? We'll enjoy it, having the news updates interspersed with music. A way to stay informed *and* distracted. Here." He clicked some batteries into the radio and turned it on. It fuzzed and warbled at him until he found the scan button. A song came into focus, a slow, stringy piano ballad, and Marlen grinned at his wife. "Oldies! See? It's nice, isn't it?"

They listened for a few moments before they recognized it—Skeeter Davis's "The End of the World." The song's lyrics were a metaphor, of course, for a broken heart, but the lyrics were too close. Marlen switched the radio off and went back to unpacking his bags.

But now Hilda has come to love the radio. She wishes she had become a radio person sooner. Radio people are up to date on current events, weather forecasts, local trading post listings. Their days contain the delightful possibility of being surprised by a favorite old song or being introduced, at any moment, to a great new one. She leaves the radio on the oldies station while she paints. It's a good mix: Billy Joel and the Beatles and Huey Lewis and the Four Seasons interrupted by only the most pressing updates. More upbeats than downbeats, and even the downbeats are often just slightly more detailed versions of news she already knows. She's developing an emotional callus, and it's such a relief.

Today, between Lesley Gore and Fats Domino, the deejay plays a clip of a scientist saying that they've been able to more precisely determine the course of things to come. "One day between hits," he says apologetically, like he wishes he could give them more time. One day when the atmosphere will be almost entirely destroyed, and the earth will feel the force of the sun in a way it never has before, levels of radiation that human beings cannot withstand. "You can potentially survive the First One," he says, unknowingly coining a phrase that everyone will use from now on, "if you head to your basement." He speaks delicately, dancing around the part about how bunkering down in a basement will not *save* a person; it will only—possibly—prolong their life by one day. This is the only good news they have for anyone now, that they might be able to put off their impending doom by twenty-four hours.

The rough estimate on the first blast is now December 27, and both blasts are expected to hit North America dead-on.

Hilda always pauses her painting during the news updates. Sits away from the wall, takes in her work while the reporter or scientist or deejay speaks. *This painting is as important as any other painting,* she thinks. It's a meditation that keeps her mind from really burrowing into reality. *As important as any other work of art, any book or poem or sculpture or composition. Each stroke of my brush is worth millions of dollars, and each dollar is worth nothing.* She realizes that this has always been true, not just now. Her art, the culmination of her life and experiences and knowledge and ability and taste, has always been worth as much as anybody else's, and everyone else's art is just as meaningless as hers. And for that reason, all of it is very beautiful, even the stuff that's ugly.

33

"Are we going to get candy, Mrs. Schmidt?"

It's Halloween, the first day of note on the calendar since the world found out about its end, and Nora is feeling apprehensive. Will parents even send their kids out trick-or-treating tonight? The streets are starting to feel precarious—not unsafe, but unnerving. Scary in a way she can't put her finger on. Still no riots, still no screaming, just that general sense of unease, like the city is coming down with the flu, turning noticeably green, but still standing, still walking around, still saying it feels fine even though it's obviously not.

"I don't know," she says. "Should we? Will anyone come?"

"Why would no one come?" he asks innocently. "Let's go to the Späti." He's coaching her. *Pretend. Like me. It's easy.*

But going to the Späti—the convenience store—only makes pretending harder. Mrs. Schmidt shudders as they enter; it looks like the set of a zombie-apocalypse movie, price stickers and other assorted pieces of trash on the floor, an open cooler with nothing in it, empty shelves. Mr. Schmidt finds one lonely package of hard candies on a rack by the cash register, next to a pack of Orbit gum. He taps on the counter, trying to get the attention of the cashier, an older lady with pretty silver hair, reading an N. K. Jemisin novel.

"Excuse me?" He offers a friendly smile. "Do you have more candy than this?"

The woman looks up and pulls her reading glasses off, letting them fall to the end of a delicate chain around her neck. She stares pointedly at the rack, then just as pointedly at Mr. Schmidt. "Doesn't look like it, hon. I'm sorry."

"Are there more in the back?"

The woman shakes her head apologetically. "Wish I could help you." But then she leans in, lowering her voice as though someone might be spying on them. "There might be more in the back. Truth is, I've been told not to restock anything. The owner wants to close." She holds up the book. "First time I've had a chance to sit still and read in as long as I can remember. My brain doesn't know what to do with this anymore." She gives a great sigh and looks around at the disheveled shop, once a labor of love, passed into entropy's lazy hands. Her voice goes down another notch. "I've even been told not to clean up this mess. He wants me to just sit here. Do nothing. I think he wants people to give up on it. Like he has."

The lady is disgusted. She's not wanting to give up yet. But this is not her shop. Not her business to revive it when the DNR has already been signed.

Mr. Schmidt leans on the counter and furrows his brow. He is determined to drag the woman into his fantasy world, which is not ending anytime soon. "Why?"

"He says it's because there's no *point*." She glares at Mr. Schmidt. "How do people decide what's pointless and what's meaningful? It's all arbitrary. And I don't think he actually believes there's no point. He's just sad."

She picks up her book, replaces the reading glasses, and tucks a piece of hair behind her ear. "You know," she says, her mouth barely moving now, "I doubt he's checking the security cameras anymore. Feel free to go back and help yourself."

Mr. Schmidt seems to freeze, clearly conflicted. "Like, steal?"

The woman turns a page. "I don't know if stealing exists anymore. The world's about to fry, and the stuff in the back room is going to burn along with the rest of us. He's just being weird and greedy." She turns another page, though she could not possibly have read that quickly. "And sad."

The woman has such a motherly air about her; it feels jarring to hear these words come out of her mouth. But she's not wrong. Is ownership a valid concept now? Up until the last second? If they get home and someone is in their apartment, do they have any right to kick that person out, to say, *No, we live here and you don't, so you have to go die somewhere else*?

"Go on," whispers the woman. "Take whatever you need."

The back room is dimly lit and full of boxes lining the path to the tiny bathroom. Mr. and Mrs. Schmidt stand next to each other, unsure of where to start or if they should.

She reaches out and flips back the top of an already opened box, revealing a layer of glossy magazines. *Der Spiegel* is written on the cover in bright white along with an unflattering caricature of a certain notorious former American president.

"Is it for sure not stealing?" asks Mr. Schmidt. In his little fantasy world, stealing is still wrong, and this still counts.

"No," she says with more confidence than she feels. She tears a strip of tape off another box and peers inside. Jewelry, cheap clay necklaces and earrings and bracelets. She holds up a necklace; it reminds her of her mother. "My mom would love this," she announces, more to herself than to him. She shoves it into her purse. "No, it's not stealing."

"Why?" He needs a good reason.

She thinks about it. "Because this store is closing, and this is their closing-out sale. Happens all the time. The prices are a *steal*. That's where the expression comes from."

He contemplates a box for a minute or two, then cracks it open. More gum.

"How much gum does this place need?"

"None anymore, apparently," says Mrs. Schmidt. She grabs a pack and sticks it in her purse beside the necklace.

It feels strange. Exhilarating. She's never stolen so much as, well, a pack of gum.

He opens another box, and another. There's a box of plastic bags. He takes one and begins to fill it, like he really is shopping a closing-out sale, one tentative item at a time.

She watches him from the corner of her eye. It's endearing, the way he looks around so anxiously, the way he's so concerned with doing the right thing even though the right thing doesn't exist anymore.

"Schoko-Bons!" he says, holding up a bag of chocolate—a brand she recognizes, but with German instead of English on slightly different wrappers. He begins to load the stolen candy into the stolen bag. "This still feels so weird," he says. Then, in an effort to stay in character: "You're right; it's such a good sale it feels like stealing."

"Stealing often feels like stealing."

This voice does not come from Mr. Schmidt or Mrs. Schmidt, or from the cashier with the N. K. Jemisin novel. They straighten. Mr. Schmidt throws his bag to the ground, as though it were crawling with spiders.

A man is standing in the doorway.

"What is going on here?" He is gruff, large, German. Angry.

Mr. and Mrs. Schmidt have no idea what to say. They're stealing—that's what's going on—but it doesn't feel like the kind of thing you own up to right away.

We're stealing?

No.

It's instinctual to deny wrongdoing at first, and it's also somewhat of a social norm—deny, or make excuses.

But we were given permission! But you weren't going to make any money off it anyway! But . . . it's the end of the world!

But Mr. Schmidt can't help but be honest. It's in his nature. He is exploding with goodness.

"We were stealing," he says quietly, his voice full of shame. "We stole gum and magazines and Schoko-Bons. She stole a necklace."

Mrs. Schmidt becomes aware of something. She's not sure when it happened, or who instigated it—it's so natural and normal, it almost doesn't feel noteworthy. The kind of mindless thing that usually means a lot the first time it happens, then less and less each consecutive time until it's an automatic reflex.

Mr. Schmidt is holding her hand.

The man in front of her fades rapidly in importance, though he is still right there, still very angry. Mr. Schmidt's presence at her side is amplified in an intangible way, like the day he entered Begonia and she felt him before she saw him. It's as though Earth's center of gravity moves into his body for less than a millisecond, everything drawn to him, everything tilting wildly to the side. There is no way everyone else in the world had not felt that happen, she thinks. But it had happened so quickly that no one would know what, exactly, it was. Millions of people are suddenly light-headed, thinking they stood up too fast or haven't drunk enough water.

And still, he's holding her hand.

The angry man comes into focus again. He is disarmed by Mr. Schmidt's hasty and thorough admission of guilt. He sweeps the room with his eyes, all those unopened boxes of stuff he will never sell. Boxes that will never be unpacked. Boxes representing his life—dreams come to fruition and a lease signed and taxes done and inventory taken and late nights and early mornings and firings and hirings and frustrations and satisfactions, all the stuff of owning and operating a business. He grunts. "I should thank you for helping me clean up this mess," he mumbles. His cashier was right. He is sad.

Then he ambles out without another word; they hear the bell over the door ding as he makes his exit. Is this permission to continue, or are they just being let off with a warning? Mr. and Mrs. Schmidt aren't sure. They look at each other. Mr. Schmidt collects the bag of Schoko-Bons from where it landed on the box in front of him. "That man said 'thank you,'" he says. "So I think that means we should at least take what we've already got?"

"Probably," she says. "I don't need anything else, though."

"Me neither."

When they emerge from the back room, the cashier is nowhere to be seen, the store left unattended.

They walk up the street, back to their apartment.

And still he's holding her hand.

NOVEMBER

34

Marlen finds his wife sitting on the kitchen floor, crying into a paint can.

"Hilda! Honey—what's up?" He lowers himself to the floor beside her—no small feat anymore. Everything hurts, joints to bones to skin to brain, and the pain is steadily becoming sharper and louder all the time, like the whistle on a train headed straight for him. Some days he's worried he won't last until the end of December, that his family will have to face that day without him. This is scarier than anything, and he is determined not to let it happen, though he's not sure it's something he can control. He has heard stories—people not dying until a loved one made it to their bedside, or until they'd accomplished some certain thing. Maybe he can do that too?

Some prophet.

"Nothing. I'm fine. I'm just . . ." She sighs heavily, wiping her eyes with the back of her hand, leaving a streak of bright blue across her forehead. "I miss Nora so much. She won't be home for another two weeks. I've done the math; it means I'm going to spend twenty-three percent of the rest of my life without her."

He glances at the wall, where a figure is taking shape—it's only one of the very first layers, but he can already see that it's Nora. Her head is turned to the side, revealing the straight edge of her distinctive nose. Hilda's an amazing artist. He's not sure about her math, but her line work is spot-on.

She picks up the brush again and takes a few tentative swipes at her two-dimensional daughter, who doesn't flinch.

Marlen sighs. "Worst timing in the world, isn't it? Her suddenly taking off to Germany just as . . ."

"Horrible timing."

He wants to ask her whether she noticed the eerie similarity in his book, but he's not sure whether she's read that far. He's begun to wonder whether his book is bothering her—beyond the shark / cruise ship thing. He watches her read it sometimes. She picks it up, a strained smile on her face, puts it down without even turning a page, goes back to her mural. Is she ashamed of him? That would be an understandable reaction if anyone else was ever going to read this book. As it is . . . maybe she just hates it that much? Maybe he's not a good writer?

What a thing to find out right before you die, that you're not good at the thing you like doing the most.

She's been working for days on the background, on getting the colors right. It's the kind of project that would look ridiculous if most people attempted it, but Hilda will make it beautiful; he doesn't doubt that for a second. He just hopes she can finish it in time. It's the most important thing on his bucket list—the only thing, really, now that places like the Great Wall of China and the Egyptian pyramids are feeling a little far-fetched—to see this mural completed.

"It's really something, Hildy," he says. He means *stunning, amazing, incredible*. But she leans into him and smiles. She knows what he means. "I was wondering, though—on your next break, would you help me with something in the living room?"

"Sure. Actually, now is good. I need to let this part dry for a bit anyway." She glances over at him, and her face falls, just for a second, before she catches herself and pulls it back into a smile. This happens almost every time she looks at him lately, like she forgets just how sick he is and is shocked every time she's reminded.

He tries to ignore it.

They struggle to their feet, each trying to help the other, laughing at their collective inability to spring up from a kneeling position without head rushes and cracking joints. She follows him to the living room, where a familiar box sits dead center, roughly the size of a casket.

She perks right up. "The Christmas tree! Are we setting the Christmas tree up early?"

He smiles. "Only this year. Next year, you have to wait till December."

The joke falls flat, given the circumstances, but she laughs anyway.

35

Iver hasn't set up a Christmas tree since his wife died. A Christmas tree is one of those preposterous traditions that gets stupider the more you think about it—a tree! In the house! The living room! *Dead*, in the living room! Dry pine needles draped with strings of plastic and wrapped in electrical wires, hung with miscellaneous bric-a-brac that doesn't make any sense—last year, Irene had a tiny Darth Vader on her Christmas tree, hanging right next to a miniature portrait of the *Mona Lisa* that had been doctored somehow so that it was Hank's face, not Mona's. Who had done this? And why? Sometimes it feels, to Iver, like people are playing meaningless, unfunny pranks on him all the time.

And, sure, a Christmas tree can feel magical, but most magic is just illusion—in this case, the tiny lights combined with the nostalgic smell of pine needles in the presence of two or more people creates the illusion of *Christmas*.

Togetherness.

Love.

When Iver lost the communal element, it all fell apart, and he saw that all he'd ever had was an oversize, flammable, rotting birthday cake that no one can eat, covered in nonsensical toys that no one plays with. And since he was alone, he had no presents to put beneath it (though he started to wonder why anyone ever did *that*, as well).

But here's an amazing thing: the magic is back. This feels like the most amazing trick yet. Iver has seen the man behind the curtain, has had the illusion explained to him, and, somehow, here he is falling for it again.

It can't be a coincidence that today, of all the days in all the months and years, Iver picked up his slacks and a nickel fell out of the pocket and rolled under the dresser. And when he got down to retrieve it, he found a box. And when he got the box out and took a good look at it, he realized that it was his late wife's memory box, coated in inches of dust. And when he opened the box, the thing right on top was a Polaroid picture of them standing in front of their Christmas tree. He takes the photograph and holds it right in front of his face so he can see her. She's twenty-seven. Beautiful, happy—a bit washed out from the flash of the camera, her smile blinding. On the back, in faded blue pen, her neat slanted handwriting: *Our First Christmas Married, November 1, 1970.*

November 1. They always put their tree up on November 1. Today.

Incredible, he thought. What were the chances this would come to him today? Like his wife was sending him a gentle nudge or a love note. A little Christmas magic. The same magic that brought his son back to life? The same magic involved in transforming spindly old pine trees into radiant Christmas trees?

Iver makes the announcement.

"We're going to get our Christmas tree after breakfast," he says.

His son looks surprised but doesn't say anything. This is to be expected; he's a quiet kid. He's always been a quiet kid. Iver sometimes worries as they eat in complete silence that the figure across the table is a figment of his imagination, wishful thinking, that he'll blink and it'll disappear—but then he reminds himself that his son has always been silent. The silence is confirmation that this *is* his son, not proof of the opposite. It confirms, it comforts; the only thing the silence does not do is explain.

"It's a bit early for most folks," Iver continues. "But we always do it on November 1. Your mother always made us do it this early. Her fault."

His son nods. There's a hint of a smile on his face, and Iver feels his insides light up. Like a Christmas tree! And for some reason this is a positive association once again.

"All right then," he says, finishing his oatmeal. "Let's go."

Ole nods and rises from the table.

He still hasn't called his parents. He imagines them at home, setting up the tree without him, and something inside him wavers. He should be there; it's tradition. Several times over the past few days he has questioned himself; they have so little time left as a family—shouldn't he be with them, even if it's not easy? He can't get to a good answer; he wants that, but he doesn't want it. He has a hard time understanding himself. He assumes this gets easier—twenty seems to be the magical age when people start to figure everything out—but as of right now it's just a mess in his head, fear and confusing feelings. He mostly tries to ignore all of that and focus on the memory of his mother leading him through traffic. Maybe that part of him, the part that clings to that memory, knows that she will figure it out for all of them, and all he has to do is wait.

And this is a good place to wait.

36

When Hank gets home from his latest hunt, the house is quiet, a silence that feels heavy like the silence in a conversation after someone has said something calculated and hurtful. He shuts the door carefully behind him and gingerly removes his boots and jacket. He's tired. He's losing hope.

The dog he found in the old farmhouse has followed him inside, as usual. The dog follows him everywhere now. Hank likes the dog; he calls it Bud, and he thinks it might actually be some kind of angel thing, something sent to keep him sane until Ole comes back. He said this out loud to his wife the other day, and she stared at him like she was mildly worried, but things like this are easier to believe these days; once you know something's for sure coming from the heavens, and you're going to meet it head-on, it makes you wonder what else is out there. Dog angels? Sure. Why not? Besides, this dog doesn't seem to have a home on Earth. Hank has tried his best to find it.

Bud the angel thing curls up on the mat beside the door and falls asleep instantly. Doesn't even touch the food Irene left out for him.

It's getting dark so early these days; Hank's not sure what time it is. Has he missed supper? He creeps through the kitchen, lit only by the yard light outside, peering down the hallway toward his bedroom, past the family pictures on the wall. They haven't been updated in years, and now he realizes they never will be—Ole, in those pictures, is still happy, his face is young and innocent.

"Irene?"

"Living room." Her voice is hushed, like she's trying not to wake someone up. It must be later than he thought. He moves back through the kitchen, into the dining room, and sees a soft red glow coming from the living room, like it's a giant egg incubator.

Standing in the doorway, he sees Irene on the couch. Her head lifts, and her sad smile greets him. She doesn't look expectant or disappointed; she doesn't expect anything when he comes home anymore.

Just the sight of her like that calms him down.

"You set up the Christmas tree," he says. "It's a bit earlier than normal, isn't it?"

Irene's face clouds. "I wanted to wait for you and Ole. But then I thought it might be a nice thing for the two of you to come home to. Besides, I needed something to keep me busy."

"Well." Hank sits on the chair across from his wife. "It's just me coming home again."

They stare at the Christmas tree.

"But maybe tomorrow," says Hank. "I'm running out of places to look, and you know what that means."

"No," says Irene, her voice suddenly icy. "What does it mean?"

"That I'll find him any day now."

"Or that he's gone forever," says Irene. "All of this end-of-the-world talk freaked him out, and now he's gone, and if we had both remained *calm*, like the Letter said, like I wanted us to, then perhaps he would be here with us right now."

Before Hank can register the words or feel surprise at where they came from, Irene is stomping up the stairs, slamming their bedroom door. He hears a tiny scraping noise as, presumably, she flings herself onto their bed.

It reminds Hank of the temper tantrums Ole used to throw when he was little. He always felt somewhat jealous of those outsize displays of emotion. Kids don't know how lucky they are that they get to slam doors and stomp around houses. He'd love to throw a good fit right now, but he doesn't want to scare Irene.

Instead, he leaves the house, shutting the door quietly behind him, walks to the truck, climbs in, drives away.

Five minutes is all it takes for him to get good and isolated. He finds a field with no farms nearby. He drives right into the middle of it; then he clambers out of his truck like it's on fire. He stands there, looks up at the black sky above him, and screams as loud as he can, for as long as he can, until his voice is ripped to shreds. He screams and screams, like *he's* on fire, like he needs someone to come save him. It feels like praying.

And then he gets back into his truck and drives home.

When he gets back to the house, Irene is standing on the front porch, waiting for him, pulling her robe around herself for warmth.

"I'm sorry," she says. "I'm so sorry."

"Me too."

"We need to figure this out before he comes home."

"I thought you said he wasn't—"

"Just talking out of fear. I'm doing everything out of fear these days. Talking. Fighting. Thinking."

"Me too. Not much we can do about that, though, is there? Can't exactly turn that off. I'm afraid that we'll never see Ole again. I'm afraid of . . ." He wants to say he's afraid of the end of the world, but that feels too confrontational. And how are they going to make this work if he can't even express his biggest fear to his wife? "I'm afraid of what this all is doing to us," he says instead.

"And you're afraid that the world is ending," she says.

He nods.

"And I haven't been allowing you to be afraid of it."

He holds perfectly still, unsure of whether admitting this is going to start another fight or not.

She opens the door, leads him back into the house. "I don't know what to do about any of it," she says. "But I'm really sorry for not letting you feel your feelings in front of me."

"Me too," he says. They go through to the living room and sit in front of the Christmas tree. Its magic is subdued without Ole here, but the little lights are trying, much like Hank and Irene.

"So what do we do?" he asks. "How do we get back on the same— you know, the same page?"

She doesn't answer for a long time. It's an impossible question, like he has just asked her if they could make two and two equal ten. It feels like giving up too easily to say it's impossible. But pretending two plus two equals anything other than four isn't giving up, is it? It's just doing math. A very neutral, objective thing. "We can't," she says finally. "I don't think we're going to be able to."

He hadn't expected her to say this. To him this is anything but neutral and objective. "Well, what then? You're just going to give up on us?"

"No, I'm just wondering," she says, "if maybe we can figure out how to love each other from different pages."

37

The day after Halloween, Mr. Schmidt comes home with a surprise. He steps into the apartment and shuts the door almost all the way behind him, indicating that Mrs. Schmidt has to guess what's out there. He's flushed, out of breath.

"I have no idea," she says. She feels ill from all the Halloween chocolate she ate last night. Schoko-Bons are a trap designed by someone who wants to teach gluttons a lesson.

"You have to guess."

"Give me a hint."

"It's taller than you."

She frowns. "A puppy."

"I said taller than you."

"And I said a puppy. A massive puppy."

"Is that what you hope it is?"

"I mean, yeah. I'd love a dog."

"We'll have to have that conversation at some point."

She nods. "After Christmas." Theirs is the most conflict-free marriage in the world, one in which all the arguments are saved for never. She has begun to think that if she were going to live longer, she could write one of those self-help books for married people on how to get along with your spouse. One rule only: always pretend like the world is ending.

"Okay. Now what do you think I've got in the hallway?"

"Taller than me? Hmm . . . a Christmas tree."

He looks disappointed. "How'd you guess that so fast?"

"I heard you lugging it up the stairs. Christmas trees have a very distinctive sound. I never really thought about it before."

"And people lugging Christmas trees up stairs also have a very distinctive sound. Remind me again why we chose a place without an elevator?"

"For the view, darling!"

Mr. Schmidt is very consistent in his adopted husband persona—it's just him, but married—but Mrs. Schmidt is all over the place. Sometimes she sounds like herself; sometimes she sounds like a fifties housewife; sometimes she has a British accent. One day she sounded like the Swedish Chef for a few hours. Right now, apparently, she's a rich, middle-aged Scottish lady. She's got a strange brogue.

"Ah yes, the view of . . . five other apartment buildings' roofs and some trees."

Mrs. Schmidt thinks the rooftops are actually very beautiful. And the tiny sliver of bird mural, her emotional lighthouse beam.

Mr. Schmidt opens the door and there it is. A bright-pink, six-foot-tall tinsel tree.

Mrs. Schmidt takes a step back. "Oh wow. Viva Las Vegas. Why is it so . . . pink?"

"Because there was a guy on the corner by Taleh Thai selling it for twenty-five euros so he could get home to his family for Christmas, and I could not pass it up, whatever color it happened to be."

Mrs. Schmidt thinks that is really very sweet, and an extremely valid reason to have a neon-pink Christmas tree this year. She almost leans over and kisses him without thinking about it, but catches herself just in time. They have not touched again since yesterday at the Späti, but she's having a hard time thinking of anything else.

He drags the tree into the living room, the iridescent branches scratching against the walls, and stands it in the corner. Magically, it seems to change the color of the room around it.

Mr. Schmidt stands there for a moment, admiring the tree. Mrs. Schmidt admires Mr. Schmidt. He, too, seems to change the room around him.

><

It's even harder to find Christmas decorations than it was to find Halloween candy. Mr. Schmidt thinks it might have something to do with the weather.

"It's such a balmy fall," he says, looking out their window, admiring their view. Snow is collecting on the rooftops, and he doesn't say it out loud, but he can't remember a winter where it has snowed this much this early, and he wonders if the earth could already be showing the effects of the thing coming at them. "I'm thinking the store people have forgotten that Christmas is coming up so soon because it's such a balmy fall. The decorations will arrive soon, I'm sure."

"You and your balmy falls," says Mrs. Schmidt. "You say that every year." She's getting better at pretending there have been other years, that there will continue to be more in the future as well.

"I'll say it next year too." Mr. Schmidt brushes Mrs. Schmidt's hand as he stands to get himself another cup of coffee, and a little firecracker travels up her arm and pops in her head. She doesn't think he'd meant to touch her; they're just getting so used to each other's presence in this tiny space. They don't give each other awkwardly wide berths the way they did the first few days, so it's inevitable that sometimes they will come into contact with one another. And yesterday? Probably a one-off. He'd thought they were going to be arrested. He was trying to comfort her. And then he didn't know how to remove his hand without making a big deal of it. And he's so, *so* good at pretending to be married.

"Christmas decorations are expensive anyway. We can make our own," she mumbles. "Petra and Sonja left behind a bunch of their stuff. There's probably loose-leaf or something we could make snowflakes or paper chains out of."

They study the closed doors to Petra's and Sonja's empty bedrooms, probably still full of clothing and band posters, makeup and hair products on the dressers, comforters on the beds, as if the inhabitants will be back someday. They haven't opened those doors since they got married; those rooms are the part of the apartment that still seem to say, "Life just ended suddenly one day, right when people were in the middle of it." Not a helpful sentiment, for their purposes.

"I'll go check it out," she says.

"Thanks," he says. "I'd feel weird going in their rooms."

He doesn't try to make Sonja and Petra part of their make-believe life. There's not any good way to do it.

Sonja's room is a disaster, as though she'd trashed it for fun on her way out the door. It feels wrong to be in here, but—why? It's not like Sonja's coming back.

Nora finds a few school binders and textbooks and stacks and stacks of sheet music, and she brings them to Jacob before venturing into Petra's room.

Petra's room is spotless, and this makes sense—she hadn't needed to be as selective as Sonja since she was driving rather than flying and didn't have to fit her life into a carry-on. She's left a few shirts in the closet, a bottle of hair spray and a hat on the dresser, and more posters on the walls of German bands Nora has never heard of.

In the closet, a surprise: an entire wall of shelving inexplicably dedicated to crafting supplies, as in a kindergarten classroom. Scissors and pipe cleaners and Mod Podge and glue and a massive roll of green felt.

She calls to Mr. Schmidt, who joins her.

"She was a crafty person?" he asks, impressed at the scope of interesting materials here.

"That's not how I would've described her," says Nora.

"How would you have described her?"

Nora doesn't want to be impolite, so she just shrugs.

They raid the closet and spend the rest of the afternoon making sheet music snowflakes for the windows and paper chains for the tree.

From the felt, Mrs. Schmidt makes a string of holly and ivy to drape over the door. They pull up Vince Guaraldi's Christmas album on YouTube and eat more leftover Halloween candy.

Mr. Schmidt is terrible at crafting and Mrs. Schmidt is amazing; they balance each other out perfectly—it's like they're meant to be! Mr. Schmidt says so out loud and then clamps his mouth shut and focuses intently on the paper in his hands, folded all wrong so that when he finishes cutting, it falls apart. Mrs. Schmidt smiles to herself and doesn't say anything.

38

Iver has received a very disappointing email.

Valued customers, it reads, Due to a shortage of drivers and workers, many or all of the pending orders from Walmart.ca may not be delivered as promised. We apologize for the invoncenience.

Iver snorts, annoyed. *Invoncenience*, indeed. They canceled his order; could they not have at least proofread their email? Everyone's just phoning it in. He'd like to think that if he had a job right now, he'd do his very best work until the bitter end. He wouldn't go around ruining people's special plans like this, not when they had so little time left for special plans. Or if he was going to ruin their special plans, he would not allow himself the idiotic decadence of spelling errors.

No arcade machines, no fancy socks. No special coffee mug for Alfie. He huffs around his kitchen for a moment, but only a moment. He doesn't have time to huff; he needs to enact Plan B.

Plan B is less technologically driven, less corporation adjacent, and therefore maybe more of a sure thing. But it's also more difficult because of the person with whom it requires cooperation, which is why it was not Plan A.

He pulls out the phone book, something that has been delivered every year for as long as he can remember, but which he has not actually used in at least twenty years (since his wife programmed every important phone number into every phone they owned). He drops it on the table, and it gives a loud, annoyed *thud* as it lands. He turns to the pages containing the names and numbers of the residents of the town an hour west of here, a place he has not visited in years. He runs a crooked finger down the center column, past the As, the Bs, the Cs . . . down to the end of the alphabet, to a familiar last name. Wallace.

He sighs. Picks up the phone. Dials the numbers.

Gets it wrong; hits a 2 instead of a 3, maybe a sort of Freudian finger slip. Alfie answers; he doesn't even know where he has called, but it still makes perfect sense that she's there. Alfie is always everywhere.

"What are you up to today, Iver?"

"Ohhhh, not too much," he says. "You?"

"Well, doesn't that sound lovely!" she remarks happily. "I'm doing the exact opposite."

She doesn't elaborate.

"I'll let you get back to it then," he says.

"I'll see you at the Pot Hole tomorrow?" She sounds hopeful, and he realizes that he hasn't been there since his son came to live with him.

"Absolutely," he says, touched that she would notice his absence.

They say goodbye, and he tries the original phone call again: gets it right, unfortunately.

"Hellooo, Elsie speaking!" She's always been very singsongy. Very bright and obnoxious in a way that most people seem to find adorable. He tries to hide his irritation. This was his wife's best friend; he needs to be civil.

"Hi," he says, his greeting landing like the phone book. *Thud.* "This is Iver."

"Iiiiiiii-verrrrr!" She is ecstatic, as always. This is the way she greets everyone, from telemarketers to grandchildren. Aggravating. Couldn't possibly be sincere. "Oh, how *are* you? I haven't seen you since . . ." She trails off.

Since his wife's funeral, yes. He knows. They hadn't spoken then, but they'd locked eyes across the church. He had been in the front row, and he'd looked up and there she was; she had given him this long, knowing *look*, the exact meaning of which he had not been able to discern, and he had stared back with obvious confusion. The moment had been interrupted by the casket, making its way down the aisle, supported by Hank and Marlen and a few other men from the community. His wife, in a box; the first time since she died that his brain had allowed him to remember what *dead* meant, the first time in his whole life that he truly understood the word *permanent*. He had given no more thought to Elsie that day—that he can recall. Maybe she came over and hugged him; he couldn't tell you.

"Oh, it's been so long—I can't even remember!" She tries to save them both. He pictures her flapping her arms, trying to get rid of the words. "How *are* you?"

"I'm well," he says stiffly. "And you?"

"I'm doing just wonderful! You've caught me baking! Muffins and cookies. I'm getting ready for my great-grandkids to come visit."

"Right." He remembers that he's about to ask her for a favor and tries to lighten his voice. "How are your—they—doing?" There's a pause. Is she waiting for him to say their names? He has no idea what their names are, but foolishly throws some out there anyway. "Emma, right? And . . . Stacy?"

"Erin and Johnny and Miriam," she says, unbothered. "They're so much fun. Erin's six and the twins are eight now. Can you believe it? They were just babies when I saw you last . . ." She trails off again. *Whoops! Can't stop bringing up that pesky funeral!*

"Riiiight, right . . . so, uh, Elsie, I have a question for you, actually . . ."

"Oh, I know you do, Iver!" She laughs. "You're a man of such few words; everyone knows that when you pick up a phone, there's got to be a good reason!"

Huh. She thinks of him as quiet, not standoffish. She doesn't seem to know how strongly he dislikes her. That's probably good, especially considering he has no good reason to dislike her. She's not a bad person; she's never hurt him or his wife. He simply dislikes her because she irritates him on a cellular level, as Marlen would say. She could just sit there in the same room as him and it would bother him. He suspects that this makes *him* the bad person, but he doesn't have a clue what to do about it.

"Well, you got that right!" He clears his throat and lowers his voice, trying desperately to sound amiable but not deranged. "I was wondering if your son still owns that arcade in the movie theater?"

"He sure does! Thirteen years now, he's been running that place! Did you know that it's currently the longest-running business in this whole town, besides the grocery store and the gas station?"

Iver can't think of many other businesses in that place, period. It's a town of one thousand. Doesn't sound like much of an accomplishment.

"Wow," he says. "That's an incredible accomplishment."

"Oh, Iiiii-verrrrrrr." He can tell she's beaming. "It's so *good* for a person's heart to watch their children succeed, isn't it?"

"Indeedy," mumbles Iver. "Is it open at the moment?"

"Is what now?"

"The arcade? Is it still open?"

"Oh, well. No, actually. He closed it down just last week, sadly." *Jackpot.* "His employees all quit after—the news—and he's not interested in spending the last of his days running it. He wants to spend time with family and all that. And none of us really need the money anymore, do we?"

Iver agrees. *No, we sure don't.* But now he's worried—he'd forgotten that money wouldn't be a motivator anymore. What can he offer in exchange?

"And you know what, Iver? As sad as it is that the world is ending, it is so nice that we've had this warning, and this time together, and that he can look back on his years as a small business owner with pride, and—hey! He won't have to worry about selling the business and having some young thing turn it into a hair salon or something! Isn't that the easiest way to deal with a business you're done with? Just—poof!—blow it up!"

This is the Elsie he remembers. Bursting with optimism to the point of insensitivity. Maybe this is why he can't remember talking to her on the day of his wife's funeral; his brain is blocking it out because it was likely so traumatic.

He can picture it now: her family gathered on the very last day of the world; her, bustling around serving baked goods, chirping about how blessed they are and how lovely everything is and how it probably couldn't have ended any better than this and how they can eat as much as they want because there is no tomorrow, while the children cling, terrified, sobbing, to their parents; and something in the sky grows bigger and brighter and bigger and brighter until it envelops the sweet little farmhouse in white-hot radiation, only a few watts more dazzling than Elsie's plastic-looking dentures, which will be the last thing anyone sees. Ever.

"Right," he says. "What a blessing."

"It is!"

"So . . . I wondered, then, if . . ." More throat clearing. "Well, so I was trying to order these arcade machines online—well, I wasn't *trying* to. I *ordered* them. But then I just got this email from, uhhh . . ." His mind blanks on *Walmart*, of all things. "The email said they can't get me my arcade machines . . ."

"Oh, that is *so* frustrating," says Elsie, so eager to console that she doesn't seem to be following. "People need to keep their word, even now. This reminds me of—"

He's going to have to spell it out for her. "Yes! Exactly, very frustrating. So. The arcade machines were kind of . . . a gift. And now, see, I don't have them."

"Ah." Elsie clicks her tongue. "That is just so sad."

"It is."

And now they sit there, Elsie obviously needing even more explanation. It would be nice, Iver thinks, if she would catch on and offer the machines before he asked so he could act surprised and demur and say he'd think about it and then, *Oh, what the heck, it's the end of the world! Why not?*

"So I was wondering if, maybe, your son . . . would be looking to sell his machines?"

"Oh no," says Elsie quickly. "What's the point in that? Like I said before, he doesn't really need money anymore, does he?"

"Right. Oh . . . okay."

"And I can't imagine anyone would even be interested in those old things," she continues. "They're not in great condition anymore. He got them all secondhand—which was a very smart move on his part, *I* thought! He was an incredible businessman!"

"Well, actually—"

"And now they can burn!" She says this gleefully, like the end of the world is just a fun bonfire that everyone's very excited about.

"Right, but I was thinking that—"

"Oh! My oven is beeping!"

Iver hears the tinny sound of an oven timer in the background.

"Elsie—"

"I should go, Iver, the muffins are ready, and the kids will be here any moment. It was so lovely to hear from—"

"Elsie! Wait!" He's so frantic he shouts at her, and instantly regrets it. *See,* he thinks, *this is part of it, lady. You don't listen.*

"Oh my. Iver. What's *wrong*? Are you okay?"

"I want the arcade machines. I was calling to ask if I could buy them—or have them—I don't mean to be pushy, but it's very important. Very important."

"Oh." Thankfully she doesn't seem at all rattled by his yelling. Just perplexed at his wanting the old machines. "Well, I'm sure he would be okay with that."

"Really?"

"I'm sure he would. I can't imagine what you're going to do with them, though, Iver."

Her voice has taken on a judgmental tone. Like a man his age wanting arcade machines is distasteful.

"I told you. They're a present."

"Okay, well, would you like me to ask him for you?"

Finally. "Would you?"

"Of course; he's the one dropping the kids off. I'll ask him right away and have him call you. This number's good?"

"This number's great. Thank you so much, Elsie. I don't know how I can repay you. Seeing how money's not . . ."

She shifts back to Chipper Elsie mode. "Oh, anytime, Iver. No need to repay friends for this kind of thing. You know, I've missed you since"—she catches herself—"these past few years. I've missed you."

Now he sees what she wants in exchange for the favor, and because he is so relieved and so thankful, it's not even that hard to offer. "I've missed you, too, Elsie," he lies, and with that the debt is paid.

He can feel her beaming from the next town over.

39

Mr. Schmidt is noisily tearing the newspaper apart.

Mrs. Schmidt raises her eyebrows over her coffee cup. "What're you doing, Mr. Schmidt?"

"I just want the crossword puzzle."

"And you need to destroy the rest of it . . . ?"

He crumples up the unwanted pages and tosses them in the garbage. "My life's too interesting to care about the boring things happening to other people," he says.

She feels a strange sense of loss, watching him throw the paper away. How many more issues will there be? What new and potentially useful information had been in that one? But she gets it; they're trying to pretend there is no apocalypse, and the paper will be full of it. Best to throw it out.

He crouches over the puzzle in concentration. "Plus, I want to keep my brain sharp for when I'm an old man. My grandfather did five crossword puzzles, three sudokus, and a Mad Lib every morning, and by the time he turned eighty, the doctors said it was physically impossible for him to develop dementia. His brain was so sharp at the end, they started prescribing trashy TV to soften it up. True story."

"Well, you're smart," she mumbles into her coffee. "I don't have anything to do, and it's weird." In an effort not to sound whiny, she concentrates on sounding tired and bored, but her words come out strangled anyway. She feels like she's sitting on the edge of a cliff, dangling her feet over; that rushing feeling in her stomach had been exciting and terrifying at first, but as the weeks go by, it's becoming a nauseating drone. People are not meant to live on the edges of cliffs.

"It *is* weird," he says, sensing her panic. He seems to understand all the nuances in her voice already; it feels like they've been married for years. "But, actually, on that note, we should probably get started."

"On . . . ?"

"Right, I forgot to tell you: I have some news." He sets the pencil down and straightens up, taking a long inhale. She notices he has to do this sometimes before he knows what he's about to say.

"Yes?"

"So you remember that I went to school for art design."

She raises her eyebrows. If this is true, it's something she hadn't known about him.

"Is that true?"

He looks offended. "Of course it's true. I wouldn't lie to you, Mrs. Schmidt."

"No, I mean, in real life."

"Is this not real life?"

She gives him a look of annoyance, but it bounces off him. He doesn't care.

She gives up. "Right. Of course I remember."

"So I got a phone call—just five minutes ago, coincidentally, while you were in the shower—from Franziska Giffey herself—the mayor of Berlin, as you know."

Mrs. Schmidt does not know, but she smiles knowingly.

"She's quite good friends with one of my old profs at the university—you know how it is in massive cities like this; everyone knows everyone else—and apparently they got to talking at one of their dinner parties, and she was saying, 'Oh, I wish I knew someone very artistic, I need to hire them for a big project,' and he was like, 'I know the exact kind of person you're wishing you knew,' and he gushed about me, and she asked for my phone number. They have a kind of guerrilla art project in mind, and they need it done by November 18, and when she described it to me, I was about to say no because I didn't know that I could do it justice in that amount of time, but then I thought—just because I can't do it as well as I'd like to doesn't mean I shouldn't try. So I said yes!"

Mrs. Schmidt can't help but laugh.

He grins. "What? You don't think I can get it done?"

"I think it's going to be very tight. Are they flexible?"

"No. November 18 is the absolute deadline."

"And what is it, exactly?" She knows he probably needs a few minutes to fully round out his ideas, but she enjoys making him work fast.

"They want me to decorate . . . Berlin . . . for Christmas."

"Berlin."

"Yes."

"Which part of Berlin?"

"As much of Berlin as I can. She wants me to decorate it just the way we've done our apartment here. She was looking at our apartment and said, Mr. Schmidt, do it just the way you've done your apartment here. I'm loving this."

"The mayor of Berlin was here? In our apartment? How did I miss that?"

"Oh no, of course not. It was on Zoom. She could see the room in the background."

"I thought you said she called you on the phone?"

"Yes, and then she said, can we do this on Zoom? I like Zoom better. And I said sure."

"Well then. You should get started right away."

"*We* should."

"Oh?"

"I told them I'd need your help. I don't know if you've noticed: Berlin is quite large."

Their imaginary life feels so mildly unhinged; the stories he invents are never outrageous, just silly. Comforting. Because it's better than

191

sulking, yes; because it passes the time, yes; but mostly because it feels like someone's taking care of her—not physically, not like he's feeding her and buying her clothes, but like he's taking care of her brain, like he recognizes that part of her isn't doing so well and he's doing everything he can to tend to it.

She checks herself. Would Petra give her that annoying smug look if she could hear these thoughts right now? Would she think Nora was weak or naive for letting Jacob take care of her?

This is the thing Nora can't quite figure out with this whole independence thing: she wants it, but she doesn't know exactly what it is, and, if it is what she has experienced so far, she doesn't particularly enjoy it. In those days between the News and Jacob's strange entrance into her life, even before Petra and Sonja took off, she felt so lonely. Is that independence? Just being so constantly, acutely aware that no one's taking care of you, no one's noticing what's wrong, pretending that's fine even if it's not?

But maybe this dependence is acceptable because it's reciprocal? Like, maybe Jacob feels the same way she does. Maybe he feels like she's taking care of him by playing along with his games. And maybe, ultimately, this is what a real marriage is: adults taking care of each other. Maybe you can be dependent and independent and have someone dependent on you all at the same time with no real problem.

40

Irene is hosting Christmas this year.

It's not exactly an apology, but it's a bridge, hopefully. Since the other night with Hank, she has become a relational architect, trying to figure out how to build bridges everywhere, since the water doesn't seem to be going anywhere.

Everyone else is expecting the world to end. They'll be distracted; they'll be hiding in their basements, eating granola bars instead of turkey and lutefisk. Christmas, Irene's favorite holiday, will come and go, and it'll be an occasion marked by fear and grief instead of joy and togetherness. Then the dust will settle, the earth will be the same as it always was, Ole will be home, and everyone will ring in the new year, sheepish and fractured and tired. They'll regret it, wasting their holidays that way.

Not Irene. Not Irene's family, if she can help it.

Irene is going to decorate. She is going to bake and cook and clean and prepare and wrap and plan. She is going to behave with grace; she wants to be like Alfie, who didn't change when she heard the world was ending and who will not change when it doesn't.

She calls Hilda to let her know.

"Hi, Irene. How're you doing?" Hilda sounds nervous, and Irene tries not to let it bother her. Hilda always sounds nervous when they talk now, like Irene is not the same person she'd grown up with, as though she's suddenly precarious and breakable and fraught. Irene doesn't want her sister to walk on eggshells around her, but—well, to be fair, her whole world is eggshells at the moment. Her missing son. Her unpopular opinions. Her strained marriage.

"I'm doing, I'm doing . . ." Irene stares across the kitchen at the fridge, once plastered with pictures drawn by Ole, now clean and empty. When's the last time Ole drew a picture? She gestures at nothing even though Hilda can't see her anyway. *How am I doing? Pretty bad, actually!*

Hilda hears the unspoken. "Any news about Ole?"

"No."

"I'm sorry."

"Me too. Any news from Nora?"

A small, guilty hesitation. "Nothing new. She's . . . just waiting. Everyone's just waiting."

"Mm-hmm."

Hilda clears her throat. "So, Irene, about that letter . . ."

"Oh, Hilda, you know what, don't worry about—"

"I read it again," says Hilda. She's eager to say this. "The whole thing. And all of the articles on the website."

"Yeah?" Irene feels hopeful, but she waits. "And? What'd you think?"

"Well. I think there's no harm in being . . . *optimistic*. But also—"

"Right. Don't worry about it, Hilda."

"I do want you to know that I seriously considered it—"

"It doesn't matter. It's not important. It's silly."

Hilda doesn't contest this. "It's okay for us not to agree on this," she says softly. "This is a very big thing, and I can't imagine everyone in the world is going to agree about it."

But, really, she had imagined agreement—right up until her sister showed her otherwise.

It's about where she'd landed with Hank, but it feels different somehow. Irene hates this tone, this glazed, patronizing voice Hilda uses when acting like the omniscient big sister, believing she's smarter than Irene simply because she's older.

So she changes the subject.

"I was calling to ask if you all wanted to come here for Christmas this year."

"Oh . . . thank you, that would be so nice." Hilda doesn't want to go to Irene's for Christmas. She doesn't want to go anywhere. It's probably the same nesting instinct that kicked in when she was pregnant with Nora, the desire to be in *her* house, cleaning and organizing—only in this case, instead of cleaning and organizing, painting. But she has broken her sister's heart already in this conversation, *and* Ole is missing. Irene could trap a live skunk and ask her to keep it in her house, and Hilda would have no choice but to say, "Oh, thank you, that would be so nice."

"Good. I'll do the cooking—maybe you could bring a dessert?"

"Love to."

"Great."

Hilda hates how strained these conversations have become. Irene sounds so nervous and tense, like she's walking on eggshells.

To be fair, the whole world is eggshells at the moment.

41

Mr. and Mrs. Schmidt have fallen into a comfortable, productive rhythm, something Mrs. Schmidt would've thought impossible only a week ago. They work Monday to Friday, nine to five.

Mr. Schmidt is getting marginally better at paper snowflakes, and they've made yards and yards of ivy garland. When they get a certain number of garlands or snowflakes or paper chains, they go outside and decorate the exteriors of the emptying shops and buildings on Käthe-Niederkirchner-Strasse. They string the felt garlands across the quiet windows, wrap them around streetlamps and trees, wind them through bench slats and bike racks. It looks festive, but also vaguely reminiscent of the Upside Down in *Stranger Things*, which feels fitting too. Occasionally people stop to watch them or give them puzzled glances, but no one asks them what they're doing or tells them to stop. Once an older woman pauses on her way past, nods vehemently, and says, "Good for you two. When all this is over, everyone else is going to feel so sad they didn't get ready for Christmas this year, aren't they?" They don't know what to say to the woman, so they smile and nod, and she continues on her way.

In the evenings they go for walks.

They try to point themselves in new directions, hoping to explore a new nook, find murals they haven't seen yet, an unfamiliar tree. Like they're looking for a blank page in a brand-new notebook, a task that should be as simple as letting it fall open—only Mrs. Schmidt soon discovers there are no blank pages. No matter how far they walk, no matter which way they go, she finds the same thing at every destination: a memory. As though she's wandered these streets for years with Mr. Schmidt.

Tonight they walk through a place called Leise Park, and Mrs. Schmidt has to hold two competing truths in her head at the same time: the first is that she has never been here before; she does not recognize the name or the scenery. The second is that this is an important place in their relationship, a place where they broke up or made up, had a first or a last. It feels important in the same way as Begonia, the bird mural across the street, her apartment—places imbued with meaning, only, unlike those other places, the context for this place's meaning is missing.

Mr. Schmidt is—or at least appears to be—oblivious to the chaos in her head. He points at the familiar landmarks and explains them as though she's never seen them before. She smiles and nods and asks questions she already knows the answers to.

"This place was once a cemetery," he says.

It doesn't feel like a cemetery. There's a jungle gym, a soccer net, what looks like a garden plot. A decided absence of seriousness; the place *feels* light.

He nods at a climbing structure, a stilted wooden lookout tower. "I played here with my friends when I was younger," he says.

"You played . . . here?" It might not feel like a cemetery, but she can't quite twist her mind around the idea of parents permitting their children to play here.

He laughs at the look on her face. "When cemeteries started charging rental fees on burial plots, people began opting out."

"Opting out of dying?"

"Of being buried. Most people do cremation here. So the demand for plots declined, and they started recycling the cemeteries."

They sit on a bench, and he drapes his arm across the back of it. It's not touching her, but it may as well be.

"Kind of weird," she says.

"Kind of." He shrugs. "But kind of nice? To grow up playing here, having birthday parties here—"

"You had what now?"

He nods. "I had a birthday party or two here. There are parts of the park that still have stones and graves, but the kids play normally; your parents don't yell at you to avoid them, like the people in them might get mad. I didn't grow up thinking of the dead as these angry people in the ground, like shushing librarians . . ." He imitates a zombie librarian, breaking out of the ground to shush the children, and his hand grazes her shoulder.

She laughs, and it feels disrespectful to laugh this hard in a cemetery. But that's what he's talking about, isn't it? He doesn't think it's disrespectful to experience joy in the presence of the dead.

"You're right. It is kind of nice," she says.

They leave the park and walk east.

"Couldn't help but notice more closed businesses today," she says. She tries to keep up the charade, but sometimes she needs to acknowledge certain things. He always listens, then quickly explains the thing away. It's therapeutic, actually.

"Yep," he says lightly. "Closed for the holidays. People are finally figuring out what's important. They want to spend more time with loved ones. I think it's wonderful. When I was younger, Christmas was very commercialized; it was all about shopping and presents and big meals and parties. It was so stressful. I'm glad society has come around to a slower pace in recent years. It feels *right*."

Mrs. Schmidt smiles contentedly. "I agree. I hope it always stays this way."

Mr. Schmidt smiles too. "It will. It will always be exactly as it is right now; nothing will ever change again. I find that comforting."

Comforting. Mrs. Schmidt adds this to the list of words that don't quite fit the present scenario.

People are very good at offering up the wrong words, and this is never more apparent than when they are faced with a tragedy.

Tragedy. The one word no one ever seems to think of, or bring themselves to say out loud.

✳

Later, Mr. and Mrs. Schmidt pass a large apartment building where a beautiful woman has been immortalized in paint, five stories tall, and goose bumps raise on Mrs. Schmidt's arms. She stops short; her mouth drops open. She is firmly pulled into reality, and no amount of Mrs. Schmidting is going to be able to get her back into their little game.

"You okay?" Jacob peers up at the painting, trying to understand what it is that has captured her attention so completely.

She isn't sure how to explain it to him. It doesn't make sense, and she doesn't want him to think she's delusional. Maybe she should ask him what he's seeing, make sure it matches up. But that would sound even stranger.

Her phone buzzes in her pocket, a text.

Thinking about you. Jeg elsker deg.

A man in a green jacket walks past, pausing briefly to see what they're looking at. Decides there's nothing *that* notable going on here and continues along, but not before the toe of his shoe catches on the sidewalk and sends him into a series of silly walks as he tries to regain his balance. Nora doesn't notice; she stares at her phone, then at the wall, then back at her phone.

"What is it?" Jacob asks.

"It's my mom."

He looks again at the wall, again at the phone. "Which . . ."

"Both."

He shakes his head. "I'm not following."

She holds up her phone. "My mom just texted me. And that"—she gestures at the mural—"is her."

As before, the mural on this wall is something she has never seen before but which strikes a note of familiarity—though this time the feeling actually makes sense: the woman depicted there is—or looks exactly like—Nora's mother. A bit younger, a different haircut, clothing Nora has never seen, but other than that . . .

"Oh," says Jacob, accepting it too easily. "I see. It looks like your mom."

"No," says Nora adamantly. "Not looks like. *Is.* Or like—is supposed to be."

Jacob nods politely. He sees both that Nora will not be dissuaded from this belief, and that it's a belief unlikely to prove true.

"What are the chances?" asks Nora. She pulls up a picture of her and her mother, taken at graduation, and shows it to Jacob.

"The resemblance is definitely there," he says charitably. Because it is. He doesn't say that it's more probable Nora's mother has a doppelgänger, that this is meant to be *that* woman.

"*Look,*" says Nora. "The birthmark on her cheek. There." She points. "And her hairline; the way it does that swoopy thing. And those freckles on her neck."

He has to admit that these small resemblances, taken together, are extremely compelling—and she hasn't even pointed out the most important bit of evidence, which is not that the woman on the wall looks like the woman in the picture but that the woman on the wall looks like *Nora.* Same mouth, same nose. This, he thinks, must be why this mural seems so familiar, even though it's one he's never seen before. The mural woman has a confidence in her face that he can see shadows of in Nora's, something she's growing into. She seems to be looking directly at him; she's smiling and she has a streak of blue paint across her forehead, as though the painter had slipped while filling in her eyes and then decided not to correct his mistake for whatever reason.

"And then what are the chances that we'd see this just as she texts me?"

"That's a thing," Jacob says. "Me and my sister have that. I'll hear a song that reminds me of her, and she'll text me right then. Or I'll pick up the phone to call her, and she'll pick up and be like"—his voice jumps up into an imitation of a woman who has smoked for fifty years—"Hey, weirdo, I was just about to call you!"

"Your sister has a beautiful voice."

"I'll tell her you think so."

She laughs. "But, seriously, what *is* that?"

"I'm just bad at impersonating women."

"No, the thing where you think about someone and then they think about you back."

"Quantum entanglement, maybe?" he says, as though that were a complete explanation.

"Totally," she says, then sees that he's serious. "That means nothing to me."

He appears to be absolutely delighted by this admission, as though he has been waiting for his whole life to stumble across someone who doesn't know about quantum entanglement. "Oh, well, aren't you in for a treat. I would *love* to be the one to introduce you to this concept. It's the coolest thing."

They begin walking again, away from the giant mural of Nora's mother. "So, okay, disclaimer: I'm not a physicist, and I might be wrong about absolutely everything."

"Okay."

"Okay, so quantum entanglement is basically when a group of particles become linked in such a way that they can't be described independently of each other, even when they're separated by great distances. Scientists have found a way to do it, which is absolutely mind blowing, but it's a thing that occurs naturally, too, without any help from people—which is maybe even more mind blowing? And once they're linked, they're"—he gestures behind them at the painting—"they're linked forever, I think, and it doesn't matter how far apart they are. Like, you could put one of the linked particles in a spaceship and send it to the moon, and whatever you did to the remaining particle on Earth would also happen to the one on the moon. They act like one particle, even though they're far apart."

"And you're implying this is a real thing that happened between me and my mom? You think the particles in my body are entangled with the particles in hers?"

He nods. "If I'm not wrong about everything. Again: not a physicist. I might just be understanding it the way I want to understand it."

Nora loves this idea, that she and her mother could be joined in an invisible way even across such distance. She looks behind them at the enormous painting, the woman who is not Hilda but has Hilda's birthmark and hair swoop and freckles. "Sounds kind of . . . *woo-woo.* If you know what I mean."

"All science does the first time you hear about it."

"True."

She texts her mom back.

I was just thinking about you too.

42

"Hi, Iver? Elephant here."

Iver is still half-asleep. His room is dark; he's not sure if it's the blackout blinds or the dead of night. And someone named Elephant is calling him? Maybe he's dreaming. He doesn't know anyone named Elephant, nor should he—though people these days *are* naming their kids stranger and stranger things. It makes him mad even though he knows it isn't good for his health, to let these trivial things get to him. His wife always told him that, over and over. But, well, she's not here now, is she? Talking to people named Elephant? Even she'd get a little irritated at this.

"Elephant?" he mumbles. His mouth feels like someone wiped it dry with a paper towel. His throat is itchy; his body aches. He has a moment of wondering if he's getting sick, but then he remembers, as he does every morning, that this is just how he feels when he wakes up now. And all day long. And into the evening. "What time is it? What kind of a name is Elephant?"

"KEL-VIN," the person says. "Elsie's son? And I'm sorry—did I wake you? It's, like, ten."

Iver holds the phone away from his ear for a moment to read the display. It's like someone rubbed Vaseline on his eyeballs; the screen looms through the fog before coming into focus, as best as it ever will. Sure enough—10:05 a.m. He feels sheepish. For a long time after retiring, he made a point of getting out of bed at the same time as when he got up for work: 5:00 a.m. Every day. No matter what.

Then she'd died, and he'd gone through a period where he stayed in bed for most of the day, and he'd come to really like it. It was the closest thing to a good long hug he could get. Over time, he developed a happy-ish medium. He didn't stay there all day, but he didn't rush out of it anymore either. He visited it frequently throughout the day. He collapsed into it as early as felt acceptable in the evenings. But then Hildy went and bought him one of those weighted blankets, and *that*. Well. Game over. That feels like an *actual* hug, and he's started slipping back into bedridden-on-purpose land . . .

"Sorry, yes, hello, Kelvin," he says, trying not to clear his throat directly into Kelvin's ear. "No, you didn't wake me; I was just . . . outside. Working."

This doesn't sound remotely true, and Kelvin knows it and Iver knows it.

"Gotcha," says Kelvin benevolently. "Elsie says you're interested in the old machines?" His voice sounds funny—tight and low and shaky, and Iver worries it's rage, that Kelvin is upset at the audacity of someone asking for his arcade machines, his passion project.

"I am," Iver says. He tries desperately to come up with a good reason, a good repayment, but he has nothing. He's already paid Elsie by lying about missing her—a payment that won't hold the same weight for Kelvin.

"Great," says Kelvin. His voice has jumped a few notes lower. He must be really angry. "I'm sure she's told you I have no use for them anymore." There's a strange, sharp squeaking noise, a lot of sniffling, and Iver realizes Kelvin is crying. So not rage—immense sadness. Iver fights the urge to hang up; he hates witnessing the breakdowns of strangers. It's bad enough when you know and care about a person, but at least then you feel like you can be helpful. Having strangers cry in front of you is akin to having strangers moon you—an experience Iver had years ago when he went to the city with his wife. Some high school kids, standing on the overpass, big white bums out in a neat little row for everyone to see, like his wife's bread dough left on the counter to rise. Iver remembers the rush of secondhand embarrassment, the shock, the incomprehension—why would someone want anyone, let alone everyone, to see *that* part of their body?

Now he's thinking he'd rather get mooned again than listen to all of Kelvin's snorting and wheezing and trumpeting, ironically elephant-like noises. Iver can hear the stuff coming out of his eyes and nose. At least the mooners stayed on the overpass while he rushed beneath them at 110 kilometers per hour; at least he didn't have to talk to them after it was over.

"She has told me that, yes," says Iver, choosing to pretend he doesn't notice the heaving breaths passing through the phone line. "And I hope she's told you, Kelvin, how much I appreciate this . . ."

There are a few more moments of ragged breathing, the distant sound of a nose being blown. "It's no problem." Kelvin's voice is hoarse and watery. "I'm just glad I can do one last nice thing for someb—"

Poor Kelvin. He can't make it all the way through the sentence. He begins to bawl again, his sobs peaking in squeaks and squeals that are painful on multiple levels for Iver. He holds the phone under his pillow for a few minutes, like he's smothering the man, but he's just trying to preserve what's left of Kelvin's dignity. He's just being respectful. He'd want anyone to do the same for him.

Soon he hears talking again and holds the phone back up to his ear. "So"—*sniff*—"how should we do this?" *Sniff sniff.* "Should we . . . uh . . . do you have a truck?"

"I don't . . ."

"Say, I have a friend with a truck. Can I bring them to you, Iver? Can I do that for you?"

"Uhh . . . well, I hate to put you out—"

"I'd really like to do that for you." More crying. "I wasn't generous enough in this life. I did so many things I regret, and I didn't do so many things I should've done . . . please let me do this one thing . . ."

"Of course, of course," says Iver. "Thank you, Kelvin. I appreciate it." He wants this man off the phone. He wants to tell him that taking some arcade machines on a two-hour round trip with someone else's truck is not going to make up for whatever horrible life choices he's currently anguishing over. But today the guilt is working in Iver's favor, so he decides to let it go.

43

It's going faster and faster now.

The kitchen mural was detailed and difficult, and progress had been slow. Several times Hilda had to go back and fix things she wanted perfect—she wanted Marlen to look healthy in the painting; she wanted Nora's eyes to be the exact right shade of blue. She even wanted to capture the sarcastic nature of Nora's cat, who would sometimes stalk past as Hilda painted, sizing up her own likeness disdainfully.

She wanted them to look happy, the way they had before last year. She wanted to fully capture what was special and important while also embellishing a little to make herself feel better, and this felt impossible and necessary—and when things feel both impossible and necessary, that's when they start to mess with you. It began to feel like she was trying to save her family, like their preservation depended on her getting their likenesses just right. Some nights she'd get up at three in the morning to change something and never come back to bed.

Marlen was concerned at first. He saw her getting increasingly frenetic, her perfectionist tendencies growing offshoots and wrapping around her arms and fingers. But he recognized that it was okay if she lost her mind a bit, that she needed this, and that though she was painting, what she was really doing was grieving. He'd been there too.

So he stopped trying to talk her out of it and began to follow her down the stairs to be with her.

Hilda pulled the recliner into the kitchen so he could sit with her comfortably, sometimes dozing, sometimes watching. Sometimes they'd chat while she painted. She asked him to talk to her about one of his many special interests, and he rambled—deep space and physics and philology and Shakespeare and pop culture and music history. Did she know that Julie Andrews learned to play the guitar for her role in *The Sound of Music*? Or that Hawaiians have more than two hundred different words for rain?

Sometimes they'd sit in silence or with the radio on, Marlen smiling to himself as he admired his wife's work, as he admired his wife, her long fingers ending in perfectly rounded fingernails, the earnestness on her beautiful face, the new lines and gray hairs that had appeared over the past couple of years. He loved all of her, so much. He tried not to think about how this was going to end and focus on the gifts—late nights and art and time.

Before they knew it, the kitchen mural was finished.

But Hilda was not.

She'd thought the last stroke of the brush would bring some closure, that she would understand her husband at last, a feeling of having cleaned a room and shut the door behind her, but the feeling instead was that of another doorway, another open door. And then she realized there *was* another doorway—the one that led to the dining room! So instead of packing up her paints and getting some fresh air, she simply hauled Marlen's recliner in there and began covering the dining room walls—a field of golden grain beneath a bright blue sky, a red combine in the distance, deer in the foreground. A comforting, familiar scene.

Just as in the kitchen, the dining room did not bring closure either. She now has to run out for more paint, and this time she buys a lot more of it. At this rate, the whole house is going to be painted, inside and out, by the time it's destroyed. And hopefully that will accomplish whatever it is that she needs it to accomplish.

44

The thing with Christmas decorating is that you can't hold back. You kind of have to attack people with the Christmas spirit. More is actually less when it comes to this. A little more is just a little more, and a lot is almost an acceptable minimum.

People do not want to gather around a sparse tree with a few twinkle lights. They want the entire room to glow; they want a certain nutmeggy smell; they want everything to be either red or green or silver—they want to feel like Christmas is an actual giant person wrapping them up in a hug, serenading them with Christmas carols, plying them with fancy Christmas drinks and fancy Christmas treats.

Irene is up to the task.

She's going to start with the garland. Years ago, she purchased yards and yards of green felt from Alfie's little craft corner at the senior citizens' center before it folded and became Alfie's little one-wall library. She'd gotten the felt on an exceptional sale and had been planning on using it as quilt batting, but then Hilda had told her that cotton was a much better option, so she stuffed it in a closet with a bunch of other craft supplies and hasn't touched it since.

It'll make perfect ivy.

She pours herself a cup of coffee, sits at the kitchen table, and begins to cut.

45

Iver is the only one awake when Kelvin knocks on the door. Fantastic. If they can get the machines moved and set up within thirty minutes, the first half of the surprise will have been executed perfectly. Kelvin grins when he sees Iver's face. He has a friend with him, someone named Zach. "Morning, Iver! Zach brought his hand truck. We're all set. You just show us where to go."

Iver studies Kelvin's face warily, but there are no signs of the hysteria from the other morning. Maybe Zach is a deterrent, being closer to Kelvin's age and, thus, more embarrassing to cry in front of; Iver certainly hopes so. "Thanks," he says quietly, trying not to appear too thankful, so as to protect Kelvin from himself. He can cry all the way home, for all Iver cares. *Subject Zach to your emotional bare butt, just leave me out of it.*

"Why are we whispering?" Kelvin asks, lowering his voice only a little.

Iver points toward the bedroom. "My son's sleeping," he whispers. "He doesn't know about the machines. I don't want to wreck the surprise."

"Oh!" Kelvin smiles, realizing that he is performing a favor for not one, but *two* people. Bonus points. "Fun. Okay. We'll be quiet!"

They've brought a twenty-six-foot box truck, and the games look comically small lined up in there. They've brought ten, but they could've brought twenty more. Iver reads the names of the ones he can see: *Ms. Pac-Man, Asteroids, Turtles in Time, Donkey Kong* . . . yes. This will do.

Zach and Kelvin begin the moving process while Iver looks on. All in all, it goes quite smoothly, and soon Iver's living room is, just as he'd hoped, an arcade, machines lining the periphery. It looks a lot fuller than the truck had, and Iver is relieved.

"We've got one more in there," says Zach. "Any other place to put it?"

"I think it'll fit. If not, you can throw it in the kitchen or some-place. Anywhere you can find a spot," says Iver, feeling like royalty.

Kelvin heads off to strap the machine to the hand truck, but Zach stays behind.

"So, Iver," he says. "How *are* you?"

Iver is instantly suspicious. "Fiiiine," he says. "How are *you?*"

"I wondered," says Zach, ignoring the reciprocated question, "if you've given much thought to what's going to happen after you die."

Iver takes a step backward, as though Zach has just pulled out a knife. There are so many directions this conversation could take, and Iver is too tired right now for most of them.

"I belong to a certain community," says Zach, and Iver thinks this is a very strange way to say you belong to a church, "and we're just, you know, trying to get the word out."

"The Word," says Iver.

"No, not the Word," says Zach. "Lowercase word—news." He has forgotten two things today: to brush his teeth and the entire concept of personal space.

"The Good News?" says Iver. He has already heard the Good News, and from people much more credible looking than this. Kelvin can take his friend and go home now.

"No," says Zach. "Not *the Good News*—though it is news and it is good. Great, even!"

Iver doesn't say anything because he has no idea what to say, and Zach accepts this as an invitation.

"The government doesn't want you to know this," says Zach, "but there have been recoveries of partial fragments through and up to fully intact vehicles of *exotic origin*."

Zach takes a step back now, as though allowing room for Iver's awe.

Iver stares blankly at him. He knows what he had been expecting from this conversation, and it was as far from this as possible. Light-years away, literally.

"*Fully intact vehicles,*" says Zach. "It's been reported to Congress in secret meetings."

"I don't . . ." Iver is just too tired. "That's incredible. Very interesting. Thank you again for your help today."

"No, you don't understand," says Zach. "I'm talking about *extraterrestrials*."

"I don't believe in that sort of thing," says Iver quickly, swatting away the notion as though it were a mosquito buzzing around his head.

"Doesn't matter," says Zach, clearly disappointed but undeterred. "That 'sort of thing' believes in *you*. Poke at the phenomenon, man. It pokes back."

Iver has never been so speechless. He has not, in all his years, ever encountered such a person as this. "Uh," he manages, "no thank you."

Kelvin returns with the last machine. "All good here, gentlemen?"

Zach, slightly deflated, nods and follows Kelvin inside the house.

At last the task is finished. Iver is relieved. Zach doesn't say anything more about aliens, and Kelvin hasn't cried yet today. Strange wins.

But on the way outside, Kelvin turns to Iver one last time. "A word of advice, Iver?"

Iver wants to tell the boy to save his advice for his strange friend, but, well, he did come all this way. "Okay." The payment for the labor.

"Time is short, you know? I just wanted to encourage you to pay it forward. What we did here today, it felt so wonderful to be able to do that for you. Don't let it end here!" Kelvin's voice has taken on an uncomfortable huskiness, and his words feel vague and infomercial-ish, like he's trying to sell Iver a magazine subscription. *Don't let it end here!*

For only $19.99, you could experience this feeling once a month for an entire year! "Pay it forward, friend. You know? It's all about love. It's always been about love." Now he rests a hand on Iver's shoulder. Iver hates this, he really does, but he doesn't show it. He would prefer to talk more with Zach about the aliens. But Kelvin's not the only one performing random acts of kindness to make up for his shortcomings. "I just thought I should encourage you to take stock. Make things right. Live out loud. *Love* out loud. Just some things to think about." He flashes a smug smile, as though he's figured everything out and is so incredibly happy to be of help to Iver, when all he has done, really, is concocted an off-putting soup of clichés and dumped it on Iver's head. He has scalded him with boiling platitudes.

But with that, they're finished, and Iver comforts himself, knowing he will never see Kelvin or Zach again. Zach shuts the door of his truck, and the three of them look at each other for a minute. Iver still feels like he should get out his wallet. He hadn't realized until now just how many day-to-day interactions end with someone getting out their wallet. Money had sneakily become the most real thing, more real than smiles or thank-yous or the desire to do obligation-free favors for people. And now that it's suddenly not real at all, what's left? Maybe guilt is the only thing left. Guilt and the desire to appear good.

"Welp. That's that," says Kelvin. He's looking a touch emotional again, and also like he wants a trophy for his great act of altruism. Iver is happy enough with what he's done—he'd give him a trophy if he had one. But he doesn't, so he just thanks him again and tries not to avert his gaze when Kelvin gets misty.

The 20 percent tip.

46

Today Hilda is painting the main-floor bathroom. The theme for this, the smallest room in the whole house, is the biggest thing in the whole world: the sky. She's done the whole room—floor, ceiling, shower, even the cabinet under the sink—in bright blue, and now she's adding cotton candy clouds all over the place so that it feels as though you are sitting in the air when using the bathroom. Marlen thinks this is a weird idea, but in a good way.

He's just outside the door in his chair; he's been asleep for an hour or so, but she hears him stirring now.

"Marlen?"

"Yeah?"

"You awake?"

"Yeah."

"Good nap?"

There's a pause where she pictures him shrugging. "All naps are good naps," he says optimistically, though she knows this isn't necessarily true for him anymore, just something he started saying back when it was.

"I'm getting bored in here," she says. "What do you have for me today?" She wishes they'd discovered this game long ago. She'd always known about his love of random knowledge, but she'd never entered into it with him, given him any kind of outlet for it. Maybe that's part of why he wrote a book behind her back.

"Have we talked about quantum entanglement yet?" he asks.

"Nope."

She shifts her position so she can paint a cloud behind the toilet, and he begins to explain it to her, how scientists have discovered that particles can become linked, that you can put one of the linked particles in a spaceship and send it to the moon, and whatever you do to the remaining particle on Earth will also happen to the one on the moon. They act like one particle, even though they're far apart.

"Can the particles in my body become entangled with the particles in someone else's?" she asks. She loves this idea, and he knows it's because Nora is so far away.

"Yes, absolutely," he says, quickly and confidently, even though he's not actually sure.

He's not a physicist.

47

Mr. Schmidt has gone from being bad at making snowflakes to competent to good to exceptional. His snowflakes have become intricate, downright ornate. His snowflakes could win awards, if awards were given to grown men for paper snowflakes.

Mrs. Schmidt is hard at work on her side of the table, sketching out a wintry mural she's going to paint on the front window of Begonia, inspired by all the hundreds of murals she has seen in her time here. The prospect is terrifying—painting something so large where anyone can see it—but this also makes it feel like the right thing to do right now, an important part of her journey of self-exploration and actualization. (Really, at this point, she's just throwing everything at the wall and seeing if something will stick.)

The mural is of the street she lives on, her apartment building with tiny people in the windows getting ready for Christmas. She'd forgotten how much she liked this. She used to do this with her ex-boyfriend; they'd take sketchbooks to the Frenchman River Valley and sit at the top of the hill, mapping out the strange topography, the massive indent in an otherwise perfectly flat landscape. They'd draw each other. They'd draw the birds, the river running through the middle of the valley like the gold seam on a kintsugi bowl.

She'd left all her art supplies at home when she moved here.

"You're getting good at that," she says as Mr. Schmidt unfolds yet another snowflake, a spiderweb of paper crystals.

He looks childishly proud. "It's my full-time job, so I have to be good at it. You're *really* good at that."

She looks down at her artwork, trying to possess a critical eye. She's not sure if she's good at it or not, and she wishes she were the kind of person who didn't care.

Her phone buzzes on the countertop. Derek. He sends three texts: The first is a follow-up to the one where he told her he hadn't cheated on her.

do u believe me?

She doesn't reply right away. She needs a moment to figure out her answer. It's not always easy to know what you believe, but the pit in her stomach is begging for further contemplation.

Then, not even two minutes later:

what ur ignoring me?

Oh, she thinks, *so he's allowed to take a full twenty-four hours to respond to me but expects me to answer within sixty seconds.* Has he always been like this, or is it his new TikTok personality?

Not ignoring, just thinking, she types back.

u shdnt have to think about it

No. I really shouldn't. And she blocks his number. Maybe she'll deal with it later, if she feels like it. Another marker on her quest for full-fledged adulthood—learning when to decisively end a conversation without feeling bad about it. Or, without feeling *too* bad about it. Or . . . should she unblock him and explain herself?

Mr. Schmidt watches her from across the table.

"Everything okay?"

"Yeah. Yes."

"You sure?"

"Totally." She sounds extremely unsure. "Just . . . someone's being stupid, and I'm trying not to let it get to me."

"A friend?"

"My boyfriend." She's not sure why it came out like that. Derek's not her boyfriend, not at all. It's a force of habit, to refer to him like that. She opens her mouth to explain herself, but now *his* phone lights up, distracting him. "My mother's calling. Excuse me."

"Of course." She'll fix this when he's done. Or—not *fix* it; nothing's broken. Not a real marriage, she reminds herself. A nonhusband should have no problem with a boyfriend, especially a nonboyfriend.

But still . . .

He speaks to his mother in German, and Nora feels as though she's watching a foreign film without subtitles. He becomes a character, someone she observes but doesn't know. These moments, when he's speaking to other people in another language, are the only ones where she feels separate from him. The rest of the time they are a cohesive unit, Mr. and Mrs. Schmidt, a couple who has been married for all of eternity, forward and backward in time.

He frowns at something his mother is saying. Nora watches the way his mouth turns down at the corners. His eyes are serious but still kind. His thumb taps on the table in soft sixteenth notes. She wants to sketch him like this, try to capture the way the afternoon sun hits the nearly invisible blond hairs on his forehead, the hunch of his shoulders, and the tilt of his head.

She moves to one of the empty windows in her sketch—her window—*their* window—and draws his outline. He's holding up a beautiful snowflake. She looks up at him again, and for a brief moment she has the strangest feeling, a sense of awe at how *real* he looks. Like she could reach out and touch him. Which is ridiculous, because he is and she could. Maybe this is the result of living with someone that you want to touch but who feels, for whatever reason, untouchable? They begin to take on a movie-star quality, like a person who exists in some other reality you're not really part of.

She hadn't noticed while she was drawing him that his conversation had grown heated. It's hard to pick up on that when the person you're listening to isn't speaking your language, but now he's pacing the room, and his voice is tight. He won't look at her, and she realizes how often he usually looks at her. The absence of his gaze is almost alarming.

It's an agonizing wait for the phone call to end, during which she tries in vain to catch his eye. At one point she thinks, *This phone call is never going to end*, which is a funny thought to have right now. Everything is going to end. But maybe not this phone call. Maybe this is the one eternal thing.

But finally the phone call does end, and Jacob faces her.

"I need to go," he says. He sits at the table and puts a hand on hers. She is too conscious of every feeling, but none of the feelings work together. It's like the bottom half of her body is wading to the hips in ice water and the top half is on fire. Then he seems to notice where his hand is, and he yanks it away. "Sorry," he mumbles. He's probably thinking about how she has a boyfriend. She needs to fix that before he leaves, but as they get further from the inciting conversation, she realizes it's going to be more awkward to bring up.

"Where are you going? And why?"

"Home." The first question is easy to answer, but he's having a hard time with the second one. "I've been . . . selfish." He sighs. "I've been neglecting people I should be taking care of."

"Like . . ." It occurs to her now that she doesn't know for sure whether or not *Jacob* is single.

"My mother," he says, "is really upset that I'm not spending more time with her and my father. And understandably so. I don't know what I was thinking." This brings up in Nora the same rage she'd felt when she read Derek's last text (u shdnt have to think about it). Why? They're not the same kinds of statements, not spoken by the same kinds of people. But she wishes she could block the rest of this conversation the way she'd blocked Derek from saying anything more. *I don't know what I was thinking? You don't know what you were thinking? Here's a thought: maybe you were thinking about me . . .*

He continues: "I went all in on this fantasy of . . ." He regrets this word, *fantasy*; she can see it on his face. ". . . on the, uh, the pretending. Us, this, you and me and *pretending* . . ." He's too flustered. He can't get back on track.

"You forgot about your family," she fills in for him. She wants him to stop; he's shattering the illusion they've worked so hard to construct, rushing around inside of it with a baseball bat. Couldn't they just bring his family into it with them?

But no, she realizes. They can't. Because there is no "them." The "them" *is* the illusion.

"You should go." She sounds bitter, like a real partner in a real marriage, not like someone pretending, someone who says goodbye to her fake spouse every night and disappears into her own bedroom while he sleeps on the couch. She looks at him, at his beautiful, serious face, and realizes that she has no business wanting anything from him. He never signed on for a real marriage. He's her coping mechanism and she's his. "That's the right thing, actually," she says. "I think this has gone too far."

Because it's hard to say what you mean at the best of times. At the worst, it's absolutely impossible.

48

Irene has taken a break from garlanding and is trying her hand at paper snowflakes to hang in the windows. She had to watch a few YouTube tutorials, but she's getting very good at them. They pile up on the kitchen table as though they're falling from a cloud on the ceiling. *Ole will love these,* she thinks. She can't wait for him to come home and see them.

49

Iver doesn't know how to make his living room look more like an arcade. He searches his memory, trying to lay his dream arcade over this living room version. Slowly, a clearer vision emerges; the differences become obvious.

It needs thumping music and a different carpet, something bright and cartoonish. It needs more of the right kind of light and less of the wrong kind, but the differences between the kinds of light are too hard to pin down. It needs a certain smell, but this is hard to pin down too—cigarettes? Bleach? Adolescent sweat? (His son can help with that last one, at least.)

It needs a lot more people. That's the one thing he can manifest. He just has to call his family.

For now this will have to do, as is. He flips the overhead lights off, and that helps a little. The machines glow warmly, like they're smiling at him. He smiles back in his own frowny way.

He hears the sound of the toilet flushing down the hall; it snaps him to attention. How long has it been since he prepared a surprise for another person? Years. Lifetimes. Not since the time he made that table-and-chair set for his wife for Christmas. He had this feeling then, too, the fluttering nervousness in his belly.

Footsteps down the hall, the sound of his silent son, and in a moment they're standing in front of each other, his son's astonishment such a reward.

"What's this . . . ?" The boy's eyes are luminous. Maybe they're just reflecting the light of the games, or maybe he is as happy as Iver wants him to be.

Iver never knows what to say in moments like this. He can feel his face smiling, and he hopes that communicates whatever needs to be communicated. All he says out loud is, "They're for you."

His son also seems not to know what to say, but the smile on his face is bigger than it's been in a while.

"Cool," says his son. "Thanks, Grandpa."

Ole feels like he's dreaming. Maybe the asteroid or whatever came early and this is heaven—his grandpa's cozy, comforting house full of vintage arcade games. He had thought he might call his parents today, let them know where he is, but now he thinks he'll wait just a little longer.

His grandpa is standing there, his smile bigger than he's ever seen it, as though the arcade games were a present for *him*. But he doesn't seem interested in playing them, just in seeing Ole play them, and once again Ole feels sad that he hadn't really connected with his grandfather before now—and not just because he gives good gifts.

He walks over to the first machine in the row. "Do I need tokens or anything to play them?"

Iver nods at a bucket in the corner. Unlimited tokens, every kid's dream, right?

His son goes straight for *Space Invaders*, just as Iver suspected he might. That was always his favorite.

The sound of the game fills the room, and now Iver is the one traveling through time. He's a younger—not young but younger—version of himself, standing with his children in the arcade, the one owned by Elsie's son, who is barely an adult himself.

Hilda's a teenager; Irene is just a little thing, a five-year-old standing on her tiptoes on the riser, pretending she knows what's going on; and Arnie's eleven. He's dazzled by the arcade, every time. It never gets less magical. His sisters love it, but to Arnie it is the most fantastical, amazing, exciting place in the universe, and Iver cannot get enough of the look on his face. Pure, unadulterated wonder. Those glowing eyes.

It's their thing. The thirty-minute drive, the two hours of arcade time, the ice cream even though it's winter, the drive back. That's what winter Saturdays are for. As a farmer, Iver is gone constantly during many months of the year, and, sure, they'll come out to the field to eat supper with him on his combine, and sometimes Irene's awake to see him off before five in the morning, but this is their golden time: five, eleven, thirteen. These numbers stick in Iver's head like a locker combination; they are very important. Because after that beautiful year, it was just six and fourteen. And then seven and fifteen.

Eleven and eleven and eleven, forever.

And this boy, in Iver's living room, it's not Arnie after all, is it? Because this boy is not eleven. This boy is not dressed like Arnie. He's a little taller, a little wider; his hair is a little redder. It's not that Iver didn't know this before now; it's that Iver didn't want to know this, so he put it off for a while. Ignorance really is bliss, even if you have to force it.

But that *is* Arnie's smile, actually, on Ole's face. One of those little miracles of genetics or DNA or whatnot, those gone living on in their relatives' bodies and brains. It's okay that this boy is not Arnie. This boy has Arnie in him, and that's a good thing, even if it's a different thing. Iver smiles, watching his grandson unknowingly play his son's favorite arcade game.

50

"Hello?"

Hank answers his phone without looking at the call display. Probably Irene, checking on him. Always checking on him. But of all the times she could check on him, he doesn't want her to check on him right *now*. He'll have to admit that he's stuck. He's done; he's run into a wall. He's sitting on the side of the road, and he's checked every possible place, and their child is nowhere; he's not in a ditch, not in a field, not in an old farmhouse. He's nowhere; he has disintegrated early.

"Dad?"

Hank is dreaming, probably. He puts a hand on the steering wheel in front of him, trying to remember if steering wheels feel this solid in dreams. It's not possible, so he is not excited at all. Not relieved. Not happy.

"Dad? Are you there?"

"OLE? Ole, is that you?"

"Yeah, it's me."

Silence. Rage. Relief. Rage. Relief. Rage. Relief.

Control.

"Where are you? Are you okay?"

"I'm fine, Dad. Don't freak out."

Rage. Relief. Rage. Rage. Rage.

"Don't freak out? *Don't freak out?* Do you understand what you're saying? Do you *know* where I am right now? Do you know what I've been doing? Do you know how . . . *angry* I am?" *Angry* feels like the wrong word. "Of course you don't; you've never had your son go missing—"

Rage, rage, rage.

Control it. Just try. Don't blow it; he'll get away again. Don't say the wrong thing. Get your voice under control. Stop yelling. His brain fills instantly with a crowd of parenting podcasters, talking in their too-calm, too-polished radio voices. Suddenly they all seem stupid. *They have no idea what they're talking about,* Hank thinks. How could they?

"Where are you?"

Silence. Ole has hung up. Hank stares at his phone in disbelief for a full minute before he thinks to check the "recent calls" screen to see where Ole was calling from. Relief again knowing once and for all where this kid went, commingled with coursing rage. He wants to punch his truck window so it shatters into a million pieces and cry. He has never felt so much of anything at once as right now.

But when he pushes the home button, he realizes his mistake. Ole hadn't hung up on him; his phone had died. It feels like a metaphor—when was the last time he charged the phone? When was the last time he'd stopped for long enough to do that?

He needs to get home, *now*. He turns the key in the ignition and sighs in relief when the truck starts. The gas tank is almost empty, too, though he hadn't noticed that until right now. The metaphors are just flying; the universe is screaming at him. He's run out of battery, he's almost run out of gas, and he's quickly running out of time.

Irene is in the kitchen when Hank's truck comes flying up the driveway, sliding sideways on the ice as he rounds the corner. She instinctively checks to see if there's anyone in the passenger seat, but there's not—just Bud the dog, pressed against the window, tongue out, eyes wide.

Lucky Bud. He gets to spend time with Hank these days, even if it looks thoroughly unsafe.

She goes back to her flat grill. She's begun some of the Christmas baking, to be kept in the garage freezer until they need it. Irene knows Hank is frustrated with how she's plowed ahead with the decorating and the baking and the planning, but it's what she needs to do; it's the page that she's on, and he's trying—she can tell he's trying, at least—to love her there.

She needs Christmas to be Christmas, not Armageddon. She needs to make lefse and krumkake, has to roll it out just exactly like this and handle the delicate dough in exactly this way. Ole's favorite part of Christmas is the lefse, so it's like she and Hank are working on a joint project today: Hank will bring Ole home; she will feed him. She has felt hopeful about this today, much more than usual, with no good reason.

Hank runs into the house, yelling, Bud right on his heels, and she is so numb she's not even curious as to what he's yelling about. This is when she realizes that she's not feeling as hopeful as she'd thought; it doesn't cross her mind that this could have anything to do with Ole. "What's wrong, Hank?" She doesn't think to ask if anything's right.

"My phone!" he gasps. "Battery's dead."

"Oh." She points at the charging dock on the counter, even though he knows it's there and is already lunging for it. He's sweating; he looks all wrong, like he's too happy and too upset at the same time, and it's going to physically turn him inside out. "Hank? Are you okay?"

"YES," he says, drumming his fingers on the counter, "and NO."

"Do you need water?"

"NO." But he can't catch his breath. His eyes are as wide as Bud's. Both of them need water—she can see that—and she rushes to the fridge to get the Brita.

"Charge!" Hank croaks at the phone, nodding at Irene as she hands him a glass of cold water. He downs it, then slams it on the counter. He's scaring her.

"Hank—"

"Ole called." Hank's face is contorted.

Her mouth drops open. Her brain is trying to protect her; her heart is flailing.

"Ole? Did you say Ole, Hank?"

She feels a drop of water on her hand, like it's raining, and she looks up to make sure she's still in the kitchen. Nothing is making sense; her senses aren't useful. Another drop.

Oh. She's crying on herself.

Hank nods. "He called. He's okay. He said he's fine. He sounded fine. He—I could just . . ."

"Hank, WHERE IS HE? WHERE DID HE CALL YOU FROM?"

"I—I DON'T KNOW. My phone died—"

"HANK!"

"I KNOW! I KNOW, IRENE! I KNOW."

They stare at each other, and then at the black screen on the counter. And then, as though they've summoned it, the little white apple appears, the phone waking up as if from an innocent little nap. Hank dives for it, trying to hold it up to his face without disconnecting the charger, worried the facial-recognition technology won't recognize this wild-animal version of him. "It's me!" he shouts idiotically at the lock screen. "It's HANK. LET ME IN."

The phone complies, after a pause, as though it wants to remind him who's in charge.

"Go to recent calls," Irene says, and he doesn't frown at her the way he usually does when she tells him to do things he's already on his way to do. Together they watch his finger, moving the way fingers do in dreams, so slowly, so inaccurately. It takes four months for him to push the button, five years for the page to load. An eternity later they frown at the screen together, not understanding what they see there.

The most recent incoming call, received exactly half an hour ago, is from Iver's landline.

51

Hilda is painting the stairs up to the second floor. Each step, top and front, and the walls all the way up, as high as she can reach without a stepladder.

(She will not be using a ladder on these stairs; she can't risk dying right now, not before Nora gets home.)

For this part of the house, she has chosen flowers. Delicate poppies, spiderweb flowers that look like they should just fall apart, lilacs so real you can almost smell them, petunias and lilies and tiny pansies at the very bottom, and thick-stalked sunflowers that reach up above her head.

Marlen sits at the bottom of the stairs in the recliner, reading his own book.

She feels immense guilt. It has now been long enough since he gave her the book that she should be finished reading it. If she were a supportive wife, she'd have read it three times by now; she'd have cried with pride as she turned the last page and told all her friends about it.

But that feeling is still there. The feeling that the book only amplifies the distance between where she is and where Marlen is.

"You want to read it out loud to me?" She says it before she really thinks it through. But maybe that would be a good bypass; maybe the feeling can't get her while she's working on her mural. Maybe his art and her art will cancel each other out.

"Are you sure?"

She hates the look on his face, the doubt. It's heartbreaking.

"Absolutely," she says. "I really am enjoying it. I want to know how it ends."

He raises his eyebrows. "Well," he says. "I think you already know how it ends. But if you really want . . . What page?"

"Mmm . . . I think I'm on page 172? Ish?"

(She has no idea.)

"Okay." He turns to page 172, clears his throat. It sounds painful, and again, she feels guilty.

"The problem with finding out you're going to die soon, but not immediately, is that there is time for the shock to wear off, and you're left with decisions to make and difficult conversations to have and, worst of all, so many mundane, ordinary life things that still have to happen up until the bitter end. Going to the bathroom. Washing the dishes. Small talk at the gas station. Making and eating food. It seems like all of that should stop, like a person should be able to say, 'You know what? I'm going to opt out of these things now. They're for people who need to exist for another forty years. They're the currency with which you pay the human rent—and why should someone pay rent when they're being evicted?'"

Hilda feels that emotion rising in her again, the resistance to these words.

"Sorry," he says, as though sensing her panic, "one second. I just need to catch my breath."

"Of course." She paints quietly for a moment. Then: "I wasn't a very good wife when you were first diagnosed."

"What? Yes, you were. You've never been a bad wife."

"I didn't say *bad*. I said not *very good*."

"Well, that's not true either."

"No, it is. Just . . . I relate to what you've written in your book. Now. But at the time you were feeling those feelings, I—I didn't know you were feeling them. I didn't ask, or you didn't feel like you could say."

"Well." He shakes his head, dismissing this. "None of us have ever gone through this before. Hard to get it perfectly right the first time."

"But you wrote this before you were diagnosed. *You* got it right."

He doesn't know what to say, so he reaches for his usual crutch.

"Yeah, but I'm a prophet," he says.

It's a joke, but she doesn't laugh.

"I just . . ." She's crying again, but she's turning her head, hoping he doesn't notice. "I'm not ready for it," she says.

"Of course you're not," he says. "It's a really big deal. You need time; that's natural."

"But I don't think I'm *going* to be ready for it. Ever. I've been doing all of this"—she points at her flowers with her paintbrush—"to try to make myself ready for it, but I don't think it's working." Her voice is rising; she's willing herself not to scream. "I'm not afraid of . . . of *after*. I'm afraid, literally, of the *dying* part. I don't want to *die*."

"Who does?"

"You!"

He stands from his recliner and inches up the stairs toward her until he's sitting on the step beside her, careful not to touch the walls or the step behind them, which is still wet. "I don't want to die either."

She sighs. "I know. I know you don't want to. But, like you said, you're ready for it. It just feels like everyone else is handling this better than I am." She pauses. "Except maybe Irene."

It's a joke, but he doesn't laugh.

"You know what it reminds me of?" he asks. "Childbirth."

"What?"

"I just remember when Nora was born, I was so freaked out at the thought of what happened to those women in the videos, of that happening to you. When they showed us the scissors in the hospital tour . . . I almost fainted then."

Hilda gives a little shudder, relieved to be distracted. "Yeah. Gross."

"And as the day got closer, I got more freaked out," he continues. "This thing was just barreling toward us—toward *you*—and there was absolutely no stopping it."

"This isn't like that, though," says Hilda.

"But it is. Because I remember back then, you were the one who should've been afraid, but you were—you were just fine!"

"I wasn't fine," says Hilda. "I was freaked out too."

"But you were *confident*," says Marlen. "You were ready. You kept saying that your body knew what it was doing. That it was designed to do it. That everything would be okay."

Hilda nods, remembering.

"I thought you were amazing," says Marlen. "I'd never been so amazed by someone. Still haven't."

He turns to face her, feeling his back come into contact with the wall behind him. Oops. "What if birth is like . . . just thinking out loud here . . . what if childbirth is a metaphor. A message. A little message to all of humanity, to remind us that our bodies know what to do, and that everything will be okay?"

52

"Dad?" It's Irene. Iver's heart leaps at her voice; he's so excited to show her what he's done. He hopes it's a good surprise, not a painful one.

"Hi, Irene! Did Ole get ahold of you?"

"He's *there*? He's with you?"

Iver frowns. "Ye-yes . . ." He has a sudden sinking feeling. He gave himself fully to a fantasy, with no regard for anyone but himself.

"How long has he been there? Where did you find him? Is he okay?"

"Oh, he's just fine. Uh . . . I guess . . . he's been here since . . . uh . . . it's been . . . a week or two? Or . . ." He doesn't have a calendar in front of him; he doesn't know how specific she needs him to be.

"A WEEK OR TWO?"

"Is there something wrong, Irene?"

"*Yes*, there is something wrong—"

Irene is replaced abruptly by Hank, who sounds equally agitated, but a tiny bit more restrained. "Iver, Ole has been missing for three weeks now. We've been searching for him. We've been out of our minds—"

Iver frowns harder. "I'm so sorry—"

"Why didn't you tell me he was with you? When I was there the other day?" It's Irene again; he pictures them wrestling over the phone.

"You never asked," Iver says simply. This is inadequate as an explanation, and it's nowhere near an apology, and everyone knows it, but he's not exactly *wrong*. She hadn't asked. He can't tell them he was lost in a fantasy, so deep into it that he forgot other people would be affected by his actions. He regrets it, but he also doesn't regret it, and maybe this is yet another thing that makes him a bad person, like how he hates Elsie for no reason.

It's not nice to come to the end of your life and suddenly realize that you're possibly not as good as you thought you were. He feels foolish and wonders if the people around him realize that old age doesn't automatically confer boundless wisdom and goodness upon a person, though he remembers believing this once, that everyone older than him should by virtue of their age automatically act better than him. At every stage in his life, he'd thought the next one would bring a feeling of having it all figured out, but it only tended to bring a feeling of having more to figure out than he had ever realized.

53

"It is just weird to me that you are not even curious." Pretend Petra is on the ceiling, sprawled out lazily like a spider. This is the strangest place Nora's brain has placed her yet, as though it's aware of an increased need to differentiate reality from imagination by making the imagined things more obvious. It's weirdly reassuring. "You meet a man in a foreign country. You have never seen him before, and yet you have all these memories with him. You know how he smells before he sits down beside you. You know what he feels like before he touches you. You know what he sounds like before he speaks. It is not déjà vu, Nora. You knew him. How did you know him? Where did you know him from?"

Nora glares up at Petra. "I didn't. It was just one of those weird things."

"Respectfully, no."

"Respectfully. *Right.*"

Petra ignores this. She walks across the room toward Nora, upside down, stepping over the light fixture. She comes to a stop in front of her and sits down, cross-legged; they're face-to-face. "You knew him, but you had never met him before. It is almost like—"

"Shut up, Petra." Nora is usually too nice to tell people to shut up, even people who aren't there.

"Nora. You are ignoring something important. Think."

"I'm not ignoring anything."

"So? Why not call him?"

"I think *we both know* I can't." This is true, not a matter of emotion. Nora's phone service provider is no longer providing phone service. She'd been using it so rarely that she can't pinpoint exactly when, but one day she'd picked it up to call her mother and found that all the amazing technology that had once been at her fingertips was just gone, reduced to a calculator, a camera, a clock, and a calendar—all things many generations past would've been thrilled to have condensed into one machine in their pocket, but that, to her, were useless and unimpressive. She has nothing to calculate or capture. Time is essentially meaningless, and she has exactly one item on her schedule: the flight out of Berlin. And now she has no way to know if that gets canceled or changed.

She'd never experienced anything quite like the feeling she'd had in that moment—a mixture of the fiercest hope that this wasn't permanent and a sinking understanding, a layer or two beneath, that it was. Like Petra on the ceiling beside the light fixture, the thing that was obviously not real next to the thing that was, her brain not quite letting her slip into delusion but pushing her most of the way there.

To be fair, the internet had lasted longer than she'd thought it would. So many things had. She hadn't given a lot of thought to the end of the world before the world actually started ending, but on the rare occasions she had, she'd pictured everything coming to an abrupt end, like a car crash. She'd underestimated humanity, the desire so many had to keep ticking along, pretending. Collective trauma was the strangest thing she'd ever witnessed.

Petra smirks at her, as though she doesn't believe the phone is out of order. Maybe Petra comes from the part of Nora's brain that's in denial. She shrugs. "I am just saying. Sometimes we wonder about things because we wonder about things. Sometimes we wonder because we already know."

Nora frowns. Someone has said this to her before. "Yeah, well," she says. "I'm just trying to stay grounded in reality."

"*That* is the stupidest thing I have ever heard," says Petra, making her point by still being on the ceiling. "What about reality is grounding? What is there to be grounded in or to? We are on a rock in the cosmos! Seven billion of us! Traveling at sixty-seven thousand miles per hour, orbiting a ball of gas, which is burning at ten thousand degrees Fahrenheit!"

Nora goes into her bedroom, lies down, and puts her pillow over her head.

But the bed sags as Petra, now apparently upright, sits at Nora's side, and the pillow stuffing doesn't completely drown her out.

"People, like you, who talk about reality like it is easy to understand and describe are just the best at ignoring what reality actually *is*, at seeing the surface of an endless ocean and pretending there is not much beneath that. Looking at a starry night sky and pretending it is one dimensional and saying it is pretty instead of realizing you have no idea what it actually is or what's in it or behind it and letting it take your breath away." Petra taps Nora on the shoulder. "Grounded in reality," she says. "It is like saying you are rooted in water."

"Stop it, Petra," Nora mumbles.

"Reality is space and time in all directions forever and ever, including inward, all of the observable things and all of the things too small or too large to be witnessed, all of the things that happen subconsciously and all of the things that cannot be seen but can be felt and sensed and just barely glimpsed: hearts beating, blood flowing, coincidence and happenstance and depthless pain and boundless joy, déjà vu and presque vu and jamais vu. None of it makes a person feel especially 'grounded,' no matter what you believe about where it started or how it is going to end. Reality is watery."

Petra is watery. She disintegrates into the walls and pours into the room when Nora is most vulnerable.

But . . . there are plants that grow in water.

Sick of Pretend Petra, Nora leaves the apartment. She walks aimlessly, past familiar buildings and unfamiliar ones that she recognizes anyway. She ends up in Leise Park, where Jacob had taken her just the other day, the place she'd recognized so vividly on her first trip there.

This place was once a cemetery.

When she'd been here with him, it had felt like a park more than a cemetery—full of bright-orange leaves and park benches and people wandering the paths, the atmosphere romantic. Now it seems like only a cemetery, and she feels morbid being here. Maybe Jacob feels comfortable being alive around dead people, but Nora didn't grow up in Berlin. Where she grew up, they buried their loved ones in the countryside, in cemeteries with old white fences around them, and your parents yelled at you to not step on your friends' grandparents on your way to lay your own to rest, and the kids told each other ghost stories about the creepy things people saw out there when they drove past in the middle of the night, and no one—*no one*—acted like death was okay.

She feels light-headed. A pinprick of pain in her shoulder, in the center of her chest, in her forehead, little bursts of lightning. She can't breathe.

She sinks onto a bench and stares at the scattered grave markers. There's only one other person in the park, on a different bench. A man, elbows on his knees, face in his hands. He seems to sense her eyes on him, and he sits up straight, catching her gaze. Jacob.

How many people live in Berlin? Three or four million? The probability of this moment is so low as to be impossible, as though Berlin were a tiny little village, like the one Nora grew up in, a place where you're constantly running into the one person you don't want to run into.

Jacob is coming toward her now, and she thinks of that day in Begonia. She'd felt that day exactly as she does now, that he was a person with whom she had history. Real history, not imagined, not a marriage of convenience. Both times it had been only an illusion, like Petra on the ceiling. She needs to remember this.

She still can't breathe.

"Nora? I was just on my way to your place," he says. He doesn't notice that she's suffocating, or having a stroke, or *something* . . .

"Thought I'd stop here and collect my thoughts, and—there you were. Maybe we've become entangled." He says it lightly, like it's a joke, but it's the weightiest thing he's said to her so far.

She puts her head between her legs.

She feels him sit beside her, his hand on her back. "Nora? Nora? You okay?"

"Mama," she gasps, "I think I'm having a heart attack."

The best person to have in your corner when you're in the ring with a panic attack is someone who has recently beaten the same opponent. They sit together until her breathing returns to normal. He's holding her hand again, and she tries not to read into it; a medical emergency calls for hand-holding.

"Thank you," she says after a while.

"Anytime," he says. "What are husbands for?"

She ignores this. "How'd things go with your parents?"

"Ah . . ." He shifts on the bench. "We had some good conversations. It's hard on them, having Anna so far away right now, and then I wasn't home very much—I get it. But they also needed to understand that I want . . ." Now he looks uncertain and doesn't finish the thought. "About what you said the other day, about how everything had gone too far—"

"I don't actually think that," she says. "I mean, unless you think—"

"I don't," he says quickly. "If anything—" He doesn't finish that thought, either, but there aren't a lot of ways that sentence could end.

"So we're good?" Why do they keep saying things that mean so much less than what they want to say?

"Yes."

The graveyard goes back to feeling like a park, like some set designer has turned up the bird sounds, warmed up the lighting, turned off some barely discernible funeral music. Nora and Jacob go back to feeling like Mr. and Mrs. Schmidt.

54

They take Irene's car. Bud sits between Hank and Irene in the front, breathing hotly into Irene's ear.

Irene calls Hilda on the way to let her know that Ole's been found, but Hilda's already received a call from Iver.

"He said he wants me there too," says Hilda, puzzled. "Is that okay? Seems weird. I imagine you guys have stuff to work through. As a family."

"Honestly, it is a little weird," says Irene. "But if Dad picks up the phone to call someone, it's not for no reason." The last time he'd called them, their mother had been headed to the hospital for the last time. "You should come. Just give us a five-minute head start? Maybe ten? Because I'm going to be a complete mess for at least that long."

When they pull up to Iver's house, Ole is sitting on the front step beside a badly decorated Christmas tree with the lights unplugged. All at once he ceases to be the crying baby on the back of Irene's eyelids and becomes himself again, a sullen preteen with his father's hair and his mother's lips. He and Hank look equally anxious, and Irene studies her family with despair. *We need to get happy!* she wants to scream at them. *We have so little time; we need to fix everything!*

Not that she believes the world is ending. But even if she and Hank both live to be one hundred, that is too little time. This is urgent. She throws her car door open and runs to her son and pulls him into a hug and a moment later she feels Hank's arms around both of them and she thinks, briefly, of the cougars and the letter and how nothing bad ever really happens. It only ever seems like it's going to.

When Hilda arrives, the family is standing in a circle on and around Iver's porch, overshadowed by a very sad Christmas tree, teeth chattering, everyone wondering vaguely why they haven't been invited inside. Ole has explained as much as he's going to for now, and Hank is relieved to feel anger replaced with hope. The thing about time being short, he supposes: they have enough time to patch things up but not enough to let it all go wrong again. They can ride this reconciliation high right to the end. In normal times? Escapism, unhealthy, a setup for cyclical failure. Now? No room for cycles! Escapism, still, but without negative consequences, only the good parts. Maybe the only perk of a gamma ray burst.

"Why's your tree on your porch, Dad?" asks Hilda, trying to steer the conversation somewhere light.

"No room for it in the living room," says Iver.

There are some shared glances between the adults that aren't as discreet as they think.

"It wouldn't fit in the usual spot?" asks Irene. In her anger, she'd forgotten about her father's apparent mental decline—but the sight of his sparse Christmas tree, with the clumped decorations and darkened light bulbs, out on the porch like this, brings her concern roaring back into focus.

"Ole and I have something for you," Iver announces, ignoring her unease. "Follow me."

So they follow their father into their childhood home, trailed by Ole and Hank. The familiar smells have mostly been replaced with new ones—dust, maybe mold—but there's still a hint of them underneath, even if it's only in their imaginations (and it probably is). Their mother's perfume, the cinnamon candles she always brought home from her favorite store in the city, her malodorous face cream.

Iver doesn't open the windows in the summer the way their mother had, and he isn't great at housekeeping. It's dark; all the blinds are drawn shut. Hilda reaches to flip a light switch, but Iver blocks her. "Nope, nope. Not yet."

There's a warm gleam coming from the living room, and Hilda feels a strange twinge of recognition, some kind of deep-seated nostalgia. Not completely out of place, considering this is the house she grew up in, until she turns the corner and realizes that the nostalgia isn't related to this house at all. It's something from farther back in her memory, from a room in her brain with a tightly shut door. And now, without her permission, the door is cracking open.

The room is lit by black-light bulbs screwed into the ceiling and lamps. Someone has draped Christmas lights around the perimeter of the room, which is lined with arcade machines, their displays glowing.

"DAD . . ." Irene bursts into incredulous laughter. "What is this?"

"It's an arcade," says Hilda quietly, respectfully, as though the living room is a sacred place. Arcades would not generally fall in the category of places people consider sacred, and Hilda might not have used this word to describe them before today, but now she sees that her father has created, not a place of frivolous entertainment, but a monument. A memorial to someone they all love and miss.

"Ole helped me with the lighting," says Iver, looking absolutely everywhere except at Hilda, who is starting to cry. He would never admit, not even to himself, that this was the reaction he'd hoped for, but deep down he's happy about it. And excruciatingly uncomfortable. He tries to move the conversation to safety. "He found the black-light bulbs at the hardware store before it closed. They just gave 'em to him. For free."

Ole is oblivious to the emotion in the room. In his mind, this arcade is all for and about him. "The games were all reset when we got them, so I have the high score on every single one," he says over his shoulder, already involved in a game of *Space Invaders*.

"Look," Irene says to Hilda. "It's Arnie." It's taken her a second longer than her older sister to fully grasp the intent behind the grand gesture, but now she does. Iver has come as close as possible to packing them all up and traveling back in time, to before everyone was so divided, before all this nonsense about exploding stars and the end of the world, before they lost their brother. A living portrait. She shakes her head in amazement. "I never noticed before how much Ole looks like Arnie."

Iver isn't sure whether he was meant to hear this or not. He breaks into one of his rare but genuine smiles. "He's like Arnie in a lot of ways. I'm sorry these past few weeks have been so hard on you and Hank but . . . it's been a dream come true for your old man."

He feels something welling up inside of him. *No,* he thinks, *I'm not going to be like Kelvin. I'm not going to cry in front of everyone.* He clears his throat, blinks his eyes. Then, when all else fails, he blurts out, "So Kelvin's friend was telling me that the government has been hiding alien vehicles."

Everyone stares at him. Irene looks concerned.

But he just shrugs. Crisis averted. "Poke at the phenomenon," he says. "I've been told it pokes back."

55

Hilda is painting her last mural—in Nora's bedroom, the only room in the house left with solid white walls. She hadn't left this one for last on purpose; she hadn't really gone into any of it with a sense of order or logic—it's been a bit like falling down the stairs. You don't choose which order you do it in; you let gravity decide.

For Nora, she has chosen birds. All kinds of birds, toucans and falcons and blue jays and flamingos and penguins. Some of the birds are adorable, some are terrifying, and some look too silly to exist in real life. Nora has always loved birds.

Marlen's recliner is in the living room, too heavy to haul up the stairs; he lies on Nora's bed instead, staring up at his wife painting electric-green hummingbirds all over the ceiling.

"I finished reading your book," she says. "I finished last night."

He raises his eyebrows, surprised. "Did you?"

"Yes."

There's an awkwardness to this that he hadn't anticipated. What were you supposed to say to someone who has just finished reading your book, your wife no less? *Did you like it? What did you think?* Ridiculous questions, because if the answers were at all negative, the other person would have to lie. Especially dangerous when the other person is Hilda, whom he can read so extremely well.

Like a book, incidentally.

"I loved it," she says, and thankfully he can tell she's not lying. He lets out a breath he's been holding since she first laid eyes on the cover.

"Yeah?"

"Yeah. I'm sorry it took me so long."

"Don't apologize for that."

"I'm not apologizing—I'm saying I'm sorry—as in, I feel sad for myself that it took me so long. It was surprisingly comforting."

"Oh?" He hadn't really expected her to use that word.

"I liked the ending."

"Like, when they all die?"

"But they don't, do they?"

He laughs. "No, I guess they never do."

"And you *are* a prophet, so . . ."

"You think I got it right then?"

"I hope so."

DECEMBER

56

Hank arrives home from what will prove to be his last ever trip to the grocery store to find Irene sitting at the kitchen table, cutting felt garlands. She has been cutting felt garlands for—days? Weeks? Years, it feels like, though this is verifiably false.

He doesn't know how to feel about the garlands, or the baking, or the snowflakes on the windows. It's only December 1, and already he feels as though he's been swallowed whole by Santa Claus himself. Any other year it would be nice, maybe, if a bit much. This year it feels like—well, it feels like exactly what it is: denial.

"Hi, Irene," he says cautiously.

She glances up at him, then back down at the felt in her hands. They're beautiful garlands, actually; it's mesmerizing to watch her make them. She has it down to an art, and her hands move so quickly it's as though the leaves form themselves. "Hi."

"How many of these are you going to make?"

"Lots. As many as I can. Maybe next year I can set up an Etsy shop and sell them."

He nods slowly. "Maybe."

Since Ole's homecoming, the family's mood has shifted, for better and worse in equal measures. They are all trying so hard. They can see each other trying. But trying, in a space where you once could just exist with no effort, is exhausting.

"Where's Ole?"

"Dropped him off at your dad's. He's hanging out there for the afternoon. I'll go get him after supper."

"Good." Irene knows she still has every right to be angry at her father, but—all's well that ends well? And he's been under a lot of stress lately, what with his whole family feeding him this story about the starburst and everything. She'd probably have cracked long ago if she believed it. She ties off the end of her garland with a neat bow.

"The delivery trucks have stopped," says Hank, as conversationally as he can.

"What do you mean?"

"I mean I went to the grocery store to get milk, and they have limits on what you can buy and how much of it, because there aren't going to be any more trucks, they said." He holds up two cloth bags. "This is all I was allowed."

This should not be so surprising. Until now, the trucks have continued coming from the cities. The shelves have been stocked—maybe with a few gaps here and there, but nothing alarming. You might not be able to get Heinz ketchup, but you could get President's Choice, and that was okay—it didn't feel apocalyptic to have President's Choice ketchup on your macaroni, unless you were someone for whom ketchup on macaroni had always felt apocalyptic.

But someone must have finally decided to call it.

He watches it dawn on her. No more produce, no more supplies, no more food of any kind. No Heinz or President's Choice or Kraft mac 'n' cheese or No Name cheesy noodles. It's not like what they've seen happening in cities on the news, where people have panicked and cleared the shelves, taking more than they could possibly use—it's not as easy to look the cashier in the eye as you're clearing out the entire canned goods aisle when you've known her your whole life and are aware that she's got five kids at home.

She has to admit, this does feel like a big deal. There is a vast difference between having to listen to people talk about the end and seeing physical evidence of it. It's like the credits have begun to roll—and the next thing is always a blank screen. She tries not to let the anxiety creep in; these are decisions made by fearful people; it will get worse before it gets better. But when the new year comes and everyone is still here, these things will work themselves out. The trucks will come back.

So she smiles calmly at her husband and says, "I have a lot of canned goods in the pantry, so many potatoes from the garden in there too. Our freezer is full. December will be a strange month, but we won't starve. The trucks will come back." He looks doubtful, so she adds, "Honey, do you know how many meteor showers I've seen? Hundreds. And I've survived every one."

He wants to believe her, but here's something he has learned very recently: you don't get to choose what you believe. It's something you observe in yourself, something you try to understand, something that explains you to yourself and to other people. You believe something or you don't, or you possibly pretend to believe it well enough to fool yourself for a while.

If he could choose what to believe, he would believe the world isn't ending.

But you just don't get to choose.

57

The night before Mr. and Mrs. Schmidt are set to leave for Canada, something wonderful happens, and it ruins everything.

Mrs. Schmidt is stepping out of the shower when she hears a knock at the door. Probably one of Mr. Schmidt's parents. They've been dropping by daily, sometimes twice a day. The four of them have achieved some semblance of balance (as much as can be hoped for during a time like this), and they are all very proud of themselves. Mr. and Mrs. Schmidt get to remain "married"; it's just that now Mrs. Schmidt has some heavily involved in-laws in the picture—but, if anything, this enhances the illusion, gives it some flavor it had previously lacked.

She wraps a towel around herself and puts an ear to the door.

"Just a minute!" Mr. Schmidt calls from the kitchen. She hears him pad through the living room, the sound of the door opening. She strains to hear who it is.

But instead of Mr. Schmidt's mother's exaggerated greeting, or his father's low, rumbling voice, there is simply nothing. Complete silence. As though Mr. Schmidt has opened the door and disappeared into thin air.

She opens the door just a bit, and now she can hear a strange snuffling sound, like someone is . . . crying?

Peering through the crack, incredibly self-conscious of the fact that she's wearing nothing but a towel, she sees Mr. Schmidt, his back heaving with sobs.

And in his arms is a beautiful young woman.

✳

Nora leaves the bathroom, slipping through the living room as noiselessly as possible, though she's certain the couple wouldn't notice her even if she were to lose the towel altogether. They are holding each other so tightly it's as if they want anything outside themselves to cease existing. Nora wishes with everything in her that she could do that for them.

She sits on her bed for a few minutes before getting dressed.

Who *is* she? Maybe a friend, a very, very close friend. So close that she is practically inside Jacob's rib cage at this very moment. *He's never hugged me like that.*

She scolds herself. Why should he hug her like that? Why shouldn't he hug someone else like that? If Derek were to show up at the door right now, wouldn't she find herself in his arms? Wouldn't she feel like she needed him all of a sudden, this familiar person who feels like home, the first domino in a long string of more and more surreal events?

There's a quiet tap on her door. "Nora? You in there?"

What else can she do? The only thing to do is open that door so her husband can introduce her to his girlfriend.

She grabs a floral button-up dress from the chair near her bed, where she'd thrown it the day before. It's wrinkled, and she cringes at the thought of looking frumpy in front of this mystery woman, of Jacob seeing them next to each other. She tugs at it and combs her fingers through her hair, and when she opens the door, there they are. Jacob has an arm slung around the beautiful woman's shoulders, and his smile is heartbreakingly joyful, the sort of smile, she realizes now, she has never seen in their time together.

He opens his mouth to speak, but the woman jumps in first. "So you must be Jacob's 'wife'!" She makes cruel quote signs with her fingers.

Nora's mouth falls open. She looks to Jacob, silently begging him to explain, angry but aware she has no right to be angry.

They're oblivious; they're just so happy.

"Nora, this is my sister, Anna."

Anna sticks out a hand, and although it is a very nice handshake, it feels more like a one-two punch. A left-hand jab of relief followed quickly by a right hook of horror. Suddenly she wishes this *was* Jacob's girlfriend. She could be his wife, for all Nora cares. Wife, girlfriend, lover—none of that would take Jacob away from Nora, because no matter what, at the end of the day (or early the very next morning), he was going to get on an airplane with her to Canada.

Unless his reason for flying to Canada was suddenly in Berlin.

It's this moment when Nora realizes that she doesn't just like Jacob; she doesn't have a little crush. It's not familiarity, déjà vu, trauma bonding—no, she is in full-blown, real, actual, chaotic, colorful, mind-blowing, mind-losing *love*. Because anyone else in this situation would be able to accept that this is the best possible outcome for everyone. Nora gets to go home; Anna is with her family; Jacob doesn't have to leave his parents. But all Nora can think of is the fact that she had thought she had one last day with Jacob, and now she doesn't have it, and it feels like someone has stolen *everything* from her, every single thing. She feels as though she's walked into the room that is her life and found nothing left in it. Only love could make fifteen hours feel this eternally, existentially important.

In light of this, it is excruciatingly hard to say hello to Anna, to sound like a normal human being.

"Hi, Anna." Nora tries to keep her voice from wavering; she pictures a string stretched between the back of her throat and her diaphragm, visualizes pulling it taut. Still, she can't help the little tonal rises at the end of every phrase. She tries to be jokey, too, but she might possibly be coming across as hysterical. "Since you're here, I guess I'm the ex-wife? This is amazing! You found a flight! You made it!"

"Yes!" The girl's eyes fill. "Can you believe it?" At the sight of the tears, Nora is overwhelmed with guilt. The one thing she has wanted from the moment she heard the world was ending is to go home and be with her family. How could she be anything less than thrilled for someone who has gotten that very thing?

She can see the realization on Jacob's face, as he understands that she isn't happy, and possibly why as well. "You know what!" Nora is either going to cry in front of these lovely people or leave the apartment quickly; there's no third option. She scrambles for her coat and purse. "I'm actually running late—" She digs in her purse for—ugh, who knows what? She pulls out a stick of gum and shoves it in her mouth. Sure. "I'm meeting Petra. For one last coffee before we . . . I . . ."

If there's anything she's learned from Jacob these past few weeks, it's improvisation.

That and you shouldn't fall in love right as the world is ending. Only an idiot would do that.

The street is strung with festive garlands and paper snowflakes, her and Jacob's handiwork. Why had they done this to themselves, to everyone around them? Decorated for a holiday when what was coming was not a holiday? This year, Christmas wasn't going to be a break from reality; it was going to be the end of it. The garlands are disrespectful, cruel like Anna's air quotes around the word *wife*.

She stops in front of Begonia, peering in the darkened window, feeling angry. Life had been so nice. So beautiful and exciting. New Everything: it had spread out ahead of her in all directions. She could stay in Berlin or go somewhere else. She could get another job or just travel for a bit. At some point, maybe she'd fall in love with someone who loved her back, but she didn't need that. Maybe have a family, maybe not. Settle down, or not. She'd been so open, the perfect candidate for a contented life because she wasn't living underneath all those enormous expectations and ideals other people seemed so weighed down by.

Or so she'd thought.

But now, standing alone in front of Begonia, contemplating her future, she realizes she had expectations too—just, instead of marriage, kids, and a big house, it was more abstract, things like good mental and physical health. Enough money to get by. People in her general vicinity that she could count on, an unexploding Earth to live on. Life, the base model. That hadn't felt like such a huge ask, and maybe that's why she felt entitled to it.

Now she sees how spoiled she's been.

She turns to face the giant bird mural across the street, the chaotic flurry of wings and beaks and talons, the colors muted in the dim light. The mural that feels as though it had been painted for her, like a present from the universe. A lovely parting gift.

She feels Jacob before she sees him, like he's a thunderstorm rolling in.

"Anna went back to Mom and Dad's place," he says when he reaches her. He's quiet and tentative. "She's tired from her trip and needs to sleep. She asked if I wanted to go for breakfast in the morning."

Breakfast in the morning. Something he wouldn't be able to do if he were on a plane. She turns to face him.

"That's great. I didn't realize she was back. Did you know she was back . . . ?" She tries to keep her voice light, nonaccusatory. *You're not a spurned lover,* she reminds herself. *He owes you absolutely nothing.*

"I had no idea. Apparently she was on some wait list, just sitting at the airport waiting for a flight to open up. She went straight to my parents' to surprise them, then to our—your place."

"Oh." Nora wants to smile brightly and tell him how glad she is that his whole family is together. *What timing! So glad your sister's not meeting her cataclysmic end alone in Montreal! You get to be together!* "Sorry for rushing out. I just had to . . ." She gestures toward Begonia, dark and abandoned and covered in paper snowflakes. She never had gotten around to painting that mural. Time goes so quickly; she'd thought she had much more of it, even after finding out how little was left.

"No, I totally get it." He lets her lie, just as she has let him these past few weeks. They're still taking care of each other, because they're still married. "Are you free now, though? Want to walk? It's getting chilly."

"Sure."

Usually this street is lined with cars, not a parking space to be found, but it seems most people have disappeared. Everyone has apparently decided to go somewhere else and stay put until it all comes to an end. Jacob wanders off the sidewalk onto the cobblestone street, walking right down the middle of the road, and she follows. It's an oddly teenaged thing to do; she feels a pang of nostalgia for late-night walks with friends down the middle of country roads, hashing out big, important things like where they would go for university and who they should ask to escort them to grad. At the time it felt like those decisions would ripple and reverberate into the future. Now she sees the truth: those decisions meant absolutely nothing. Tonight means nothing too. Maybe this knowledge will be helpful as she tries to navigate this last conversation.

"I'm happy for you," she says finally. It took a while to get it out, and it's almost a lie, but there it is.

"Thank you."

She can't properly read his expression; he looks uncomfortable, or apprehensive, or maybe just confused. His shoes are silent on the cobblestones, but hers click loudly. It sounds like she's by herself.

He nudges her with his elbow. "So then . . . what's bothering you?"

"Oh, where do I begin? So many things!" She's trying to keep it light, like she's rattling off a to-do list. "I don't love flying, the world is ending, I have to get up super early tomorrow, and I'm anxious about missing the plane. You know. Lots—" Her mother has always had this special talent for laughing brightly when she should be crying. Nora tries to emulate it. "Lots to be bothered about!" The snow is so dense it's soaking through Nora's toque and jacket, dripping down her face and neck and back. She's shivering violently, but she doesn't feel cold.

"But you'll get to see your boyfriend soon?"

"I don't have a boyfriend," she says quickly. "I misspoke the other day. I have an *ex*-boyfriend. I don't think I'll run into him back home. He's already dating someone else."

He gives a quiet, exasperated sigh. "That would've been good to know."

"Why? What would you have done with that information?"

"I mean . . ." He shrugs. "I've just felt bad, wondering if your boyfriend hated the thought of you living with me."

He's holding back, but maybe he's just trying to go easy on both of them. Hindsight really is twenty-twenty, and right now this feels like the cruelest thing. Hindsight should be completely blind, so you never know what you've missed out on. What good is hindsight at the end of the world? She thinks of all the times she has wondered why he didn't make a move, finish a meaningful-sounding sentence—it's been her fault, all this time? Because she'd led him to believe she was unavailable?

"The decorations look nice, though," he says. "We did a fantastic job of that."

She nods. "We did a really good job."

"Maybe we could do it again next year?"

Nora shakes her head. "I'm sorry. I don't think I can pretend anymore."

A car drives around the corner, and they sheepishly scoot onto the sidewalk as someone yells at them in German from the window.

"What did they say?" Nora asks, sinking onto a bench.

Jacob tries to make a joke. "Roughly translated, like, 'What a beautiful night for a stroll! Thank you for the decorations! Merry Christmas!'"

"I'm fairly certain I recognized at least one word, and it wasn't any of those."

"I may have misunderstood." He shoves his hands into his pockets. "I do tend to misunderstand things. From time to time." He looks sideways at her, like he's asking her a question.

"I think you're pretty perceptive, though," she says, trying to answer the question she hopes he's asking.

He sits next to her. The cold seeps into her legs from the bench; the warmth spreads from his shoulder into her arms and chest.

He's quiet. Maybe he wasn't asking a question. She tends to read into things.

"You happy?" she asks.

"Hmm?"

"About your sister. I bet you're really happy."

"Yeah," he says. His voice is hoarse. He doesn't sound happy.

"I'm happy for you," she reiterates. She will keep saying it until it convinces one of them. Either one of them; she's not picky.

58

Ole doesn't know how long he's been sleeping. He crawled into bed around ten, had lain awake for what felt like hours. The clock only says eleven thirty. But this is how time has felt for him lately, like flimsy fabric—a shirt that stretches and shrinks when you put it on and take it off, that can be turned inside out or crumpled. Minutes contort and touch and stretch and shrink. He tries to pinpoint exactly when it started feeling this way, but he can't. Maybe it's always been like this. Maybe you just don't think about time when you're a little kid, same as how you don't think about love or death.

He gets out of bed and creeps down the stairs. He needs something to eat.

He hears someone in the kitchen and knows it's his father before he gets there. This is what he means about the minutes touching. It's like he's already seen the thing that's about to happen, sitting at the kitchen table with his father. And maybe this is how time has always worked; maybe time is all over the place, only perfectly linear in a person's memory, like a deck of cards being thrown into the air and then gathered and put in order after the fact. There's no way to know for sure.

"You're still up?" His father looks concerned, like it's abnormal behavior for a teenager to be awake in the middle of the night but perfectly normal for a middle-aged man.

"Guess so." Ole sits across from his father. It's the first time they've been alone since Ole came home, and they're remembering how it was before he left. They don't know how to talk to each other anymore, and maybe this had begun before the news, before Irene and Hank started fighting. Possibly they'd wanted something to blame it on, but really it was just those weird teenage years, where parents and kids forget how to talk to each other or relate to each other or offer each other grace.

The clock is louder than usual; they hear the snowflakes hitting the ground like someone's throwing bowling balls from the sky.

Amazing, thinks Hank, how much he has wanted this—more than anything he has ever wanted—and now that it's here, his instinct is to say it's late and he's tired and to go upstairs to bed.

What did the parenting podcasts say about this? Nothing. They covered defiance, bad behavior. Lying, sneaking out. What to do when your kid was exposed to bad influences, how to talk to them about drugs.

On how to be comfortable in each other's presence when you're both quiet and introverted and awkward? Nothing.

Hank clears his throat. He thinks of that night in the field, screaming into the sky. That version of him would give anything for this moment. What would that version of him do, though? If he asks anything too vague or open, Ole will answer in kind, and the conversation will die; they'll sink into it and drown. He knows this from experience. He can't say, *How're you doing?* Or *What are you thinking?* Or *Where's your head at?* Or *I'm so happy you're home.* They can't do ocean conversation. Hank needs a stream. A puddle. A drop of dew on a leaf. He thinks hard for a moment.

"I'm hungry," he says. "Are you?"

Ole looks relieved. "Yeah."

That's it. Okay. Next question: "What are you in the mood for?"

"Whatever."

Hank tries not to feel irritated. His fault, too vague and open. It seems unfair that parents spend all those years nurturing this relationship with their kids, only to have to start from scratch again when they become teenagers. But if it's what he has to do, he'll do it.

He remembers when Ole was little—five or six—and always had a specific, enthusiastic request ready on the tip of his tongue. They used to bake together, Ole on the stool, Hank trying to show him how to measure out a cup of flour without dumping it everywhere. There was a stretch of time when Ole wanted to make cinnamon buns every Saturday morning. Hank almost never felt like it, but Ole had been so excited—about the process, about surprising Irene in bed with fresh baking.

Hank has an idea. A good idea.

"Well, I'm in the mood for cinnamon buns."

Ole looks around the room, as though cinnamon buns might appear on the counters at the mention of them. He looks open to it.

"Would you . . . want to help me bake some?" Hank tries not to say it like he would've to five-year-old Ole, like he's one of the Doodlebops and baking cinnamon buns is the! Most! Exciting! Thing! Anyone could ever do! It needs to be the opposite, he's found, when he's talking to teenage Ole. He tries to sound like it's something he could be talked into. At gunpoint. He holds his breath.

Ole looks at his father with that usual blank expression for a moment, and Hank feels the all-too-familiar plummet in his gut. But this time, a small smile appears at the edges of Ole's mouth, like a crack of light in a dark cavern.

"Sure," he says. It's not an enthusiastic reply but the smile is comforting. The smile is everything.

Hank is emboldened. "Hey, you know what we should do?"

Ole raises an eyebrow.

"When they're done, it'll be, what"—Hank tries to remember how much time to allow for the dough to rise and all that—"two in the morning? Three? We should wake your mother up and serve them to her in bed. Like old times."

The crack of light grows; Hank feels the warmth on his face. Ole thinks this is funny. It's like a prank for them to wake Irene in the middle of the night with fresh cinnamon buns.

"Okay," Ole says. "Yeah."

Hank could cry. He absolutely cannot, but he could.

They launch out of their chairs, as though each is afraid the other is going to change their mind—or worse, ask a harder question than *Are you hungry?* Hank finds a recipe in a weathered cookbook and reads the ingredients as Ole paws through cupboards. He's lost, Hank realizes with some amusement. He doesn't know where anything is. But he's trying. It's a metaphor for them. Lost but trying.

Baking requires just enough discussion to keep them from hearing the snowflakes falling outside, to drown out the ticking clock. Once, though, Ole pauses before he adds the teaspoon of salt and recounts the Saturday years ago when they'd brought a fresh cinnamon bun to Irene who, unknown to them, had a stomach bug. "She puked on me," says Ole, and suddenly he's laughing so hard there are tears in his eyes. Hank has to lean on the counter, and it kind of hurts his back to laugh this hard, and Ole has to get a new teaspoon of salt because he's spilled the one he had all over the kitchen floor.

59

Nora does not wake up on the morning of her departure because she did not go to sleep the night before. When 12:01 a.m. arrives, she's still wandering the empty streets of Berlin with Jacob—overtired, racked with dread, and strangely euphoric. They should say goodbye; she should get some sleep. She has a flight in the morning; he has breakfast with his sister. They're delaying the inevitable. Around 2:00 a.m. they sit on the crumbling steps of a bright-yellow residential building that seems to glow in the dark, and, for the very first time, she kisses him. Or he kisses her. Or it's exactly, perfectly mutual.

(Too close to call.)

Three things cross her mind during this kiss:

1. Wow,
2. I have less than a month left to live, and still I'm not sure I can go the rest of my life without this man, and
3. Déjà vu.

60

At three in the morning, there's a soft knock on Irene's bedroom door. She looks around in the dark and throws an arm out to the side; Hank isn't there.

The door creaks open, and two figures appear, one large one and one small, accompanied by the smell of cinnamon and butter. What's going on? She looks at the clock again—8:00 a.m. That makes more sense. The sun is streaming through the open window along with a sweet breeze. She'd been sleeping the first time she looked at the clock, having the strangest dream about the world ending, Ole going missing, a fight with Hilda over . . . what? She can't remember. It doesn't matter.

"Mommy!" Ole runs to the side of the bed and scrambles up. His hair is sticking out in all directions, and he's still in his Spider-Man footie pajamas, but he's covered in flour—he'd obviously gone straight from bed to the kitchen, and Hank never makes him wear the little apron she got him. She bites her tongue to keep from scolding Hank, for letting him get the comforter all dirty. Both of them, dad and son, are so proud of themselves. "What's up, buddy?" she says, stretching her arms overhead.

"We baked cinnamon buns!" Ole curls into her side, and she snuggles down into her pillows with him. This is her favorite way to wake up. She's surprised she hadn't heard them banging around the kitchen, music up, Hank trying to keep an overzealous four-year-old from emptying the entire bag of flour into the mixing bowl. She must have been tired. Slept like a rock. Strange dreams. They had a dog in that dream.

Hank sets the plate on her nightstand along with a cup of coffee. "Sorry, it's cold now," he says. "Poured it too early. Misjudged the timing."

"It's fine. Thank you so much."

"Okay, bud." Hank holds out his arms. "Should we let Mom eat in peace?"

"No!" Ole yells happily, still nestled into her side.

"It's *fine*," says Irene again. Most mornings the idea of a quiet breakfast in bed while her family cleans the kitchen really appeals to her. This morning, for some reason—maybe because of that dream—she just wants them here.

She takes the plate on her lap, careful not to jostle Ole too much, lest he realize he's snuggling and put an end to it, and tears the tail off the spiral of dough. It's warm and gooey, covered in more butter than she'd ever put on herself—which is completely fine—and she closes her eyes. "Mmm," she says. "It's amazing. You guys are amazing."

She opens her eyes. The door creaks open and two figures appear. The lamp clicks on, illuminating her husband and son, standing there by the bed looking equal parts sheepish and pleased with themselves.

"Wake up, Irene! We baked you something," says Hank. She's confused for only a minute; then she sees what it is. A cinnamon bun. It's like the arcade in her father's living room, something that is what it is to everyone else, but to her, it's a whole bunch of other things.

"What time is it?" she asks groggily.

Ole starts laughing (and it feels like a miracle; it's been such a long time). "You don't want to know," he says. But then he adds, "It's, like, three in the morning."

She shakes her head. "You two are so funny," she says, but there's a lump in her throat. The idea of her husband and son in the kitchen, conspiring to wake her at three in the morning with baking. At the sight of Ole perched on the end of her bed, far enough away that she can't even hug him. She can almost feel the memory of him curled into her side as she eats her cinnamon bun, the smell of his hair, still a little sweaty from sleep, the pride emanating from his body at having so successfully surprised his mother. Like it was only a moment ago and not years. How unfair that time only goes one way, that by the time you understand how much you will miss something, it's only because you're already missing it.

61

The goodbye was difficult, and this is the biggest understatement in the history of the universe (though *this* might be a very small overstatement). It came shortly after their first kiss, shortly before their last kiss, and was interjected all throughout with second and third and fourth and fifth kisses. All the kisses felt like unanswerable questions, frustrating and confounding but demanding to be asked anyway.

They had to go back to the apartment so she could get her bag and her cat; then he drove her to the airport, at which point, in her sleep-deprived state, she toyed with the idea of not getting on the airplane. But there was an inevitability to getting on the plane, not dissimilar to the feeling she'd had when he asked her to get married, like tripping at the top of the stairs and knowing that you're about to fall all the way to the bottom, everything happening so fast there's no time to comprehend or wish for anything else. Time began to move at an unreal speed. The drive to the airport should have been long enough to have one last conversation, but it was over before she could form a complete sentence in her head.

Jacob didn't say anything either.

And now he's gone. She can't even remember what she'd said as she climbed out of his car. She's not sure she'd said anything at all. Maybe she had simply opened the door, gathered her pet carrier and her backpack, and walked away. What's wrong with her brain, that chunks of memory are disappearing into nowhere like this? Not the usual things, like what she had for breakfast last Tuesday or what shirt she wore yesterday, but big, important details, like, *What were the last words she spoke to the love of her life?* It's as though that memory has been removed, cut out cleanly like a biopsied mole, the skin sewn together where it had been, leaving a tiny scar so she won't forget that something was there even if she can't remember what it looked like.

She sits in the airport, facing her gate. There's a desk in front of her, an older woman behind it with her head down, organizing something. She has long silver hair gathered in a low ponytail and burgundy fingernails that make soft clicking noises as she shuffles things around behind the desk. After a few minutes, she straightens and walks over to Nora, lowering herself heavily into the seat next to her. "It always feels nice to sit down," she says, "once you reach a certain age. My feet don't love high heels anymore." She leans over and peers inside the pet carrier at the cat, who lifts its head and glares back at her. It's not here to make friends.

"My feet have never loved high heels," Nora offers, "if it's any consolation. I guess I wouldn't have made a good flight attendant."

"Isn't that interesting," says the flight attendant.

Nora is unsure of what the flight attendant could possibly find interesting about feet that don't love high heels. It's probably rarer to find feet that do.

The flight attendant sticks both legs straight out in front of her and rolls her ankles in small clockwise circles. "I've been noticing a lot of people doing that."

"Doing . . . what?"

"Referring to themselves in past tense. The way you just did—you said you wouldn't *have made* a good flight attendant."

"Oh. Yeah, I guess that is interesting." When *had* she started doing that? She has no idea.

A middle-aged man with a large black suitcase nods at them as he heads toward the gate. He's got a small child trailing him, tiny legs taking five steps for every one of his, pulling his own miniature suitcase.

"Morning, Raymond!" calls the flight attendant, her legs still in front of her like a kid sitting on a too-big chair, rolling her ankles. "Morning, Alexander! Aren't you two all bright eyed and bushy tailed this morning!"

The child doesn't slow down—he has clearly been taught how to walk in airports—but he yells over his shoulder, "I lost another tooth!" and then opens his tiny mouth as wide as it will go so the flight attendant can see what's not in there.

And just as the small boy knows how to walk in airports, the flight attendant knows what to do when kids tell you they've lost teeth. She gasps, slaps her hands on her legs, yells back, "No WAY, Alexander! Third one this month! You're going to be rich!"

Alexander nods; they're almost out of sight and earshot now, about to disappear into the gangway. "AND! The tooth fairy raised her price! Five dollars a tooth now!"

The pilot confirms this with a little eyebrow wiggle over his shoulder. A father still trying to do what he can to make life magical for his kid, who will probably never have to find out the tooth fairy isn't real.

The flight attendant turns back to Nora as the pair disappears. "That's the pilot on our flight today. He's trying to do as many as possible before the end without sacrificing family time. Beautiful way to go out, isn't it? Alexander gets to see the world and hang out with his dad and meet new people. Raymond gets to help people get home to their families. A lot of the flight staff are doing that."

The whole scene is comforting to Nora. The little community these people have carved out, the shared sense of duty or charity or whatever it is now. She hadn't considered until this moment that for her to get home, perfect strangers would have to be looking out for her, giving something up themselves. You tend to think of airplanes as machines, don't you? Not people driving machines. Not men with sons, remembering to show up for flights while also remembering to pay for teeth.

The flight attendant sets her feet back down. "Plus," she adds, "it keeps you busy, keeps you from losing your mind. That's why I'm still working. If I didn't have something to do, I'd be a total wreck. But that's how I've always been, so I guess nothing's really changed for me. Human nature, isn't it?"

Nora's lost again. "Sorry—what is?"

"You think things like this are going to change you into someone else, but generally they make you more of who you already are. That's true of lots of things. Tragedies. Weddings. Ends of civilizations."

"I guess so," says Nora. But she doesn't think it is true, or she hopes it's not, because that would mean that she's always been delusional, lonely, and needy; she just hasn't been enough of any of those things to notice until now.

There's a stark difference between the way air travel had been and the way it is.

Before: heavy on security and order and lineups. A fairly even spread of people—vacationers, business professionals, dreary folks headed home for funerals or to visit sick relatives. Excited, mourning, annoyed, bored.

Now: no security, no order, no lineups, and no recognizable emotion. Just a mass of people shuffling around like zombies. They don't expect organization from anyone else, so they come prepared, and they go where they need to without help. There's a sense of dulled panic, like a loud sound that has been going on for so long that you stop paying much attention to it.

A man plunks himself down where the flight attendant had been before she got up to go take care of something else. He's probably a solid decade older than Nora, and he's clutching his backpack in front of him instead of wearing it on his shoulders, like a little kid on a school bus on the first day of kindergarten. He's wearing pants that zip off below the knee and a *South Park* T-shirt. He peers at her out of the corner of his eye, as though she might not notice him looking at her if he doesn't move his head.

She meets his gaze, annoyed. She has no desire to interact with anyone for the duration of this trip. He can't possibly know that she's just said goodbye to the love of her life, but still, his attention feels disrespectful, like he's hitting on a brand-new widow. How does one convey this with only a look? She tries.

She is unsuccessful; he misinterprets the look she gives him as an invitation—though he seems like the kind of man who could turn any look into an invitation.

"Hey," he says. He is oozing with a quality Nora has witnessed only on television to this point in her life. A level of confidence surprising for a man seemingly unable to commit to one length of pants for an entire day.

"Hey."

She can hear him swallow; she considers going over to the desk, pretending she has a question for the flight attendant.

"So," he says. "You from Canada?"

"Yup."

"Hey, me too!" He sounds excited, as though being from Canada were not a prerequisite for boarding this flight. "Which part?"

"Halifax," she lies. Like there's going to be a future in which she would not want this stranger to know where she actually lives. It's some variation on the old "not even if you were the last man on Earth." Only, in this case, it's more "not even if there were an Earth."

"Me too!" he exclaims. He has relaxed a little, sure they're hitting it off. "Seems like we have a lot in common."

"Well, one thing."

"Two!"

"Ahh . . ." She isn't sure whether his assertion is sincere or whether he thinks this is flirtatious banter. It's all still so foreign to her. "Halifax is *in* Canada, so. One." She looks around for that flight attendant, or the pilot. Even Alexander would do right now. But the only person in their vicinity is Jacob, walking toward them, and he's certainly only a figment of her imagination. She thinks of Petra on the ceiling, her fried brain taking such great pains to separate fiction from reality.

It would be helpful, she tells herself, *if you would put him on the ceiling.*

"Want to sit together on the plane?" Zipper Pants Man has begun to do an annoying sort of lean, melting into her side as though physical contact might actually help his case. She's not sure where he got this idea.

"No, thank you," she says, melting in the opposite direction.

"Aw, come on, gorgeous," he says. His face is very close to hers. "I'm sure your boyfriend won't mind."

She stares at him. It shouldn't surprise her, that creepy men would be creepy even in end times, but she'd thought they might be somewhat distracted. Maybe that flight attendant had been right, though—the end of it all doesn't change you; it just makes you more of whatever exactly it is that you already are. Maybe this man hadn't been *this* creepy until he found out the world was ending. Perhaps he feels desperate to have someone at the very end, and could anyone blame him for that? Who wants to die alone?

Imaginary Jacob is standing in front of the man now. He doesn't look angry, but he doesn't seem pleased either. "Excuse me," he says to the guy. "This is my spot."

She almost doesn't dare entertain the possibility of Imaginary Jacob being Actual Jacob. It would be too heartbreaking if it turned out she was wrong. But he must be real, because Zipper Pants gives a big snort. "She doesn't need you to come over and save her," he says. "Guaranteed I walk away and you think you're going to sit down and pick up where I left off."

Jacob looks at Nora, amused. She realizes he's waiting for her to say something.

"This is my husband," she says to Zipper Pants. "I don't need saving, but—that *is* his spot."

Zipper Pants makes a big show of looking at the empty seat on the other side of Nora. "You could sit on *that* side of her," he says belligerently.

Nora shakes her head. "But then you'd still be *there*, is the problem."

"I see no problem," says the man.

"Now boarding," calls the flight attendant, who has reappeared behind her desk. She winks at Nora. "Flight TS2123."

"Okay," says Jacob. "Great. You stay. We'll go."

She looks at him uncomprehendingly. "Go . . . where?"

"Onto the plane."

He picks up the pet carrier and starts walking, and suddenly she's following him toward the plane, Zipper Pants bringing up the rear.

"You're getting on the plane with me?"

"I do have a ticket."

"But your sister—"

"Is with my parents. They're together. They're okay. I want to come with *you*."

"But . . ." She grabs his shoulder and he stops. Zipper Pants stops, too, once again acting like they won't know he's watching the whole thing if he pretends to be looking in a different direction. They ignore him.

Jacob's face is clear, not conflicted at all. "I was thinking that this was a really difficult choice to make, but as I watched you walk into the airport, I realized that was the wrong way to think about it."

"As a difficult choice?"

"No, as a choice, period. It's not a choice. I can't *not* come with you, Nora."

They're in a nineties rom-com, where a shocking lack of airport security allows the declaration of love to take place right at the gate, right at the last possible moment, where the declaration of love is ardent and inexcusably cheesy, but it's also something that can't be said any other way. More importantly, it's something that can't *not* be said.

Zipper Pants is rolling his eyes, but Jacob doesn't notice or care. "Nora, this is going to sound absolutely—you're going to think I've lost it—but that day we first met, I *remembered* you. I felt as though we'd already met. And every day we've been together has felt new, but also comfortable, and I'm not sure if that's just"—he wavers, but only for a second—"love, or if something weird is going on, but I've loved every minute. And I know we don't have a lot of time left, but I can't imagine spending any of it without you. I don't have a choice; I *have* to come with you."

Nora nods. "It's like falling down the stairs," she says.

This is not the most romantic sentiment a person could convey in a moment like this, but Jacob seems to understand. "Yes. Exactly."

62

The flights from Berlin to Frankfurt and Frankfurt to Toronto are as close to an out-of-body experience as Nora has ever had. From space or heaven or another dimension, wherever you go when you leave yourself, she watches herself reach for Jacob's hand just as he reaches for hers, and she sees the shy, naked joy on both their faces. She feels happy for them and confused by them. How can anyone look so hopeful and excited at a time like this? She can't understand—but maybe that's why she's watching from out here. There's not enough room for so much conflicting reality, for logic and hope, love and grief, eager and anxious anticipation of both the end and the beginning of the same thing.

On the plane everyone looks more fearful than they had in the terminal. That makes sense—the terminal had been only a holding place; this is a vehicle, moving them forward again. Some nod or try to smile at others, but most seem singularly focused on stowing luggage and sitting in seats, anxiously rearranging neck pillows and trying to settle their children, like absolute perfection in the most minute, controllable detail has become extremely important. Maybe they're all thinking about how little security there was in the airport, how even if this flight isn't hijacked and flown straight into the ocean, it's probably the last flight they'll ever take, and they need to get it exactly right.

Nora's just observing. She doesn't need to get it right; she needs to see it. That does feel important. She watches as Jacob tells the person seated behind them that they're on their honeymoon. The person looks stricken. "What's the point in that?" he says, jamming yellowing earbuds into his large, rubbery ears and proceeding to ignore them completely as he fusses with the zipper on his jacket, the carry-on that won't quite fit all the way under the seat, the window shade. For a moment Nora finds herself in her head again. She misses the apartment, the pretending. They can't pretend here. There are too many people worrying in such close proximity. But then she floats out of her body again, and she feels fine. Someone rolls their heavy suitcase over her foot, but it doesn't hurt at all. It occurs to her that nothing has ever hurt, that she can't remember what pain feels like.

Jacob puts an arm around her and kisses her forehead. She curls into his side and falls asleep before the safety announcements. She already knows what to do if they crash, and she already knows it would be pointless to do it.

They land in Frankfurt. They take off in a different plane. They cross the ocean and land in Toronto in the middle of a blizzard. It's midmorning, but the plane has the feel of a movie theater late at night, the last few stragglers collecting their wrappers and soft drinks and coats, everyone looking around with dazed expressions, trying to come back to reality after spending a few hours in some other world.

As they walk into the familiar Canadian terminal, her overtired brain sags in relief, and she settles into her head again. There's the Relay store, the fragrance kiosk, the familiar magazines lined up on racks with headlines she can read, people she recognizes—famous people she has never met, but she's as happy to see them as if they're her friends or family.

It feels like nothing that has happened has happened; it's all impossible and fuzzy and absurd. Berlin, Jacob, Sonja, Petra, Jori, and Yannick and the fake marriage and the end of the world—all a dream, like she'd fallen asleep on the way to Toronto, on her way to Berlin, and her subconscious had drawn up a whirlwind couple of months based on the time she'd spent planning the move. Tomorrow she'd arrive in Berlin and meet the real Sonja, the real Petra, people she'd conversed with only via email to this point. Sonja would be as sweet in real life as she'd imagined. Maybe she'd meet someone *like* Jacob.

But then . . . actual Jacob wouldn't be standing beside her, holding her hand. It's a useless question—would she rather the world were not ending and Jacob was a dream, or have Jacob but know the world is ending?—but she asks herself anyway. It seems like a question that should be easy to answer, a question that tells you something important just because it's not.

63

The people in the small towns and villages have cleanly split into two groups: those resigned to this whole end-of-the-world thing and the small-but-vocal subsection of people who have decided to ignore it completely, as being *against* it would imply some level of belief. The believers and the agnostics. No atheists.

For the most part it's a civil split—probably because the only thing to do in either case is wait and see. The harvest was good this year, and it's hibernating time in any case. With only a couple more weeks left, the panic over food and supplies is past its peak—it died off as people figured out what they needed and distributed their leftovers among those who had nothing. The Hutterite colony shared its eggs and meat. There is no drama, no hysteria, just the practicality of farmers and the kindness of neighbors.

Now things are hushed, almost normal, and Hilda has been trying to enjoy it. She is ready, the food is ready. Soon Nora will be home. The only thing not tied up and taken care of is her relationship with Irene but she has to believe that will happen in time too.

The Christmas decorations are up on Main Street, snowflakes and candy canes suspended from the streetlights. An elaborate Santa's workshop has been sketched on the grocery store windows with red and green dry-erase markers, and the wooden Nativity scene is illuminated by spotlights in front of the church. Baby Jesus, as usual, is not in the scene—the church secretary will add him on Christmas Eve if she's not already fried to death. People are indoors, congregated together, and the streets are quiet.

So when Hilda arrives in the city to get Nora from the airport, it's like jumping into a frozen lake. A gasping moment where you're surprised out of your mind even though you should've known, more or less, exactly what to expect when you jumped. The snowplows haven't touched the main roads in days. There are cars in the ditches, having gotten stuck, pushed to the side, abandoned, and Hilda's thankful Marlen urged her to take the truck. Most of the businesses are dark and closed up; no one has bothered to board the windows, and many of them are smashed in. The city hasn't put up a single snowflake or candy cane. One church has its Nativity displayed, but Baby Jesus is already there. That secretary is probably already holed up in her basement, hiding more from people than heat rays.

There's a large group of protesters in front of the airport with signs about the government. The signs make no sense, don't seem to have anything to do with gamma ray bursts, and the people are angry. They're screaming at everyone, at each other, at Hilda's truck. She wants to roll down her window and challenge them. *Why are you yelling at me? I have nothing to do with anything. I just got here.*

But it probably wouldn't be a fruitful conversation.

The airport itself is comparatively empty.

People drift around the terminal like windblown snow, unsure of absolutely everything, a few steps this way, then back that way, rethinking. There's one couple at the arrivals gate, a couple with a baby. The monitors that usually display information about arrivals and departures are blank. Thankfully there's a woman sitting at the information booth, and Hilda approaches hesitantly. Everyone seems so fragile and volatile; she's nervous to speak.

"Excuse me?"

The lady's head swivels slowly toward Hilda, and she gives a great sigh, as though she carries the weight of the airport on her shoulders, but her eyes are kind. "Yeah?"

"Hi, sorry, I'm waiting for my daughter. She's flying in from Toronto, and, as I'm sure you're aware, cell phones aren't working—"

"Right." The woman smiles comfortingly. "Well, I'm just . . ." She looks down at a stack of papers and scratches her head. "I don't know what I'm doing here anymore, to be honest. I don't know how helpful I can be at this point, what with everything crashing . . ." She's mumbling at the desk, not at Hilda. She flips through some papers, peering over her glasses. "As of last week, I can tell you there was supposed to be a flight coming in today, from Toronto, within the next half hour. If nothing's changed, it should still happen. They're trying."

Relief washes over Hilda. "Thank you so much."

The woman sighs. "I'm really sorry I can't be more help. I'm doing what I can. We're all trying."

Outside, the sun moves behind some clouds and the airport darkens. The shadows seem deeper, like in a dream, like Hilda's brain is powering down the parts that aren't important for survival to preserve battery life.

She thanks the woman and moves to the arrivals gate.

Until the moment Hilda lays eyes on Nora she doesn't realize how much she expected something to go wrong, that she actually believed she would never see her daughter again. Hugging her is the best feeling in the world. This is one of those things people say about a lot of feelings, but those people don't mean it the way Hilda means it. She feels whole. She feels happy. She feels eternally optimistic.

"I brought you something," says Nora, after they've both had to pull away and dry their faces on their sleeves. "A little souvenir." She looks sheepish, like she knows that souvenirs are maybe a Before Times thing. Hilda doesn't think this is necessarily true. She accepts the small box, handmade from green felt. Inside, a small silver locket.

64

Jacob hangs back and lets Nora finish hugging her mother. Finally she pulls back and tips her head toward him, indicating that he should step forward and introduce himself.

"And who's this, a friend from the plane?" Nora's mother turns to Jacob, and he at first offers a meek wave, then self-corrects and gives a proper handshake.

"Yes, a friend," he says, a knowing smile in Nora's direction. "Jacob."

"Yes, and now . . . um . . . we're . . ." Nora, flustered, turns to Jacob for help.

"We're sort of married, actually," Jacob says brightly, his voice quavering. Poor guy. They'd had so much else to consider when making this huge decision, and so little time in which to consider it, that they had not stopped to think about the sheer awkwardness of Jacob meeting her parents.

Nora watches the news play out on her mother's face. She's probably wondering what Nora could possibly be thinking, bringing a guy home with her at a time like this, wondering if either of them realizes how hard it is to get a flight back to Europe right now. *This kid's poor parents! They're never going to see him again!*

"A friend from the plane," says Hilda slowly, "and now you're married."

She hasn't quite gotten as far as all that yet. She's still processing the bare bones of the issue.

"Oh," says Jacob. "I see—no. There was a lot more time between the first thing and the second thing. And—not a friend from the plane. A friend from Berlin."

"Only married on paper!" Nora chirps.

"It was my mom's idea," says Jacob, as though this endorsement will mean anything to Hilda.

They should have rehearsed this, they're realizing.

Jacob swings an arm around Nora's shoulders and grins. But then he notices the way Hilda bristles and quickly moves his arm back to his side.

"And let me guess," says Nora's mother, sighing, "you didn't tell me this before because you wanted to tell me in person?"

"I guess . . . yeah? It's easier to explain in person, for sure. And—and in person you can see that he's not a scary guy or anything. It's . . . it's just Jacob."

"But does *Just Jacob* have parents? A home?"

"Yes. And a sister." Jacob is trying to look appropriately sad without also looking as though he hasn't made this gigantic sacrifice completely on purpose. The speech about how it wasn't a choice, for example, would probably not be as effective on Nora's mother as it had been on Nora.

"And you are going to try to get back there before . . . ?"

"No," says Jacob. He hopes he doesn't look as frantic as he's starting to feel. "I was hoping I could—and I didn't really consider the fact that we were springing this on you—and it's really okay if—"

"Oh no, that's not what I meant." She touches his shoulder in a motherly way. "You're more than welcome here. I just know how heart-broken I would be if Nora couldn't be with us at this time . . ."

"I know," says Jacob. "It wasn't an easy choice." He takes Nora's hand, and she smiles at him.

"Well, shall we?" Nora feels as though a weight has been lifted from her shoulders. She is home—or close to it anyway. She has Jacob. She has her mother. She has her cat. They head to the car to begin the long drive to the farm.

65

In the end it's not NASA or the news anchor or the radio deejay who shares the news that the world is ending early: it's a farmer.

Of course it is. Who has a closer relationship with the sky than someone who grows things for a living?

Hilda and Nora and Jacob are seven miles from home when they notice a sign for a garage sale at the end of a neighbor's driveway. EVERYTHING MUST GO, it says in bright red.

"Everything must go," muses Hilda.

"They're not wrong," says Nora. "Everything must go." She glances over her shoulder at Jacob; he has fallen asleep in the back seat, snoring quietly.

"What do you think?" asks Hilda. "One last garage sale, you and me?"

Nora and Hilda had always loved going to garage sales together. It feels like the right thing to do now.

They pull up the horseshoe-shaped driveway, and the little green farmhouse comes into view.

The house appears to have thrown up its contents. There are piles of stuff everywhere, all over the lawn. Not stacked neatly, not arranged nicely—thrown. Clothes, photo albums, children's games and toys. Knickknacks, bowling trophies, coffee cups, tablecloths, bottles of shampoo and conditioner and lotion. Books. Hats. Knitting needles . . .

An older couple lives here, Harry and Judy Kreike. Harry is a farmer. Judy is a seamstress. They're a sweet couple, everyone likes them very much, and right now they're standing among all their earthly possessions, screaming bloody murder at each other.

Nora and Hilda can't hear what's being said yet. They watch as Judy picks up a shoe from a pile beside her. She doesn't throw it or raise it or anything, just holds it, but it's sending a clear message.

And now Harry's yelling. He doesn't need a shoe; he stands up a little straighter and points at the sky.

Hilda wonders if she should turn the truck around, but it would be extremely conspicuous at this point. Judy has noticed them now anyway and lets the shoe fall to the ground at her feet. She plasters a smile across her face and waves at them. Harry hoists a stack of old *Country Living* magazines onto a table, trying in vain to create some sense of order in the yard.

"Howdy, neighbors," says Harry as Hilda climbs out of the truck. His face is still flushed with exertion.

"Having a garage sale?" Hilda had hoped the garage sale was meant as a little joke, a last-ditch effort to connect with the neighbors—surely they don't think people are actually going to be out hunting for deals right now?—but that doesn't seem to be the case.

"Yes," says Judy firmly.

At the same time, Harry says, "Oh, for Pete's sake."

"Everything is twenty-five cents," says Judy.

"She's trying to sell my tools," grumbles Harry.

"You don't need your tools," says Judy, starting to yell again. "The world is ending!"

"Yes, but I can't help but notice all of your jewelry is still in the bedroom. I'm not seeing any of your fabric out here either." Harry is making a big show of peering into all the piles with his eyes bulging, the veins in his forehead popping out, his cheeks sucked in; he looks like one of those bulbous fish that live at the very bottom of the ocean.

Hilda and Nora do an awkward, silent lap as the couple argues. Nora purchases a tiny jewelry dish shaped like a cat, and Hilda pays twenty-five cents for a coffee mug with UFF DA! written on it.

"Thank you," says Hilda. "It was so nice to see you again." The subtext here, of course, is "goodbye," and Hilda feels unexpectedly emotional about it. When you live in a village this size for long enough, you fall in love with everyone, even the people you don't like, even the people you find very strange. Maybe there's something invisible that happens; maybe it has something to do with Marlen's quantum entanglement.

"Yes, dear," says Judy, who is quite out of breath and pulls first Nora, then Hilda in for a hug. "I'm so glad you could make it."

"A tip," says Harry. "They say it's ending on the twenty-seventh, but—" He looks up at the sky and shakes his head. "Tomorrow. I don't think we have longer than that."

Hilda and Nora look to Judy to see if they're meant to take this seriously, and she nods matter-of-factly. "Harry's never wrong about the weather," she says. "But the meteorologist *always* is." She leans in and whispers as though someone might be listening. "And we all know we can't trust *NASA*." She doesn't even say *NASA* out loud, just mouths it at them, her face deadly serious.

Hilda isn't sure why we can't trust *NASA*, but she nods anyway. "Absolutely," she says.

They climb into the truck, clutching their last garage sale purchases, and creep down the driveway, watching Judy and Harry yelling at each other again in the rearview mirror.

"You okay, Mom?" asks Nora.

Hilda nods, sniffling. "I love them," she says. "I wish we had time to go around and say goodbye to everybody."

66

When they arrive home, the reunion is complicated. Marlen is noticeably unwell, and Nora is angry that no one warned her. But she gets it, too, because she would've done the same thing in his shoes. And, anyway, as they've been learning these past few months, forgiveness has to come fast, before anger or even instead of it, because there is so little time.

Marlen shakes Jacob's hand, a puzzled look on his face. "I've met you before," Marlen says, and it's not in any way a question.

"No, I don't think so," Jacob replies, but this *is* a question.

No one has any answers.

There are easier surprises too—the best one being Hilda's murals. They walk through the house, admiring them room by room, as if it's an art gallery. The family portrait in the kitchen, the clouds in the bathroom, the birds in Nora's bedroom.

This one is Nora's favorite. "I've never seen anything like this," she says. "Why didn't I know you were an artist?"

"I'm not," Hilda says modestly.

Marlen rolls his eyes. "Your mother is being ridiculous," he says, and this, her parents' good-natured arguing, is the thing that makes Nora feel like she is really, finally, home, and everything is as it should be.

"I hear you ran into Derek," Nora says to her father, laughing at the sheepish look on his face.

"Hilda! You told her?"

"Not me."

"Derek texted me." Nora shakes her head at her father. "Said he thinks you hate him."

Marlen shrugs. It's the time for truth telling. "Well I do," he says honestly. "I hate him *a lot*."

"Marlen!" Only a few months ago Hilda would've smacked him on the shoulder playfully; now she knows how sensitive he is to touch so she just clucks at him and shakes her head. A small adjustment that few would pick up on. Nora tries not to notice.

Then it's time to tell Marlen about Harry's prediction. Someone else might have shrugged it off, but Marlen knows Harry's track record so they grab their go bags and head for the car. There's no way to let Irene know that they're coming with the phones down; they'll just show up.

Hilda thinks, as she pulls her seat belt across her chest, that Marlen was right all along. This *is* an awful lot like having a baby. There's the hospital bag packed well in advance, there's the due date, and there's the baby, despite everyone's best plans, throwing convenience out the window, coming early—coming *now*.

Ready or not.

67

The Pot Hole is closing.

It's time. No one has told Alfie, but she knows somehow. It feels self-evident, the way things do sometimes if you're really paying attention. The sky is medallion yellow; the wind is picking up.

Alfie has always been interested in being helpful, and to this point she has felt that the Pot Hole has been a helpful place. It's given everyone a place to go in a town with nothing going on, something to do, something to look forward to—people underestimate the power of something to look forward to, even if that something is just a coffee date in mismatched chairs in the back of a small-town gas station. The Pot Hole might be one of her best contributions to the village. She knows she should feel proud of it.

And now it's time to shut the doors for good. She locks them behind her, even though, to an onlooker who knows the situation, this might seem like an absolutely ridiculous thing to do. It's not like someone's going to go in there and mess the place up or anything. It's more a point of ceremony, a symbol of finality. She pockets the keys and steps back for a moment of solemn reflection. The Pot Hole is part of her legacy, along with the library, the church, the many showers and parties and organizations and charity events she has organized. It feels fitting to stand here and take the time to acknowledge all of it.

Is that it? All of that, and I'm still alone?

She feels surprised at the thought. She has given everything to this town, yes, but she has never asked for anything in return, and she has never felt bitter or overworked or annoyed. It's actually shocking to have these emotions pop up now. How long have they been lurking in the back of her mind, pretending to be other, happier feelings? Masquerading as contentment, selflessness, joy?

Alfie looks around at the quiet Main Street, the post office, the bank, the grocery store. She has given and given and given, oblivious to the fact that maybe some part of her was giving out of loneliness, out of a place inside her that assumed if she gave and gave and gave, that at the end of it all, her repayment would be . . . family?

But no. She's going to walk back to her trailer and spend the rest of her life there, alone. Elsewhere, a woman might be thinking about the wedding shower Alfie threw for her in the church basement, with thoughtful centerpieces and funny little skits and her favorite desserts. A couple might fondly recall a date at the Pot Hole where they fell in love. The family of the young woman who passed away a few years back might remember the funeral luncheon, planned by Alfie, where an astonishing four hundred people showed up and were well fed.

But none of these people will be thinking about Alfie.

She pulls the keys out of her pocket again and drops them in the dirt at her feet. It's not that she'd take any of it back. It's not that it wasn't a beautiful, worthy way to spend a life. She just wishes . . .

"There she is." Hilda breathes a sigh of relief. They'd gone by Alfie's trailer, but she hadn't been there.

"Oh good," says Nora. "I hated the thought of her alone for this."

Iver shuffles over in his seat to make room for Alfie, thrilled that they've found her.

They pull to a stop in front of the Pot Hole, and Hilda jumps out of the car. "Alfie!"

Alfie turns. She's been crying, and this is somewhat shocking. Hilda has never thought of Alfie as someone who cries.

"Hilda." Alfie's smile is so sad; Hilda wants to reach out and wrap her in a hug—but she doesn't, because Alfie's not a hugger. Though now Hilda's wondering: Is this assumption based on anything other than the fact that she's never seen anyone hug the woman?

"Harry says it's—the—you know what—it's happening early. It caught us a little off guard, honestly. Do you have somewhere else you'd rather be? If not—do you want to come with us? We're going to Irene's."

Alfie's face is doing all sorts of things Hilda has never seen her face do. She doesn't answer, just does a lot of nodding. She stoops and picks something up out of the dirt at her feet—keys?—points at Hilda's car. Still nodding.

Hilda takes a chance and throws an arm around Alfie's shoulders as they head back to the car together, feels her melt into the side hug, realizes she might have been wrong. Maybe, all this time, Alfie was a hugger and no one knew it.

68

A storm is brewing. The sky is golden. It's not like the start of any storm Irene has ever experienced out here. Not like the tornado of 2009, or that midsummer hailstorm three years before that. This feels final in a way that's hard to describe. Like standing at the top of a tall flight of stairs, knowing you're about to fall down them.

She's in the living room, hanging snowflakes from the windows, when she notices the sunlight reflecting through them has changed color, intensified. She rushes into the kitchen, where a copy of the Letter is stuck to the fridge with a magnet. She reads it from time to time, when her faith—or lack thereof—begins to waver, like it's a holy text reminding her of what she doesn't believe. She reads it and recites her private liturgy in a whisper. *None of this is true or logical. The world is fine, the end is far away, it's all hysteria.*

She'd read it when the grocery stores stopped selling groceries, and again when the gas station ran out of gas, and again and again and again as friends left town and the cell phone towers went down.

And now, as the sky turns the color of a field of wheat, she reads it with tears streaming down her cheeks.

Hank comes into the kitchen and finds her like that, and they stare at each other for a moment before he walks over and gathers her in his arms.

"Are you okay?"

"I don't think I am," she says. "I don't think any of us are."

He doesn't say I told you so; he doesn't even think it. To his surprise, he's disappointed. Maybe he had believed her, a little. Maybe, though you can't choose what you believe, you can also believe something without knowing it, even while believing something contradictory at the same time. Maybe the entire concept of "beliefs" is just something too complicated to be understood by human beings.

Ole comes into the kitchen. He's crying too. They pull him into their arms, wishing they could keep him safe between the two of them.

"What do we do?" Ole's voice is so small; Irene thinks of him nestled into her body on Saturday mornings, eating cinnamon buns.

"We have to finish decorating for Christmas," she says, swiping at her eyes. "Everyone will be here soon. Hilda promised me we'd celebrate Christmas together." She knows, somehow, that they will be here in time. Hilda has never let her down.

She bursts into action. "Ole," she says, her voice calm but commanding, "you need to grab the garlands and the snowflakes. Hang them up all over the basement, make it look nice." As she speaks, she marches into the living room and grabs the Christmas tree. "Hank, get the stuff from the freezer in the garage, get it into the basement—and the microwave and all the stuff from the pantry." She drags the tree noisily down the stairs, losing half the decorations on the trip. They're going to spend Christmas in the basement with Iver and Hilda and Marlen and Nora, and it's going to be *nice*, and it's going to be *festive* and *magical*, and they are going to *like* it.

Irene steps onto the porch as they come up the driveway: Hilda and Nora and Marlen and Iver and Alfie and an unfamiliar man—or is he unfamiliar? Irene has the feeling she's seen him before.

They spill out of the car, eyes wide, looking up at the sky.

Irene pretends to smile and greets everyone with a hug. Hilda hovers at her side as everyone files past them into the house, catches Irene's arm before she follows them. The wind is so loud she has to yell.

"IRENE! I NEED TO TALK TO YOU!"

Irene sighs inwardly. She knew this conversation was coming. She'd thought they could at least get in the house first, have some lefse and something to drink.

"I'M SORRY!" Hilda is yelling louder than she really needs to. Maybe that's why she'd wanted to do this out here, so she could scream her apology. There's not really any other scenario in which this would be acceptable.

"DON'T WORRY ABOUT IT!" Irene yells back, also louder than she needs to.

"BUT I DO, THOUGH! I *DO* WORRY ABOUT IT! I HAVE BEEN WORRIED SICK!"

"YOU KNOW WHAT, HILDA?" Irene has to get right into Hilda's face now. If someone in the house were to look out the window at this moment, they'd think the women were about to start throwing punches. "NO MATTER WHICH ONE OF US ENDED UP BEING RIGHT, I WOULD BE SAYING THE SAME THING RIGHT NOW— ALTHOUGH IF I HAD BEEN RIGHT, I WOULD BE SAYING IT IN A LOT QUIETER VOICE, I THINK—LET'S NOT WASTE THE REST OF OUR LIVES ON THIS! PLEASE!"

It's even harder for Irene to make her voice heard now; the wind is absolutely screaming, and she has a lump in her throat, but Hilda understands, even though she hadn't heard a word her sister said. She'd thought this would be a much more difficult conversation, a much more complicated fix. They should've done it sooner. But then . . . it would not have been half as guttural as it is now. "I LOVE YOU, IRENE!" Hilda is screaming from the very bottom of her stomach, and it feels wonderful, cleansing, healing.

"I LOVE YOU TOO!" Irene screams.

The wind sounds less frightening now, just passionate, insistent, howling along with the sisters on the porch. As if the universe itself has a message too.

I love you! I love you! I love you!

69

The radio, the last of the voices from the outside world, has gone silent. They can no longer see the lights of the neighboring farms, and the roads are dark, no headlights, no sound of old farm trucks in the distance. The only visible light and movement are in the sky above them, nature making up for the failure of modern technology. The twinkling stars seem to be moving closer, like the universe itself is drawing in. The northern lights are out, too, electric-green sheets of it. Alarming warning lights or a beautiful last show. Even at the end of the world, perspective makes a difference.

In all the years they've lived in the middle of nowhere, none of them have ever truly felt isolated, until now. Their house may as well be floating into deep space.

They're sitting in the basement around the Christmas tree. Hank has brought the couch and chairs down, as well as the dog bed for Bud. The room is festive; Irene has done a beautiful job. There are strings of ivy and holly cut out of green felt draped all over the basement, with twinkling Christmas lights and intricate paper snowflakes in the window wells. It's a bit much, but it's Christmas, so it's okay.

Jacob admires Irene's snowflakes. "I've never been able to make those," he says to her. "I always cut them wrong and they fall apart."

"I'll teach you," she says. She likes this boy. He reminds her of someone, but she can't think of who it is. "They're easy once you get the hang of it."

"What day is it?" Ole asks. He has lost track.

"December 24," says Marlen. His voice is raspy; his head lolls back in the chair. Still, he smiles at his nephew. He has a strange wisp of a memory, where he is here, in this spot, with this family, but this boy is still missing, never came back.

But that can't be right, can it? He's right there, real as anything.

"No, it's not," says Hank. "It's December—"

"Yes, it is," says Hilda. "December 24." This might be the first time Hilda is wrong and Hank is right. But it's not going to work out in Hank's favor, because everyone decides to believe Hilda anyway. Sometimes you do get to choose. "It's Christmas Eve."

"What, no presents?" Ole is only half joking. He's not sure why he even wants presents. What good would they do, since they'll just blow up in the morning? But tradition is important, pressed into him since birth, and presents are fun. He's still a kid, especially at Christmas.

"I got you all a little something, actually," says Irene, to Ole's great relief. Because Irene is ready. Turns out she was right to focus on Christmas. The rest of them have gained nothing by not focusing on it.

It's such a cliché, to wake up one day and realize how much you've taken your spouse for granted, to think of all the ways you could've treated them better, cherished them more, but that's what's on Hank's mind right now. And it is thoroughly too late to do anything about it—anything he says would come across as wooden; it would seem like he was just trying to make himself feel better in the face of death. *Next time,* he thinks, *I'll do better.* It's an abstract thought; he doesn't dwell on it.

"Can we open them now?"

Irene hesitates. Tradition is important to her, and tradition says you wait until Christmas Eve. Then she laughs. It is Christmas Eve. It's the only Christmas Eve they're going to get; she knows this.

"Sure. I'll go get them."

Hank follows her, and they return with armloads of presents wrapped in shiny red and green paper. Books for Marlen and Nora, a Nintendo Switch game for Ole, earrings for Hilda, new slippers for Hank and Iver. There are even, peculiarly, presents for Jacob and Alfie and Bud. No one seems to think this is strange. Maybe they just have that much faith in Irene. She doesn't miss a beat, even an impossible one.

Iver leans over to Alfie and quietly tells her that he had ordered her a present, but Walmart had failed to deliver. "A mug," he says. "It said VVVVVVIP on the side."

She looks puzzled.

"Very, very, very, very, very, very important person," he says.

She pats his hand. "It really is the thought that counts," she says, and he can see that she means it even if it's a very, very, very, very, very, very cliché thing to say.

"Marlen has a present for everyone too," says Hilda, pulling out the box of books.

It feels a little sad, giving everyone a book they'll have no time to read, but Marlen finds he doesn't actually mind. It might be awkward to have them read something so personal anyway. This way they can be proud of him and that will be that.

So the books are passed around; the covers are touched; the spines are cracked. Marlen is congratulated on his accomplishment.

"When did you find time to write this?" Irene asks, impressed.

"Over the past year," he replies.

She nods and flips it over to read the back; there's quiet in the room as everyone else does the same. Hilda smiles to herself, watching them, waiting.

Ole is the first to notice.

"Wait. *When* did you start writing this?" he asks.

"Last year."

Ole frowns.

"And it was about this right from the beginning?"

"Yes."

"About what?" says Hank, still reading the back. Then: *"Oh."*

Everyone looks at Marlen incredulously. Irene is so scandalized as to seem almost insulted. "*How?* What are you, a prophet?"

Hilda laughs. "That's the running joke in our house."

"How does it end?" asks Ole. He's not really asking about the book.

Marlen shifts in his seat uncomfortably. This is the downside of releasing a book this way. You can't just say, "I guess you'll have to read it!" That would be especially cruel under these circumstances.

"Everyone dies, I guess," says Hank.

"No, actually," says Hilda. "They don't."

Irene is hopeful. "Oh? What happens?"

Everyone looks to Marlen like he really is a prophet. He's always been on a bit of a pedestal to them, the man with so much random knowledge, but now he's leveled up.

"Well, they do actually . . ." He finds he suddenly can't say the word, despite the fact that the topic has monopolized his entire life for the past year. He clears his throat. It's easier to talk about the mechanics of it, the things that happen to the fictional people in his book instead of the real people in front of him. "Okay, so you know how they say your life flashes before your eyes right before you die? Scientists have studied the brain wave patterns of dying people and collected the stories of those who've had near-death experiences, and they're fairly positive, almost one hundred percent sure, that it's true—in the moments before you die, you experience a flood of emotions and memory, like vivid hallucinations, as powerful as a drug trip but still only as reliable as a human memory can be, full of holes and problems, things repeated and absent. An entire life condensed into a thirty-second replay that feels as real as reality."

He has to pause and catch his breath. Breathing never used to be so hard.

"So the premise of my book is, essentially: What if this isn't a limited experience? What if it's infinite, or near infinite? I was thinking about, like, when a person gets to the last thirty seconds of the replay. Would their brain know it's only the replay? Or would the same thing happen as the first time, restarting the process? And if so, the dying person's life would flash before their eyes *again*, right, and then, like a nesting doll of time and memory, it would just go on and on and on like that. So that's what's going on in the novel. The people experience intense déjà vu, and they sometimes experience the sensation of being able to tell the future, and sometimes they remember things that have happened before, in other, I don't know what you'd call them, *life cycles*, and they re-create those things, or change them, fix them . . ." He trails off. He needs to catch his breath again.

Iver doesn't say it out loud, but he likes the idea of a chance to fix things. Who wouldn't?

"So everyone does die," Ole clarifies.

"Yes?" Marlen picks up his book. "But they never actually *experience* dying? Everyone only appears to, from the outside. But *inside*—inside of *them*, I guess you could say, billions of lifetimes fly past, like blades of grass viewed from the window of an airplane."

"I found it quite comforting to think about," says Hilda. "You die, but also, you're immortal. You never die."

"But you do, though," says Ole.

"I guess death is in the eye of the beholder," says Marlen. He sets the book down on his knee and takes Hilda's hand, the way he's done so many times before, the way he hopes he will do again and again and again. "So to answer your question, Ole: the way the book ends is, essentially, that it starts again, and the idea is that on the next iteration, tiny things will change. Memory is imperfect, and maybe this is a feature, not a bug. The couple that chose to break up the first time around will get back together, a relationship that fell apart will be fixed, a person who was lonely will find family, a person that was lost will be found. And like erosion, the effects of all these tiny changes will eventually wear away at the rough edges of the characters' existence, until, at last, it reveals something perfect. Maybe that's what happens: everyone gets to live their life over and over until it's perfect."

They stay up as late as they can, dropping off to sleep one by one where they sit, on the couch, on the floor. Marlen and Hilda sit together, nestled into an oversize armchair like a couple of teenagers, a blanket over their legs. Marlen's reading the book Irene gave him, and Hilda's dozing off and on, enjoying the groggy feeling pulling at her, the comforting sound of her husband's heartbeat in her ear.

70

The battery-powered Christmas lights strung around the walls are their only light. The windows are covered, one last futile swat at survival by people who know full well that they won't make it. But it feels wrong not to try.

The air is thick. Everyone wonders if they're imagining it. It feels harder to breathe, and it makes them sleepy. Nora thinks about Petra, about everyone holding their breath, waiting to see what comes next.

For a while they're unexpectedly bored. They wonder if it will hurt. They wonder if they'll feel anything at all. Sometimes the mind wonders about things because it wonders, and sometimes it wonders about things because it knows.

Iver doesn't want to sit in silence, so he breaks it with a lovely story about his late wife, and it sets them off. They talk about the past, mostly. Embarrassing stories, happy memories. They ask Alfie questions about herself, and they tell her funny stories about their family. There's a celebratory feel to it, like a memorial luncheon for someone who's lived well.

Jacob and Nora are seated beside each other on the floor, laughing at a story Iver's telling about Hilda as a three-year-old. Irene has taught Jacob how to make a paper snowflake that won't fall apart; it's a nice distraction. He has a neat little stack next to him, snipping away as they visit. Nora's thinking about how both of them had known they'd end up here. Magic? Delusion? Memory? She's thinking about Leise Park, too, the children learning to experience joy as they play near the dead. This basement is their own personal Leise Park. Translated into English: Quiet Park. A place that is not irreverent, not dismissive, but still joyful and silly and beautiful. Like paper snowflakes and ivy garland in a basement shelter.

Alfie is elated; she has never been such an active participant in this part of a memorial luncheon before. She's always been in the kitchen, cleaning tables, comforting someone in the bathroom. Now she has been set free; she's working the room, hugging everyone. Maybe even she hadn't realized that she was a hugger until now. Hilda watches her. Is it tragic that she's waited until the bitter end to experience this kind of joy, or beautiful that she found it in time?

Hilda marvels at how quickly a person can settle into a reality, even a horrible one. She knows what Marlen means now, about being used to dying. She places a hand on her husband's shoulder and feels his reciprocal reach from somewhere in the darkness. "You okay?" His voice rumbles against her. This is interesting, too, how the right person can make you feel safe even when you know you're not.

"I'm okay," she says, and she means it. Her daughter is here; her daughter is tangible proof of a truth she learned twenty years ago. *My body knows what to do, and everything is going to be okay.*

"Should we uncover the windows?" Hank's voice floats through the blackness. He doesn't sound quite like himself. "It's not like we're going to be safer with them covered. It's just a mental thing."

"I agree," says Irene. Her voice wavers; she's trying very hard to keep it together. "I want to be able to see you all."

"I kinda want to see what it looks like," says Ole.

"Only if everyone's comfortable with it, obviously," says Hank. "Does anyone just feel better with the windows covered?"

Silence.

"I'm okay with uncovering the windows too," says Hilda. She puts her free arm around the nearest person; it doesn't even matter who it is at this point. She thinks it might be Ole. A memory flits into her mind, like a fleck in her eye that darts away when she tries to look at it. She can't get at it, and she lets it go.

No one else speaks up, but no one argues, either, and within a few minutes there are shuffling noises and then the sound of something ripping, and a triangle of strange pink light appears. To Nora it looks like the light in Berlin, reflecting off those beautiful old buildings.

More ripping, and the triangle becomes a rectangle. The room is bathed in a soft glow, like the sun has been replaced by a giant ball of Christmas lights. Hesitantly they move toward the window.

"Don't get too close," says Jacob, stopping them in their tracks. "It's probably like how you shouldn't look directly at a solar eclipse."

Nora's cat ignores this advice; she climbs into the window well and basks in the glow of the incoming blast. Everyone else stays back, straining to see out the window into the yard.

"Oh. It's foggy," says Nora. She hasn't let go of Jacob's hand since they woke up this morning. Now she grips it tighter.

"It's not fog, exactly," says Marlen. "It's photochemical smog, is what it is." Marlen sounds impressed with himself, which is fair. There is nothing left to be but impressed. Hilda leans her head on his shoulder again. "I got it exactly right."

"Déjà vu," says Ole, staring out the window, though there's not much to see. Just thick pink smog and vague shapes where they know there's a line of trees. It's still; the wind screamed all through the night, but now it's moved into the distance. It reminds him of the summer they had all those tornadoes. He remembers hiding down here then, watching the window fill up with gravel, not feeling afraid until he saw his mom's face and realized she was trying not to cry. It's why he's not looking at her now—instead, he takes her hand. "I have that feeling like I've been here before."

Irene looks away from Ole; she doesn't want him to see her holding back tears. She wants to be strong for him. Kids don't realize how hard it is to be the adult, how courage doesn't just show up, how life is actually more frightening when you're older because the stakes get higher and higher. You love more and more people and also understand more fully how fragile and temporary they are.

Strangely enough, these aren't tears of sadness or grief or fear. She's immersed in this moment, and just so thankful he's here. His fingers are still so small; she can't help but think of taking him to the city when he was a toddler, holding his hand as they crossed the street on a sunny day, pointing at the traffic lights and signs and explaining what everything means.

Red means stop. Green means go. But don't just look at the lights; look at the cars too. They don't always listen to the lights. You have to keep your eyes peeled, buddy. This place is dangerous. Hang on to me.

The balance between instilling caution and provoking anxiety. She'd never quite figured that out. Now it doesn't matter. The only part that ever mattered was that they were together.

He was so young then; he probably hasn't thought of that trip since. One of those bittersweet things about motherhood, how those special early memories become so precious to you and lost completely to your child.

The basement is getting warmer—they're not imagining it—and the air is getting thicker. Hilda bites her tongue so she won't mention the thing from Marlen's novel about how this air, at the very end, will turn to plasma, and their lungs won't be able to make use of it. She is proud of herself for knowing this, even if it's a little macabre. She picks up his book and turns to the last page.

There's a bright flash and a crash of what sounds like thunder, but the sound is much bigger than thunder. It comes from absolutely everywhere; there is no place the sound is not.

It's in their heads and feet, traveling down their arms into their fingers and to the end of every hair follicle. It's in the attic and the basement and the silverware. It's in the trees the kids climbed growing up and in every single stalk of wheat in the fields. It's in the sun and the core of the earth and it's coming out of their mouths.

The sound, in all its furious power and blinding light, turns out not to be the end. It's the beginning of the same as last time, but better.

Just the tiniest bit better.

Acknowledgments

Deepest, loudest, lovingest, heartfeltest, and most sincere thanks to the magnificent Alicia Clancy and the whole Lake Union team, who are all so lovely to work with; Victoria Cappello, my fabulous agent; Laura Chasen, to whom I owe my sanity, I'm not kidding; James Gallagher, Heather Rodino, and Sarah Vostok, who edited this book with magical eagle eyes; Philip Pascuzzo for the dream cover; Barclay Krause for just, like, *everything*; Sarah Ann Noel for the daily encouragements and trickle-down therapy; Kiersten Taylor for being able to take a picture of me that is not awkward, purely because I don't feel awkward around you (and bless you for that); and Kate Evenson and Rachel Del Grosso for reading that weird early draft. Oh, and Becky Zaleschuck! For all the weird conversations that made it into this book in various ways. Glad to be entangled with you.

About the Author

Photo © 2023 Kiersten Taylor

Suzy Krause is the bestselling author of *Sorry I Missed You* and *Valencia and Valentine*. She lives in Regina, Saskatchewan. For more information, visit www.suzykrause.com.